The Ruins at Uxmal

By

Jeremy S. Wood

Copyright © 2001 by Jeremy S. Wood
All rights reserved.
No part of this book may be reproduced, restored in a retrieval system, or transmitted by means, electronic, mechanical, photocopying, recording, or otherwise, without written consent from the author.

ISBN: 0-75961-792-9

This book is printed on acid free paper.

1stBooks - rev. 3/12/01

Table of Contents

Chapter 1 1

Chapter 2 9

Chapter 3 12

Chapter 4 18

Chapter 5 24

Chapter 6 26

Chapter 7 31

Chapter 8 35

Chapter 9 41

Chapter 10 46

Chapter 11 55

Chapter 12 59

Chapter 13 69

Chapter 14 82

Chapter 15 97

Chapter 16 100

Chapter 17 107

Chapter 18 114

Chapter 19 127

Chapter 20 138

Chapter 21 148

Chapter 22 154

Chapter 23	170
Chapter 24	174
Chapter 25	178
Chapter 26	187
Chapter 27	192
Chapter 28	196
Chapter 29	206
Chapter 30	211
Chapter 31	214
Chapter 32	226
Charpter 33	230
Chapter 34	248
Bibliography	254

Chapter 1

On the morning of the day of the party held to honor Dr. William Moore, a physician of repute in Manhassatt, Long Island and the father of her lover, Sally Parks heard the telephone ring in her den. Anxiously she picked it up. After recognizing her brother David's voice, she suddenly glowed at what good news he told her. Hearing that he had just been promoted to a junior partnership at the prestigious law firm of Olds and Ruel climaxed her vacation! Marvelous! An opportunity to entrap her sweetheart in marriage was now hers. She hung up the phone and flounced gaily to the window seat to review her scheme.

As her devoted brother would do anything for her, she knew she could induce him to use his influence to have Kirke, a law student, hired as an associate when he was ready. She could definitely count on that. She felt that his influence would be tantamount to certainty. And as the firm was expanding she felt additionally certain that there would be no problem. Very good indeed! However! —fearful of losing her elusive boyfriend, to get him—really, she acknowledged, blushing—to lure him—into marrying her, she would have to first appeal to his immense ambition with the promise of a job in the firm. Then, after succeeding in her matrimonial aim and when he had been hired, the way would be open for him to have a brilliant career and for the two of them to rise to the top of New York society—just what she wanted!

She paused a moment, realizing that her parents would be opposed to her scheme as they would say it would be very incautious to marry a man before he was installed in a job and one whom she had only known for a short time—eight weeks. But never mind that—she had always been rebellious! In her job as a reader for Bosworth Publishers there had been Kirke, who had been working there since June before his final year at Cornell Law School, and—Don Juan that he was—he had been charming. And she had fallen body and soul for him!

And equally as important as that, he was the kind of a guy she was looking for—he had the drive, the connections and when he had completed his studies would have the education to attain the social and financial heights she very much desired. Very much indeed! Reflecting on her relatively modest circumstances, she now wanted life in the top drawer. So one move had led to another, and now, lying before her, was the realization of her hopes.

The next question—when could she tell Kirke the news and broach her plan? And how? He had not even mailed her a postcard since he had been sent out of town these past ten days—was he growing distant? —and even if she could secure his address from the company, a letter or a phone call would hardly do for information as significant as this. He must be told personally. Thinking hard she then realized that he would surely make every effort to be at his father's celebration. Of course! Fly in from somewhere! He was devoted to him.

And—what luck! The opportunity to see Kirke was at hand! As Mrs. Moore had learned from him that she, Sally, was his latest favorite, she had invited her to the party so it would be entirely in order to attend unescorted.

Having prayed all afternoon that the evening would satisfy her hopes, Sally was overjoyed when Kirke made an eleventh hour appearance in the ballroom of the Sewane Country Club. However, she knew it was too late to raise this matter of vital concern then. If only she could induce him to see her the following day—Saturday. So tonight it would be best to guard against any revelation whatsoever.

"Are you on the lookout for another Miss Lonelyhearts tonight, Kirke?" she asked facetiously, as she greeted him, knowing of his popularity with girls.

He looked embarrassed. At first, he flushed, then answered coolly, "I'm hardly a boor, you know."

Although slightly annoyed by his distant attitude, she continued, "Well, there are advantages to not being one."

"What do you mean?"

Recovering, she parried. "Tell you later, dearie. Your mother and father are just returning from the bar, and it's too important—very important—to cover in a few words now. As the weekend is coming up, can we meet then?"

As he did not immediately reply she felt she had moved too fast. She changed the topic and asked him how he was doing in his hobby of writing.

"Oh, quite well," he said, off-handedly.

Resuming her flip manner, she riposted.

"You've got it all figured out, haven't you—both your avocation and your career?"

"My avocation is my second vocation. And ever since I've been born, chum, I've been career-oriented. My parents saw to that. You see, then I'll be able to support a girl like you in the manner you've been accustomed to."

"Am I to be flattered that you've already picked me out?"

"I'll have you know my career comes first," he rejoined airily.

"How insensitive can you be? I suppose I'll have to wait. What an insult! But I assume that when you return to Cornell, you'll have me up to graduation?"

"I would consider that."

"If a hard-to-get rogue like you undoubtedly are would do that for me, I'd appreciate the courtesy."

"I couldn't think of anything less."

She appraised him with a glance. His demeanor matched his looks which were excellent. Six feet of height, a trim, muscular figure which, together with his superb poise, made him most appealing. And his gay debonair manner—charming. She thought that he would make a fine catch. Then she continued, "Since you said you wanted to write, I can be your critic. I'd like to try my hand at that."

"The only things I've done are a couple of stories last year. Would you like to see them?"

"Of course, hon, of course!"

"Well," he said, grinning, " I suppose I could let you look at them."

She seized her opportunity again.

"How about this Saturday? I can look at them and also tell you that important news I mentioned a moment ago."

He hesitated again. Finally, "I'll see you around two o'clock," he replied, nodding his head.

She received him at the home of her parents, with whom she was spending the rest of the week. She thought its tasteful New England style—wooden, painted white except for a gray roof and shutters—and its stunning setting—a tree-shaded greensward overlooking Long Island Sound on the outskirts of Manhassatt—were sufficient reasons to regard herself as a lady of some standing, not one to casually cast aside after an affair. She greeted him graciously, yet proudly, led him into a sunlit parlor, motioned him to a wicker chair and asked for his stories. Deliberately she concentrated, intending to make him anxious to hear her when she was through. "You're not lacking in ability, " she remarked quietly, looking up at him.

The Ruins at Uxmal

Delighted when he said, "You certainly deserve to rate with me after that comment," she reflected further that what with her liveliness and looks with its clean cut features, auburn hair, very white skin against which her gold bracelets shone plus her sterling background, she would indeed make him a nice wife.

After this she took the opportunity to bring up the important subject. When he told her he was returning to New York the following week, she said, "It's fortunate you're going to be here because I need you."

"You do?"

"Yes."

"Well, I'm hardly the type to run away from damsels in distress."

"I'm glad to hear that," she said gravely. "It makes me happy. It causes me to hope that you won't back away from what I have to tell you."

He laughed, a trifle uneasily. "Well, come on now, stop being so mysterious."

"Kirke, this is serious. I do hope you just didn't regard me as a fling when you made love to me this past month. I love you very much, and I certainly hope you love me."

"Well?"

"The news, Kirke, is very important, that is, it's very important to you."

"I don't follow—"

"Listen carefully." He waited expectantly.

"Look, dear, what would you do for an offer of a brilliant job? Everything you want?"

"Well—," he laughed, "plenty, I guess."

"I sincerely hope you mean what you say. Because I'm taking you up on it."

"You are? How?"

She took a deep breath. "I can make you an offer of that job."

"You can?"

"Yes. I can." She hesitated for just a moment. "But I have a price."

"You do? What?"

"It really isn't much of one." Then she played her lead. "After all, we've been crazy about each other from the moment we've met. That's the only condition I have, upon which my offer depends."

"What the devil do you mean?"

"It should be obvious."

"You mean that I should marry you in order to get the job?" he asked, amazed.

"That's it," she said incisively. "Precisely that! And—is that too bad? As you know, I'm very much in love, and I've reached the time for decision. Frankly, I'm out to get what I want."

"My God!"

"Think, Kirke, of the opportunity!"

"The opportunity? What?"

"You'll be an Associate in the law firm of Olds and Ruel!"

He swallowed hard, "You can do that? " Then, "Well—how in the devil are you going to get me a job?"

"Through an important personal contact. This person, I'm very sure, can get you in with ease."

"You do? You really know?"

"I'm very sure. But trust me—you're aware I'm not reputed to make statements which are half-cocked—not when important decisions are involved. That's all I'm going to say. Now you think of it! You'll have a splendid position—a terrific future—everything you want, including me. Now that isn't so bad, is it? After all, we've hit it off pretty well, haven't we? All you have to do to get it is consent, and when you're ready in a year's time—well, you leave it to me. Really, the only thing that would hold you off is a sense of losing your freedom—and is that so important to you now? I feel it's high time you married and settled down. You're everything I want."

She watched closely as Kirke, nonplussed, stared at the floor. Finally he said, "It's a devil of an opportunity. But my God—the responsibility. I hadn't figured on that."

"I'll be a good wife to you, Kirke. I swear I will."

.Yes, you would. But all this is so fast." He strode across the room, hands behind his back. "You're a fine girl, everything I could want in a woman."

"Then why not?"

"I've never been faced by anything like this before. Can't you understand?"

"Neither have I. Oh, but of course I understand. As you said, you don't want the responsibility."

"That's not really true." He hesitated, turned about, and faced her. "I'm only trying to make a tremendous decision."

"Under the circumstances that shouldn't be too hard."

He nodded, hesitated again and then spoke resolutely, "Yes—you're right—," she waited, hoping—"what a chance—but I don't know..."

"Don't you love me?" she asked point-blank.

His defenses shattered, thunderstruck, "Oh—why, of course!" he spluttered. Then, after a prolonged moment, he spoke with extreme tenderness, "Yes, darling, I will marry you."

She got up, put her arms around his neck and kissed him Then, "We have a lot of planning to do."

For a moment he deliberated. "Tell you what," he said, "let's think about that for a week. Why don't we take next Saturday and go out to Montauk Point for a picnic and hash things out? We have a lot to talk about."

"A good idea. Montauk would be perfect." Then, tremendously elated at having jumped the first hurdle on the road to success, she joyfully kissed him, took his arm and led him to the door.

Chapter 2

As Montauk was crowded with automobiles and throngs of pedestrains during the summer season, she couldn't help admiring Kirke as he skilfully piloted his Chevrolet through the streets on the way to the beaches at the farthest reaches of the town. Another of his appealing features. It showed he was a take charge kind of guy, the kind who could compete with her, and she liked that. She was lucky to have landed him. They'd have a glorious future together. Now enjoy the day.

"You know," she then commenced, recollecting the brochure she had acquired when her uncle had taken her there on a fishing trip the previous summer, "although Montauk's essentially a fishing village, those beaches closest to the lighthouse on the other side of town will be just great for our picnic. And later we could finish off the day by having dinner at a fine local restaurant—Gosman's—where we can dine on seafood on the roof overlooking Montauk Inlet. It'll be nice."

"All that would be surperb," he replied, stepping on the gas.

As they approached Montauk Beach, she felt slightly nervous as she anticipated her further plans. Then, as they alighted from the car and spread a blanket on the sand, she realized that he was ready for her to begin talking seriously.

"Well," she began, "How does it feel to be engaged?"

"I still can't get used to the idea, you proposing to me." He grinned. "I thought the hallmark of a lady was reticence."

"Dear, it's 1960. I hope you don't have any second thoughts about it."

He shook his head. "No, hon, you did the right thing by taking the initiative. You're perfect for me—energetic, forceful, impulsive, and I need that as a check to my caution. Your temperament is ideal for me. You'll be a fine wife."

"I agree. And when you graduate from school this year, you can thank me for putting you on the track to a marvelous career."

She then sized up the situation. The job was half done. He was ready to get married so don't waste time; he might slip off the hook.

"Now, do you really think we need to go through a long engagement?" she continued. "I think we ought to dispense with that and get married as soon as we decently can. Lengthy engagements are for kids who are still on Mom's apron strings."

"True."

"Well, then, the first thing is to set the date of our wedding."

"Yeah—you have any plans?"

"How about September 15? That would give us a brief honeymoon in Atlantic City—say a week—and then allow us time to look around in Ithaca for an adequate apartment before school starts on the 28."

"A good idea."

"And as for the marriage, I would like to make it a private affair—you know, have only our parents and a few friends for the occasion."

"Why?"

"Well, neither of us is a church-goer, so what's the point of all the ceremony? However, I think we should have it in a church. I don't feel like having a shirt-sleeved city clerk perfunctorily going through a ritual which is very important to us."

"I agree. Have you one in mind?"

"Yes. There's a small Presbyterian church which is just lovely—you know, painted white, with a steeple—New England style—over in Oyster Bay which would be ideal. I've met the minister—Bosworth did one of his books—a collection of sermons—he's a nice guy, and I'm sure he would be fine for us. Mother and Dad know of it, and I'm sure yours do as well."

"Does he require us to be counseled?"

"I don't think so. I'll call and beg off if necessary."

"Ok. Now how do you think your parents will feel about our marrying on such short acquaintance?"

"I hope they won't be too worried. After all, you're going to be a lawyer with good financial prospects, and that will impress them."

"And mine?"

"Same thing."

"What about the fact that I don't have a job right now?"

"Don't worry. I'll tell them all you need money for right now is to complete school. Now, as your parents are wealthy, they'll have to continue to foot the bill, except what I can contribute by working. My doing that would help some, but with both living expenses and tuition costs we'd have to rely on their assistance."

Again Kirke nodded. Feeling then that business was concluded, she said, "So most everything is jake. And let me say I think you're a real man for the way you've behaved."

"Now that is a most fitting comment. Thank you. Now let's go see that lighthouse. You interested me. Then, after a swim, what say we finish off the day at Gosman's? It'll be a good way to relax after all this fuss and feathers of the past week."

Chapter 3

That night, as she entered the house of her parents, she noted the time by the grandfather's clock in the front hall. It was two a.m. The late hour reminded her of their strictness during her girlhood.

"Thank God, they can no longer wait up for me," she exclaimed to herself. "But how worried will they be when I tell them about Kirke and me? Probably a bit." She ruminated a moment. "Now what can I say that might relieve any anxiety?"

Continuing her thinking, she mounted the hall stairs, thoughtfully cocked her head and went to her room.

She rose the next morning devoid, however, of any plan in spite of a sleepless night spent trying to think of one. But she dressed herself well, for it was Sunday, and if anything was to succeed, she must first cater to their old-fashioned notions of Sabbath decorum. Next, she emphasized the haughty arch of her eyebrows with a facial pencil and, with a regal air, descended the stairs to join them in the breakfast alcove.

Her mother, dressed in a morning outfit, her silver grey hair carefully combed, her matronly features composed, paused from mincing an omlette and posed an unexpected question.

"Darling, may I ask you to do a small favor? Can you entertain Paul Bloomfield for the weekend of August 31? We'd so like it if you would. It would be a nice gesture on your part to return the courtesy the Bloomfields showed us last year when we were the guests at their anniversary dinner in Philadelphia. Paul is coming up here to see his uncle and aunt and, as you know, he is an awfully nice boy."

And, thought Sally, you wouldn't be beyond hoping that a more than casual date might occur, would you? The Bloomfields were a wealthy and highly respected family, prominent in Philadelphia real estate circles, and a match between her and Paul would be all that her parents could hope for. But boy! — what a surprise she had for them.

But as she heard this request of her mother's—blam! —the idea struck that what excellent reasons it suggested for selling Kirke to them. Kirke, like Paul, had all the desirable qualifications—he was upper-class, he would, sometime, undoubtedly inherit a great deal from his parents, he was most acceptable, and he was on his way to a fine career—and the top.

And as far as she was concerned, he was one swell guy. Aside from the rashness of their marrying so soon, he was an ideal candidate. But she felt a bit worried about that obstacle. Then she suddenly became aware that her mother was awaiting her reply. Picking up her napkin, she addressed her.

"I'm sorry, Mom, but I can't see Paul. I have a very good reason for turning you down. I've met a boy who is working at Bosworth's for the summer—and I''ve been seeing a lot of him these past eight weeks and what do you think—I've fallen in love! Romance has blossomed in my lfe—and it's great! I've been knocked for a loop! So I'm not interested in having anything to do with Paul Bloomfield."

"Well, now—this tale has caught me napping," cried her mother, her urbanity broken but replaced by a rapturous smile. "However, I'm delighted for you, dear. It's about time for you to marry—after all, you're twenty-two. Now, tell me, what's the name of the boy? Where is he from?" She leaned forward, on the qui vive, to hear her daughter's answer.

"Kirke Moore," began Sally hopefully. "Now, listen to this: he's the son of Dr. William Moore, the distinguished neurosurgeon who lives right here in Manhassatt. You know of the doctor, don't you—at least by reputation? Now that indicates background, doesn't it? It's first class, of course. Also, and this I know to be extremely important to you: I expect that his parents will give him a considerable inheritance when he marries—most likely some cash and property out in Syosset."

"That does help," commented her mother dryly.

Her father pondered, then asked, "How old is he?"

"Two years older than me—twenty-four. And last but not least, he's as handsome as they come."

"Well, of course, that is nice to hear," said her mother with a lively twinkle in her eye, "Now, what does he look like? Describe him to me."

"Mother, he's just gorgeous! He's got wavy brown hair, the most entrancing hazel eyes, regular features; he's six feet with a beautiful build he got from being on the swimming team during his undergraduate years at Columbia and all the manners, personality and polish I could want. I'm very lucky; I've landed a superb guy."

Her father rose to his feet, crossed his arms and strode back and forth the length of the breakfast room.

"Well, all this, as your mother has just said, is very nice..."

"When did he propose?" interrupted her mother "A week ago."

"I'll bet that was an exciting moment."

"And we want to get married real soon," said Sally hurriedly. "Opportunity like this rarely knocks twice, and we want to turn it to good account." Then she plunged ahead. "Now look here," she continued, "I have to tell you something you're going to be rather worried to hear."

"What the devil is it?" anxiously inquired her father.

"Well, as everything is happening so fast..."

Her father anticipated her. "You mean he doesn't have a real job in prospect?" Sally nodded.

As she said this, her parents stared straight through her.

"Well, this does pose a problem," said Mrs. Parks.

"You're in for a heck of a ride," admonished her father.

Sally retained her poise. "He's a very fine young lawyer-to-be; he's in the top fifth of his class, third year, at Cornell Law School. I don't think there's too much to worry about."

Her father said only "H-m-m," put his elbow on the arm of his chair, then leaned forward and remarked, "I hope the young man is as promising as you say he is—for your sake! But to me—well, I dunno." Then he made a sally. "Knowing your impetuous nature, M'dear, I'll bet you're as much to blame as he may be for rushing into this thing."

Sally blushed and laughed. "That is perfectly true." she agreed.

"I don't think you can be as optimistic as you think," interposed her mother. "I would suppose—contrary to what you intend—that Kirke cannot continue with law school. Won't he just have to go to work," she concluded wearily, "and give up every chance he has to be a lawyer?"

"And after he's driven a truck for awhile he'll get thoroughly fed up with that and everything else including his marriage," declared her father.

"We're not that weak!" exploded Sally. "Kirke is going to finish law school." Then she exclaimed, "Kirke's parents will see us through. After all, they've paid his bills so far with both tuition and living costs. And I'll make a contribution; I'll go to work to help out."

"Oh—I see you've thought of everything," said her father rather waspishly. " For the immediate future, anyway."

"And as far as a job is concerned, we're no worse off than a lot of young couples. I have an ace in the hole. We'll make out allright."

"What's the ace?"

"Nothing more than a probability, at present, but don't worry—I have confidence."

Assuming his full professional diginity, Reverend Parks reflected for a long moment. Then he spoke in a tone of benign resignation. "Well, now I guess you've given us no grounds for objecting—at least, not too strongly."

She raced to him. "Thank you, Dad! You're a peach." She flung her arms about his neck and kissed him.

He stroked the back of her head. "And so are you—in spite of yourself." She then ran to her mother.

"Thank you, too," she cried, bending over her chair and embracing her. Mrs. Parks responded by returning her hug and speaking to her most affectionately.

"Although both of you are very young—well..." Then dismissing further objections, "Now, when can we meet Kirke?"

"This weekend."

"Have you set the date for the wedding?"

"It'll be during the middle of September." Then she faced both of them.

"Don't worry, either of you. We'll be allright." Then, utterly worn out, she suddenly grasped the table edge and slumped into the chair beside it.

Mrs. Parks poured them all a cup of coffee. After a sip, she sat back and announced, with a touch of pride, "It's time to leave for church. And isn't it a most appropriate time to go?"

Sally then broached another surprise.

"Listen," she said, "you know the gossip which will attend our wedding, if it were a big one. It's so sudden, people would wonder. Why don't we just have a private ceremony at which only you, Kirke's parents and a few close friends would be present? I think that would be best."

To this proposal her parents, after consulting, readily agreed so that Sally, having surmounted all problems so far, felt so euphoric that she considered the final topic—the discussion of finance—with Kirke's parents with the utmost confidence.

Chapter 4

On Thursday night, Sally accompanied Kirke to the home of his parents. Dr. and Mrs. Moore received them cordially. However, when Kirke informed them of the proposed circumstances of their marriage, Sally was dismayed to see a worried expression flit across Mrs. Moore's face and his father become mildly irate.

"What in the devil are you attempting to do?" he cried. "Your idea, Sally, of Kirke's being able to step into a cushy job right out of college based on the mere fact that you think you can appeal to somebody in the firm, is most problematical. In my opinion, it's crazy."

"That is what I think," said Mrs. Moore most emphatically.

"Well," countered Sally, "As I have an excellent record, I don't think I'd have any trouble landing back at Bosworth's until Kirke could get something, so the risk is not as great as you think."

"Well, that may be true, but it's still too much of a rush," objected Mrs. Moore. "'Too much of a rush. For Heaven's sake, wait for the next year until Kirke finishes school. After all, you two haven't known each other for long, and you may have heard of the old saying, 'Marry in haste; repent at leisure.'"

Sally emphatically shook her head in disagreement as Kirke replied "We don't want to wait for a year. We're both of age, and we're very sure we want to do it right now."

"Is that the only reason?" asked Dr. Moore sarcastically.

Even as she blushed, Sally thought it was impossible for him to avoid thinking like that. "Yes," she replied evenly. "You know that people don't wait for years nowadays. That's old hat."

The Ruins at Uxmal

"I suppose that's true," said Mrs. Moore.

""Oh, bosh!" said Dr. Moore. "Why not wait?"

"Because we have confidence in ourselves and our futures, if you must have another reason. I've just explained why we don't think there's much risk. And, last but not least, we're two young people in love. That should be enought to convince you."

"You think that takes care of our objections," said Dr. Moore. He shook his head. "Your financial status—"

"That'll work out, I'm sure," said Sally.

"Is that so?" snapped Dr. Moore.

"Why shouldn't it?" said Sally. "Kirke will be an educated lawyer, and I'm a skilled worker. We'll have a fine future. Frankly, I think we're approaching this thing quite sensibly."

"Well, I don't," Dr. Moore continued in a tone of finality, "and to insure that you actually do be sensible, I won't support Kirke and you for this final school year. The two of you can go to work immediately and earn enough to complete your education by yourselves."

"Dr. Moore," said Sally expostulating, "that would only set us back, and we're anxious to get on with our lives..."

"My dear," he replied exasperatedly, "I'm doing this because what I think you both need is a good strong dose of reality. You, Kirke, haven't a job, you both want to marry too soon—the whole idea is ridiculous! I think you'd both be better off finding out what the score is—in real life, out there."

"I agree with what your father proposes," said Mrs. Moore.

"But—," said Sally, protesting.

"Now that makes two of us," said Dr. Moore. "For Heaven's sake, listen to us- and do as we say. And understand—we're adamant about how we feel." As he rose to his feet, signifying the end of the interview, Sally noted Kirke's crestfallen features, but only disregarded them and became more determined than ever to achieve her goal.

As she walked with Kirke down the driveway to his car, he turned to her.

"That finishes us, as far as getting married right away, I guess. We'll have to wait a year. It's too bad, hon, too bad."

"Not yet," retorted Sally, "I have one final card to play."

"Really? What is it?"

As they stood by the door of the car, Sally realized that if she lost this final gamble her marriage—and everything else—would go by the boards. To wait a year—that was out! In a year's time, she might lose Kirke. That loss must somehow be prevented! David must confirm—he must confirm—that he could place Kirke in the firm—now! But could he? That is what she had to find out.

"Before I play it," she said, "remember your promise to me."

"Yes, I remember my promise. And your certainly worth taking a risk for! You were magnificent! —standing up to my parents the way you did. I would be an absolute fool to walk out on a woman like you!"

"We can do it by eloping," she finished quite calmly.

"Elope?" he cried, startled. "My Gosh! You mean, to hell with our parents..." She nodded. He blinked, astounded, then dubiously, "Well—you may be right. But I don't know..." He tossed his head, then, "And after that the problem of the job—"

"Listen, I'm pretty damn sure I can get you that job. But first, you'll have to marry me."

"You sonuva gun, you're making up my mind." Then, "Well, I'm willing. But—Mother and Dad will be—"

"I can take care of them. Leave it to me."

"How in the devil?"

"I'll simply do it by making a phone call. You can watch over my shoulder." She paused.

"But first, let's locate a justice of the peace. We'll take tomorrow off and do it that way, let the church go. Come on, now."

After she had located the justice at the county courthouse the following morning and arranged for them to meet with him at 1 p.m.,Sally said, "You're going to become a married man." She smiled.

She expected the ceremony to be disappointing—and it was: a perfunctory service performed by an indifferent official, a casual routine taking only a few undramatic minutes from their lives. After it was over, she willed the vivid recollection of its mundaneness from her mind, took Kirke by the hand and made a journey to the nearest phone booth in the lobby where, summoning her nerve, she made her important call.

"David?" she said, "This is your sister." Then she spoke straightforwardly. "You know, hon, you're so good I feel—I really do—that I could ask anything of you, and if you had the power, you'd do it for me. Is that right?"

A chuckle on the other end of the line. "What are you up to, now?"

"I have to ask you to do something important for me—real important."

"You do, eh? Well—what's on your mind?"

"I have to make a request of you. Understand that it is very important. It's about a job in the firm next year for—"she laughed self-consciously—then her voice rose, intensely, tremulously, "Listen, Dave, this man is much more than a friend of mine!"

"A job—you say for much more than a friend of yours?"

"Dave, this person—this gentleman—his name is Kirke Moore—has just become my husband."

"Well, I'll be damned!"

"Yes, he has. Now what do you think of that?"

"What do I think of that? Well—consarne! —what you've just said is enough to sink the duck! Give me a sec to recover! I'm fit to be tied! Married! Hell—I can't think of anything to say! What the devil—Oh, well—oh-naturally, I'm delighted for you, dear. Please accept my best wishes."

"I felt you would be pleased. And you'll be pleased more to learn that Kirke is the son of a distinguished neuro-surgeon right here in Manhassatt. He's all class."

"Well, that's just great. But what does the family say to all of this? They must've been terribly surprised."

"They don't know about it yet. We eloped, so we did it in a jiffy—for reasons I'll tell you about someday, but not now."

"Won't they be surprised? Hope the house doesn't fall down. However, I feel sure they'll be pleased—Mother especially. They'll take it allright. But it's just like you—to stir things to a boil. But now, to you, kiddo—good luck, my best—and all of that. And extend my congrats to the fellow—he's getting a rare gal. He certainly is. But now, didn't you say something about a job?'"

"Listen, dear, as part of that good luck, we need a bit of it right now. And I hope you can give it to us."

"How?"

The Ruins at Uxmal

"Dear, this fellow I'm married to is going to be a lawyer. And here's where you come in. I'm very interested in having him go to work for you."

"Oh, I see."

"Listen, Dave, he has everything you'd want: he's one of the top men in his class at Cornell Law School, third year. He's on the editorial board of the Cornell Law Review. He's a magnificent prospect, just the kind of a man you and the firm could use."

"Well, good."

"Now, I've got to know if the prospect of a job in the firm is definite—by this time. When you first told me of your appointment to your new position, and later at dinner, a good job for somebody, from what you said, was pretty certain. Have things happened in the last three weeks to make it absolutely definite? I have to know; our future depends on it."

For a moment she listened intently to his reply, then suddenly squealed, and cried, "Oh hon, that's great—thank you, thank you so much! Oh I could just love you to pieces! But now—oh, listen, hon, I'm sorry but I've got to go. I've got to say good-bye, I've got to run. We're in the county courthouse, and Kirke is waiting." She then hung up, her face radiant.

"You're in," she said to Kirke. "Absolutely." Then clapping her hands exultantly, "Your parents won't have a leg to stand on to bar you from finishing law school."

"You're right," said Kirke. "They'll consent. I have a sure feeling they will. So we can stop worrying and thinking we're defeated. We aren't."

"How right you are!" Sally exclaimed. "Tomorrow we'll go tell them the news. Then it'll be clear sailing until graduation next year."

Jeremy S. Wood

Chapter 5

On September 23 Sally joyfully arrived with Kirke at Cornell. Here, she thought, is the bedrock to our future. Everything is dependent on Kirke, and Kirke is dependent on his education. It was so vital, nothing must interfere with it. Then, while Kirke registered for rooms at the student center—the Willard Straight Hall—situated on the middle of three ascending plateaus covering an area four miles square in the mountainous region of the Finger Lakes in upstate New York, from its terrace she commanded a bird's eye view of half the campus—also to be her way station enroute to her preparation for the role she was to play as the educated wife of a big-time lawyer. She thought, thank God, the financial wherewithal to reach their goal had been assured. Gazing to her right was, first, the library, the intellectual Mecca of the university, a big potential aid on their road to success—with a tall clocktower and beyond that, in the shape of an immense rectangle, the arts and engineering campus. She was going to audit two classes in the arts in that campus if, as she intended to work, her schedule permitted. Then, peering up and rearward she saw a rising hillside, two buildings and much shrubbery which concealed the agricultural school, stated in the university bulletin to be as large as the arts and engineering campus. This, while intriguing because it gave her a rounded picture of the university, did not have for her the relevance of either the arts campus or the Myron Taylor Law School, located in one gigantic building about one hundred yards to the left of the Straight. It was in this latter structure, she realized, that the foundations of a glorious future for her family would be laid, to be achieved by the success of her husband. Then, looking further to the left down the road which ran before the student center was Collegetown, an area of rooming houses and a few small restaurants, inhabited by students who chose to live off-campus during their upper-class or graduate years. And it was there she and Kirke would reside and prepare for their daily adventures. As she reflected further on her potential future, the surrounding physical beauty of their world struck her. She recalled that on approaching the university from the nearby town of Ithaca, she had delighted in the fall splendor of the countryside. There was Cascadilla Gorge, bordering one side of the campus, a chasm resplendent with cascading waterfalls and whose rocky sides were dotted with small bushes in full bloom. On the horizon she had noted Cayuga Lake and hills over the whole surrounding area dotted with greenery. As she thought on how lovely the scene was, she felt that there was no more entrancing locale for them than this university. The entire spread confirmed her belief that she would be entering a magnificent place where Kirke's studies would prepare them for an ascent to the social and financial pinnacle she ardently desired. She then decided that they should first make inquiries about student apartments for couples, and, after a long search during the rest of the morning, they picked one near the campus in Collegetown. After completing that job, to satisfy her curiosity, she proposed visiting the arts campus. This feature was most engrossing to her. She saw that it fulfilled her idea of what the setting of a university campus should be. Six gray stone buildings enclosed a huge, grassy square which was crisscrossed corner to corner by sidewalks with a bronze statue of the university's first president, Andrew Dixon White, at the center. A number of trees adorned one end of the square and lent a countrified air to the scene. Sally felt a new surge of enthusiasm in the courses she expected to take, together with a marked determination that her children should also have the same educational opportunities.

As the day ended, walking the distance with Kirke to the Straight for dinner, Sally felt overjoyed with their new surroundings and looked forward to what the future might hold for them.

Chapter 6

On waking on the morning of September 28 Sally really rejoiced. School starts, she happily thought. She rose early to prepare breakfast. As she did so, she thought that with the rapid sequence of events in her life, the occasion of her marriage—such a brief affair—was only minor to what lay before her. Her nuptial ceremony now seemed more a preparation for the time to come than anything else. Therefore, she paid no undue attention to the recollection; her concern was for life at Cornell. Kirke's life and hers! Her ideals would be fulfilled with a man she was crazy about. She kissed Kirke good morning and, as he arose from the table, gaily said, "Remember, bring only good news when you come home."

He saluted her. "Of course, Madam, of course."

After Kirke had left for his eight o'clock class, she felt in the mood to enjoy the day. As she had only secured a part-time job, she had the mornings off. She decided to mosey up to the Straight for another cup of coffee and doughnut before ten o'clock class. Arrivng at nine, she found the place crowded. Boys, usually tieless, wearing corduroy jackets and slacks and coeds in oversize sweaters and saddle shoes caused her to note humorously the individuality of her own clothes—a dress, stockings and low-heeled Oxfords. It troubled her not at all that her apparel was unlike that of other students. She felt too old to be a Josie College; furthermore, she was just here to get all she could out of her chance to learn so as to help provide the best possible preparation for her future status. Now how would her professors impress her?

After arriving at Goldwyn Smith Hall, the major arts building on the campus, bursting with curiosity as to what this academic center of her life was to be like, as she entered the

The Ruins at Uxmal

classroom for her English course she was confronted by the ugliest man she had ever seen, seated at the instructor's desk. She was so astonished she could scarcely ask where she should sit.

In profile the professor resembled a fish. A long bony nose was the most prominent feature of his face from which both chin and forehead receded at acute angles. Pale, slightly grayish cheeks, like an overcast sky, and two cloudy blue eyes which, when he looked at her full face seemed, in spite of their tendency to stare, not to be observing her because of their opacity which strongly suggested a dead sea denizen. His angular, though large-boned body was dressed in a worn gray sport jacket with leather patches at the elbows, unpressed gray slacks and wide, unshined shoes. The only prepossessing trait he had was his hair which, while thin in spots, was turning an attractive iron gray and was carefully combed with the tip of a lock touching his forehead.

The face was very large, however, and the cheekbones high, making him look quite forceful in spite of his grotesque appearance. Sally, utterly amazed, wondered if this creature would behave in as unique a manner as he looked. If he did, well—he would almost certainly be a most unusual individual—with undoubtedly a most unusual mind—which would most definitely shape hers. She waited suspensefully for him to say something uncustomary—and something intellectually intriguing.

She was not disappointed in either respect. When all the class had arrived, the professor languidly swiveled about in his chair and, seeming to ignore the class, said not one word while writing, "Waydon," on the blackboard behind him. Then in a move so effortless as to make him appear utterly supine, he turned to the class and remarked, most casually, even almost indifferently, "That's what I go by."

He then continued, "As my name begins with "W," I have always had the misfortune to be seated in the rear of any class I ever attended. I am, therefore, going to exact revenge for past misdeeds by seating those whose names begin at the end of the alphabet in the first row. The first to be so seated is Mr. Wright, followed by—"

What a manner! She was then surprised even further as he very offhandedly made the assignments for the course, although allowing the students ample time to copy down the name of the text which was a collection of short stories about which they were to write a critical paper "of not more than three pages" on the one assigned for each class—but then said, "For your training in critical thinking." At that Sally gasped with excitement...

Failing to note any other names except her own because of being so fascinated by Professor Waydon's appearance and manner, Sally made here way to her new seat. She expected to spend a very interesting forty-five minutes, but the professor did not oblige.

"As you haven't anything prepared for class, there wouldn't be much point in holding it, would there?" he asked, revealing a set of horse teeth. Then he raised a red hand, displaying large, ugly knuckles and perfunctorily remarked, "You may go."

Sally barely had time to recover from this experience before her next class at eleven in Fine Arts. In this class, Professor Frederick Ward was quite a contrast to Professor Waydon.

Soft spoken and unassuming, very well dressed in a highly conventional manner—light brown suit, polished shoes and figured tie—and with an understated, delicate sense of humor, he induced Sally to feel perfectly at ease and, therefore, stimulated to pay the closest attention to the lecture on the art of ancient Egypt.

The Ruins at Uxmal

It began with architecture. Raptly Sally listened as Professor Ward spoke with an air of authority about the pillar called an obelisk. This man is knowledgeable, she thought. Then for a moment she reflected on what life as a museum curator would be like. She was so fascinated by this art world opening before her that she knew she would retain most of the lecture, even though her notes were scrappy compared to those of the girl seated next to her.

After lunch at the Straight, she went to her job. It was not at all exciting, just a routine filing job. But when she returned home, she was still in a state of euphoria about her two classes.

Excitedly she told Kirke about her professors. Waydon—what a presence! He was not only unusual in appearance, but also different both in dress and manner. And he had promised intellectual stimulation. Here was a person, she felt sure, who was undoubtedly a man who was his own man, who did his own thinking! What a priviledge—and pleasure—to study under him! Her intellectual training would be so uncommon it would definitely fit her to move in any society—any society whatever! And Professor Ward! More conventional, yes, but oh, so knowledgeable! She would be amply repaid for her association with him. He was certainly no slouch. No, nothing must ever interfere with this chance at these opportunities to make herself fit for the life she wished to lead.

She found her husband equally stimulated by his session at law school. His reaction to his professors was also most favorable. Both were equally pleased about Cornell University, and she felt once again that Kirke had made a wise selection in his choice. It seemed to her that their happy future was assured.

As the semester continued Sally felt that her initial enthusiasm was fully justified. As she sat for three months in the English course, she realized even more the true value of the way Waydon conducted it. During every forty-five minute period, there was no lecture at all; the session was devoted entirely to question and answer until the meaning was unearthed. When it came her turn to answer she was literally trembling, both out of fear that her answer would prove unacceptable and a marked curiosity as to the manner of Professor Waydon's reply.

"Wh-a-a-t d'you make out of the theme of this piece of writing?" Waydon would first ask the class. Then, turning his head slowly to gaze penetratingly at her—"Mrs. Moore?"

She gave her answer. Waydon inclined his head slightly in a nod, said nothing as he felt her answer unsatisfactory and nodded again at another student. He followed this procedure until the correct answer was given. Then he slowly smiled in approval and continued to the next point of discussion.

What was always sought was the most penetrating reply which would capture the elusive idea behind the theme of each story. It was all intellectual cogitation; no credit was given for memory—only pure thought counted. Sally reflected again that it was the finest kind of intellectual training to be had; it would establish habits of thought which would be lasting. And this training was to be had only by associating with the type of mind one encounters on the faculty of a major university. She was even more convinced than ever that any child she might have should have this kind of education.

Her feelings about the Fine Arts course were equally enthusiastic. Although being strictly lectures, requiring only note-taking and memorization, it proved fascinating because it introduced her to the history of ancient civilization as presented through their art. She enjoyed it all—from the study of Egyptian culture through that of the Mesopotamian in the Fertile Crescent and, later in the semester, to that of the Greeks and Romans. And as the semester progressed she became even more impressed with the value of her cultural education for the status she hoped to eventually assume. The only interruption to her thoughts occurred as Christmas approached, which she looked forward to spending with her husband at her parents' home on Long Island.

Chapter 7

When the festive Christmas day had come and passed, Sally still anticipated the further joy of the annual New Year's dance at the Sewane Country Club. On that evening, after donning her formal dress, she judged her appearance before her husband in the bedroom of her parents home and was thoroughly pleased.

"Don't you like this expensive dress?" she asked him. "What a Christmas gift from my parents! With the white pumps with roses across the toes, I am really dressed." She imagined herself a member of the beau monde.

She delicately rubbed her shoes on the backs of her stockings to remove any specks of dust and carefully checked the arrangement of her hair. She saw she was absolutely bewitching. She knew her dark brown hair, cut in bangs, framed her comely features and her white skirt slit to just above the knee and a blue blouse with a decolletage neckline trimmed in ermine appealingly clothed her chunky, rounded figure. She felt really ready to party.

As she left the house, she paused only on the hall stairs to shout, "We're going," to her mother when she took her husband's arm before continuing to the garage. In the gayest of moods, she remarked, "You're the handsomest man ever, dressed up in your white tie and tails, you look like a top-flight lawyer on your way to dinner with the Governor," while slipping into the seat of the car beside him.

A crowd had assembled at the club when Sally and Kirke arrived, accompanied by her sister, Eileen, whose date, a young doctor, had been delayed by an emergency at the hospital. Sally recognized a number of her high school classmates among the becomingly coiffed women in elegant gowns and their escorts dressed either in tails or black suits and was rather amused— being so dressed up they looked somewhat out of the character she remembered.

"What they're wearing tonight reminds me of your father's party," she remarked. "There, everybody was ready for the dress circle at the opera."

"Well, he's quite an old bird," replied Kirke. "He deserved it."

"My father told me he was very highly regarded for his competence," commented Sally.

"He earned many honors," replied Kirke, "but one in particular stands out in my memory. You know, in 1939 the Nassau County Medical Society, in a deciding vote to elect the Physician of the Year for New York State, chose him. When I think of the letter of commendation Dad received from the mayor, I just can't tell you how pleased I was."

"He's somebody you can be proud of," remarked Eileen.

As Kirke said "Yes," rather wistfully, Sally felt that he was thinking deeply of this tribute to his father. She realized how high the standards were which he felt he had to live up to. That accounted for his ambition, upon which her hopes rested. The doctor had graduated from Harvard as a Phi Beta Kappa, had held a notable string of appointments at Columbia Presbyterian Medical Center, had made a number of significant contributions in medical research and had served his practice steadfastly in Manhassatt for thirty years.

"In addition to all that he does," Kirke then said, "he is outstanding in other respects as well. He is a good father. And he is a good person. I recall my Mom once characterizing him as a saint, and as far back as I can remember, he always has been.. He almost never loses his temper. Everybody who knows him loves him."

"In short," said Sally, "he is an exemplary man."

"Nevertheless, having that kind of an old man," said Kirke, confirming her deduction, "doesn't make for an easy life for his son."

"Because, as you've been given everything, much is expected of you, eh?"

He nodded.

She knew he had been very privileged. He had undoubtedly been introduced when young into the finest circles in local society, academically prepared for the best universities and always shielded against condescension and economic hardship. Unquestionably contingent upon all this, however, was the presumption of his parents that he would do well in whatever he attempted. She reckoned that he had learned early that to be a lotus-eater was not in his family tradition.

But is that such a tough condition, she asked herself. Having been protected against any setbacks she knew that he felt, with the egotism of youth, that he could attain any goal he really desired. She knew he felt quite confident that the world belonged to him.

She nudged him. "I'd like to circulate and say, 'Hello,' to the gang here. Take me around, will you?"

She admired his savoir faire as he took her arm, and they moved towards the crowd in the lounge. She figured that if their lives worked out the way she assumed they would, she and Kirke would gain entree to the social life of the New York business aristocracy, an aristocracy much much higher on the social scale than the one with which she was familiar. She knew that they spent their summers at fashionable parties in imposing homes in Glen Cove, Oyster Bay or Northport or sojourned in cabanas on the beaches in the Hamptons and attended the polo matches at Westbury. She hoped to have all those stimulating experiences in the future. Yes, she had done right in snagging him as a husband; she was absolutely sure of that.

Chapter 8

The music of the orchestra was wonderful, the pianist performed a lilting solo arrangement of "Ain't Misbehavin'," but the dazzle of the man she was with totally preoccupied Sally. When Kirke left for a minute to order some drinks, she tried to think of some way she could please him. Stymied for the moment, however, she turned to her sister, Eileen.

"What could I do that would really please Kirke?" she asked her.

"Get his stories published," said her youthful but quick-minded sister.

"Now that's an idea," agreed Sally. When Kirke returned she said to him, "I've been wondering if I could help get those stories you showed me in print. I know a few publishers, of course, and if I put in some good words about your things, they might possibly be willing to give them a more careful reading than some flunky who'd just get 'em together with a whole lot of other stuff he'd have to read."

"Why that's sweet of you, honey, to think of that," exclaimed Kirke.

"Just a favor to help budding talent," she remarked matter of factly, and threw a look of appreciation at Eileen. Her sister was pretty good. Only seventeen and with a Radcliffe scholarship next fall. Sally had all the affection of an older sister, and it was reinforced by Eileen's warm regard for Kirke. Sally knew Eileen regarded him almost as a big brother and greatly admired him for his dash. She even laughingly acknowledged that her sister was a trifle envious of her. In addition to this flattering tribute to her taste, perceiving that the offer had put Kirke in an even more agreeable state of mind than ever, she thoroughly enjoyed a most pleasant evening until the clock on the wall in the lounge told her it was time to go home.

When they gathered to go, Sally saw that Eileen's date had already left, having unexpectedly been called back to the hospital. She was happy to see however, that her sister's spirits were not dampened by his departure; they remained high as their car entered the Sunrise Highway between Bethpage and Manhassatt. But although traffic was light and the night clear, she was a bit nervous. She realized that those conditions, in spite of the wet pavement from an early evening rain, in combination with his exuberant feelings had made Kirke more than a trifle heady. Unthinkingly he had accelerated the speed of the car. Even though she voiced a warning cautioning him to slow down at an intersection, he failed to heed the danger of excessive speed.

Suddenly she felt the car skid. She screamed as it left the road; a tall steel pole, placed in the center island to assist snowplows, appeared in front. As the automobile struck the pole a glancing blow; she saw Eileen, seated next to her, lurch forward against the windshield; she, herself, thrown violently against her door, had a fleeting glimpse of Kirke being flung out his side as the car careened wildly for a hundred yards, ground up an embankment on the opposite side of the road, turned over and stopped, right side up, badly battered.

After a few moments Sally, recovering from her stunned condition, thought first of her sister. She saw that the windshield was streaked with a red smear where Eileen had been thrown against it. Fear made her aghast. Then a gaping gash in Eileen's head which was twisted askew and rested unnaturally on one shoulder almost made her faint. Lying in the seat, her sister seemed lifeless.

She saw Kirke, staggering, appear in the doorway of the car.

"Are you hurt?" he cried hysterically.

The Ruins at Uxmal

"No. But—My God! Look at Eileen! Oh, Kirke, what'll we do?" She clutched frantically at him. "Are you allright?"

"I've got a pain in my right knee, but I can move. I think I'll be ok."

"Thank God!" Then, in a flurry of desperation, "Get some help!"

"How the devil can I do that?"

"Oh, God, I don't know—go out to the highway and flag somebody," she cried frenziedly. Then she turned to her sister.

As Kirke, reeling, left, a man's yell startled her.

"My God, he's walking away from it."

Sally saw a bearded individual followed by a woman run up from their car which they had stopped when they saw the accident happen. Too dazed to comprehend their excited questioning as they looked inside the wrecked vehicle, all she heard was one caution from the woman, "Try to keep calm, dear; try not to lose control of yourself."

Sally managed to peer intently over the man's shoulder as he looked at Eileen. Eileen still made no movement. She felt her stomach turn over as he said, "It looks as if she's badly hurt. My God—she might even be dead." Then she heard him order his companion, "Honey, drive back to that allnight cafeteria we passed and call the hospital."

Getting out of the car left her exhausted. Then, although managing an "I'm allright," to the man's questioning look, she could only watch numbly as he addressed Kirke. "I see you're hurt, buddy. You wait here. I'll stand in the road and flag the next police car."

"No," replied Kirke, "I'll get some flares from the trunk of the car and help you"

Left alone, the thought my God, what has he done rushed into her mind. Looking again at her sister, she whispered pleadingly, "Eileen, are you allright?" Eileen did not stir. Feeling sick, she retched and then, terrified, cried, "No, please God, no! She isn't dead."

Brakes squealed as a car stopped, interrupting her anxiety. "Thank God," she thought as a state trooper got out of a police vehicle. Then she saw the bearded man tell the trooper what had happened and that his wife had gone to call the hospital. Next as the trooper approached her, she felt it incumbent to tell him, "My husband's knee has been hurt..."

"If neither of you are bleeding, we'll wait for the medics to take care of you," he said. Then he turned from her, looked at Eileen in the wrecked car, took out a pad and started making notes.

In a few minutes, she saw a second patrol car arrived. Another officer got out and joined them. His first question was, "How bad?"

Sally listened intently as the first officer summarized the situation. "This fellow's been hurt, but he's still walking around; this girl seems ok, but there's one in the car who looks all done in."

At that moment the ambulance arrived. When two medics got out; she saw the first go to the wrecked car, the second, as he approached the group, look first at her.

"Although I look allright, I'm ready to faint," she then said.

The attendant took a small packet from his pocket. "Take this,"he ordered, handing her a pill. "You look as though you need it." Then he turned to Kirke.

Sally winced when Kirke gritted his teeth as the attendant manipulated his knee.

The Ruins at Uxmal

"No break." he said. "It's probably just severely wrenched. But go with us to the hospital so they can x-ray it and see if anything's really wrong." He turned away and joined the other attendant who had procured a stretcher by the wrecked car; the two of them loaded Eileen on to it and put her in the ambulance.

Another car drew up. Sally saw that the officer did not notice it as he continued examining the wrecked vehicle and that Kirke said nothing. She felt a surge of disgust against her husband and was impelled to take over.

"That's your wife, isn't it?" she said to the beared man as a blonde woman got out. As the bearded man said, "Yes," the officer turned to them.

"What's next?" asked Sally.

"We'll have to file a report on this, of course, but you won't have to come to the police station in Mineola." replied the officer. "Have you any relatives living in this area?" Sally nodded. The officer continued. "Well, give me their phone numbers. They'll undoubtedly join you at the hospital. Leo will call the station and tell it to contact them."

She then looked at Kirke who was distraught. "Courage, dear. Courage."

"It was all my fault," he blurted out, apologeticallly. "I wasn't watching the speed limit and..."

"Yeah," said the officer, agreeing, "and that pole you hit—it would stop a plow."

"What do we all do now?" Sally then inquired.

After taking the phone numbers of their parents, the officer continued. "You two'll be taken to the hospital." Then he indicated the bearded man. "We'll need him and his wife as witnesses. They'll be contacted to appear at the hearing."

"Ok, I understand. Now would you please, tell them"—indicating the attendants—"to hurry, Officer. My husband...His knee..."

The officer nodded and spoke to a medic. Then, "Bub, get into the ambulance."

"I'd like to ride with him," said Sally.

"Ask them," said the officer, indicating the medics.

As they made no objection, Sally got into the ambulance. Kirke looked at her and wailed, "What if she dies?"

At that she almost broke. Looking at the officer standing in the open rear doorway of the ambulance, she saw that he was also irritated, by the question. Then she thought his responce was only appropriate, "Buster, this is no time for that. Just sit tight, and we'll soon know all the answers."

The driver then started the engine, and Sally, clutching Kirke's right hand, seated herself beside him as they left for the hospital in Mineola.

Chapter 9

On the way the hapless Sally, ready to collapse, her mind whirling with terrifying imaginings, huddled with Kirke on a bench in a corner of the ambulance while the interns ministered to Eileen. Finally, after she had waited some torturing minutes, one glanced at her.

In a somber voice he said, "This accident was very bad." Then, "Is she any relation to either of you?"

Sally nodded. "My sister." Then she felt the pressure of his grip on her shoulder.

"She's dead, I'm afraid. From a broken neck." In a gentler tone he added, "I'm terribly sorry, but there was nothing we could do."

"Oh, my God!" cried Sally, her head whirled and she felt terribly faint. Kirke broke down completely and began sobbing.

The intense compassion in the intern's voice became even more evident to her.

"She went very quickly. She didn't suffer. That should be some consolation to you."

Then he bent over her and raised his voice slightly.

"What if she had survived as a cripple? Unable even to get out of a chair. Take it from me—it's better this way."

Sallly, in shock, only moaned while Kirke continued to shake. The intern turned away and pulled a sheet over the body of Eileen.

When the ambulance had drawn up before the emergency room entrance, Sally saw two attendants waiting with wheelchairs for both of them, and she and Kirke were wheeled into the reception room. As one of the interns spoke to an attendant at the desk about transferring Eileen to the hospital morgue, Sally lapsed into obliviousness.

After a few minutes the arrival of the police caused her to raise her head. One approached her and said gruffly, "The parents of you two will be here pretty quick."

Over the officer's shoulder Sally saw a nurse. As she came up to them she handed them pills and cups of water from a tray. "Take them," she ordered. "They'll calm you down." Then Sally listened fearfully as the nurse told Kirke she was wheeling him away for an examination. Afterwards she closed her eyes.

A few minutes later, Kirke returned and tapped her on the shoulder. "Dear, my parents are here," he muttered.

Sally looked and saw Dr. and Mrs. Moore on the other side of the reception room. Dr. Moore was addressing the officers. Sally looked intently at them. Intense worry showed on both their faces. Then his father turned away from them and addressed Kirke and her.

"What happened to you?"

"I'm allright," said Sally, "but Kirke—"

Kirke pointed to his knee. "The x-ray showed that it has been wrenched."

His mother crossed herself. "Thank God, it's only thatl" she exclaimed and then her pent-up feelings erupted in a harrangue.

"How did you lose control of the car? My God, you know how to drive. D'you realize—oh, my God!" She clapped her hands to her face and broke down, weeping.

His father attempted to interpose calm.

"Dear, please, please, try to calm yourself! Please now, please calm down."

The Ruins at Uxmal

"Yes," said Sally, "I can't stand any more. Now, for God's sake, what happens next?"

Dr. Moore turned to the police officers. Mrs. Moore, tightly clutching a wadded handkerchief, stood stock-still, her attention riveted on the exchange taking place between them.

The first officer supplied the information, then concluded by saying, "Your son will be arraigned within seventy-two hours. You won't have to wait long."

At that moment Sally's parents arrived. Jim Parks, white-faced and tieless, looking as if he had received a death sentence, first looked anxiously at Kirke and her, then accosted Dr. Moore; his wife, coatless and with scarcely any make-up, first uttered a deeply sympathetic,"You poor children," as she saw them, then sank into a chair, seemingly unable to observe what was taking place.

Sally heard Kirke's father, as he spoke to Jim Parks, seeming almost to plead for mercy.

"Jim—my God—my boy was at fault. He was driving too fast, the car skidded on wet pavement and—," he wrung his hands—"Eileen—," he wrung his hands again, "was killed.

The other acknowledged his utterance with a benumbed look. "Awful, just awful," he muttered.

Events transpired in a bustling pattern which Sally was almost too dazed to follow. All she remembered was a jumble of orderlies and nurses hurrying about, the police officers talking to all the parents and then the latter exchanging pathetic comments with each other.

After a few minutes her father took her mother's arm and resignedly announced, "There's nothing more to do here," and then to Kirke, "With your crutches you can walk, can't you?" Then to Dr. and Mrs. Moore, "Let's all meet at our house."

As her family arrived home first, Sally next saw Mrs. Moore in the vestibule as she turned suddenly to her husband and asked a searching question.

"What if he is convicted of manslaughter?"

Sally cast a frightened look at Kirke's father, but he ignored it, led his family into the living room and motioned for them to be seated first. She then saw that her father was too distraught to say anything. He just picked up a decanter from an end table, poured six glasses of sherry and, after handing them round, sat down heavily on the sofa. His wife, numb from shock, just sat in her chair, staring blankly at the wall.

Sally thought Kirke's father appeared somewhat doubtful as he answered his wife. "I hope it will not be that...manslaughter..." He shook his head.

Looking upward, as if to God, Mrs. Moore ignored his reply and immediately asked, "Isn't that terribly serious?"

Slumping wearily back in his chair, he replied, "Well, it's not murder—be glad of that." Then he forced himself to revive and continued, "But, depending on the degree of culpability—which I hope will be slight..."

Sally's voice betrayed her anxiety as she interrupted, "How can you hope that?"

The doctor collected his thoughts. "Because the officer said there was obviously no deliberate intent." Sally nodded, sat back and stared at the ceiling.

The doctor then added, "Let's all hope he will be tried for negligent homicide." He reached forth his hand and gently stroked his wife's shoulder. Then he addressed Mr. and Mrs. Parks.

"As I presume—and hope—you will not be vindictive, bail bond presumably will not be required, and he will be released on his own recognizance—temporarily, of course." He drew a deep breath. "The trial will be held probably in a month or two."

"Will he have to go to jail?" asked Mrs. Moore.

"I hope not," replied the doctor, his features grim. "But he will almost certainly be put on probation."

Mrs. Moore looked down at her hands.

"Still, he will have to bear the burden of this for the rest of his life. I pray it will not break him.

His father only slumped into his chair and uttered a poignant sigh.

Chapter 10

On the fateful day of Kirke's arraignment, as the family car proceeded along Mineola `Avenue on the way to the courthouse, Sally observed their parents muttering exchanges betraying their anxiety that he might be tried for manslaughter. Their misgivings immeasurably augmented her own. And when she got out of the car, the leaden-colored stone steps and the heavy bronze portals of the entryway seemed to symbolize the oppression weighing heavily on her. As she climbed the steps, her tension mounted even further.

Inside the courtroom, she gasped when Kirke had to grasp the arm of his attorney, Robert Johnson, as the judge summoned them before the bench. Next, she saw his ashen appearance as he waited for the judge.to speak.

In a peremptory manner the judge questioned him.

"Are you aware of the charges filed against you?"

"Yes sir," he answered meekly.

"Do you wish to have them read?"

Then she saw Robert Johnson raise his hand. "No, Your Honor," he said. The judge nodded.

"Your Honor," said Johnson, "the sister and parents of the deceased wish the District Attorney to be informed of their petition for leniency for the defendant."

The judge nodded again, made a note and then spoke in a more kindly manner.

"Because, as the police report says, there was no deliberate attempt to commit the crime, the mandate will be made to the

The Ruins at Uxmal

District Attorney to give your petition his full consideration in the indictment."

He then took off his spectacles. "The trial will be held six weeks from today's date on February 15. That is all. The court is adjourned."

Being quite relieved, Sally took the arm of her husband, leading him, utterly drained, before Johnson from the courtoom.

Outside, she tried to comfort him.

"Look darling," she said, "you know that if you're tried for negligent homicide, it'll just be for comitting a misdemeanor. That'll only mean a maximum fine of one thousand dollars, plus a year of being on suspension from a jail sentence—you'll probably get that as we requested leniency for you."

He looked at her agonizingly. "I hope so," he said as he walked unsteadily to the open door of the car.

Three days afterwards, as they sat in church for Eileen's funeral service, Sally thought of the future. What would happen to that? She felt almost at her wit's end. Was this funeral the end of all her hopes? Then she looked at Kirke and thought about her immediate problem. Kirke seemed, at first, hardly in a condition to sit through the minister's eulogy. However, as he listened to it, he impressed her as gaining surcease from the morbid thoughts of what he had done. As he nodded his head, he seemed to her to believe its theme that Eileen's life, although incomplete on earth, would be fulfilled in Heaven was really true. But as for her, she was too distressed over the death of her sister to believe anything; all she felt was that she was hearing a lot of eyewash. After all, what did the minister really know? Then, for the first time, she felt a surge of anger against her husband. He had killed Eileen. He had ruined all her hopes! Out of pure carelessness. Damn him! But then her conscience spoke to her, and she reverted to the attitude of Christian piety which had been

47

Jeremy S. Wood

instilled into her since childhood and which overcame her independent thinking.

But at the burial site her resentful mood returned when she saw the coffin being lowered into the grave. She felt the tragedy of Eileen's death so deeply—it contrasted so starkly with the joy of the radiant winter day that it immeasurably increased her anger; she became barely conscious of where she was until her father, seeming to sense her mood, nudged her to rouse her from her thoughts.

Then as the car drove down the road which led from the cemetery to the highway, he spoke to her.

"Look at all the small trees by the gravestones, dear—they're so prettily spaced—she'll be happy here. I know she will."

Sally just gazed fixedly at the floor of the car and shrugged her shoulders. She thought, everything—all their hopes had been destroyed. Was this Christian funeral service anything but a sop in compensation for that loss? Kirke, seated beside her, grasped her hand, but she remained unresponsive. Her mother leaned over him and gently patted her knee.

That night after dinner, as their families were seated in the living room, she again had to put up with the consolations of her father, as he spoke to her and Kirke.

"Look," he said, "what is done is done. Try, please, not to look back on this tragedy—nothing can be served by it. You, Sally, have always been wonderful that way in the past. Try, I repeat, try now, for your own and Kirke's sake, to apply it to this terrible instance. You must. All cannot be over for you. And your mother and I will always be behind you. As for you, Kirke, I know that your parents—" he nodded at them—" feel the same way. The entire future is still ahead of both of you. You must make a go of it, in spite of what has happened."

The Ruins at Uxmal

To this Kirke's father added a cautionary, "If you don't, who knows what will happen to the two of you," as Mrs. Moore nodded in assent.

Then, as Sally thought Kirke was speechless with despair, she was suddenly surprised as he began speaking .

"Jim and Pat," he said in a stiff manner, "I hardly know what to say, but I realize I have to offer to do everything I can..."

"No, that's not necessary, son," quickly replied Jim Parks, speaking very soberly.

"You can't do anything. The loss is irreparable. Besides, you're suffering enough as it is. You can't take on anything more." He cast his head down and looked fixedly at the pattern in the Chinese rug on the floor.

Mrs. Moore seconded him. "Jim's right, Eileen is gone. All we can do is carry on." She took out a handkerchief and dabbed at her eyes.

"If only—only I could make it up to you in some way," said Kirke, looking at Mrs. Parks.

"No, don't try," she replied. "It wouldn't help. Now you and Sally musn't live in the past.

That is over. It's no use to brood over it. You must try not to."

"Yes," said Dr. Moore. "You have your own lives to live, as Jim has just said."

"However, I almost feel like my life is over," said Jim Parks. "Yes," he added reflectively, "but then I wonder—I hope— against Fate that it isn't."

"It's terrible to have you think like that, Dad," said Sally, breaking the agonizing silence that followed. But Jim Park's voice was comforting in reply.

"Don't say that, dear. Although I feel that the Devil has the upper hand for the moment, we, of course, believe in the Almighty and hope he'll pull us through." Then he said weakly, "I think we'll be allright. We'll just have to pray that we recover..."

"I will pray for you, believe me I will," interrupted Kirke.

Mrs. Parks shook her head.

"You're expressing hope—God bless you—but no, that won't happen. The loss, and you really know it, is forever—it's inconsolable. Whatever solace time will bring will be superficial. You never get over something like this." She began to cry.

Jim Parks touched his wife's shoulder. "There, there dear. Try not to cry." He nuzzled her and patted her gently. She responded feebly by drying her eyes and attempting to compose herself. Then Jim Parks said, "It's been a long day. I guess we all ought to turn in."

Sally indifferently shook their hands as Dr. and Mrs. Moore rose to bid everyone good-night and take their departure.

Several days elapsed before Sally could pay attention to anyone. She alternated between sorrowfulness and morosity. All she did was sit in a chair and stare at the floor, occasionally throwing her head back to cry "Christ!" or "Jesus!" or else giving way to a fit of weeping. Kirke was in an equally somber mood, but he retained his self-control, sitting quietly, looking out the front window seeming only to brood. But eventually he said, "I have something to say."

She roused herself to listen attentively to him.

"You know," he said, "since this tragedy has about finished me off, I can't go on with law school This term is just about to start—that's too soon—and no! —definitely! —not even for the next. I don't want to be a lawyer anymore—at least not for the immediate future. It would be too much of a tax. I couldn't possibly concentrate on the work."

"Well, that's understandable," Sally replied indifferently. Then, making an effort, "Do you think the mood will last, be permanent?"

"Possibly, even probably."

"Well, what on earth are we going to do?" she then cried, almost snapping. "You just can't go to pieces! And, for that matter," she then affirmed, "neither can I!"

"I know that," he responded weakly, "but the way I feel—"

"Well, how do you think I feel?" she wailed, breaking into tears. "With you a wreck—not to mention me! Oh, Kirke, are we all washed up?"

His only response was, "I don't know, I don't know."

She realized then that she had to shoulder the burden of responsibility. She made a great effort and got a grip on herself.

"Well," she said, "We've got to live. We've just got to keep going. We just can't go to blazes." Then forthrightly, "You've got to get a job. And so do I."

"Of course, you're right," he agreed. Then, putting his head in his hands. "God, I hope I'll be able to hang on to mine."

"You'd better."

As his attitude reminded her of the loss of their aspirations, her distress welled up again.

"Look at what's happened to the wonderful life you and I had hoped to lead!" she shouted. "Our glorious future together. What's happened to that?"

"I know," he said despondently, "but, dear, I'm just not up to much of anything."

Her testiness increased. "Well, what are we going to do? Think, man, think!"

He put his head in his hands. After a few moments he looked up at her.

"You know, right after the trial, which comes up in five weeks, I guess I'll have to start looking for that job, that is, if the judgment of the court is what we hope it will be."

"You will do that?"

"Yes. I need some job—just some job—to fall into and get my mind off of what's happened."

She nodded her head. "Since you feel that way—understandably, just some old job that, I guess, is all that is open to us. And since we can't keep living off our parents forever, can you think of a line of work you might get into?"

"No, I can't."

"Well let me see," she said. She tried to think.

"I'd like to get away from this pattern of being the well-educated man out for a career," continued Kirke. "That's what any corporation looks for."

Sally suddenly flashed with inspiration.

"True—it's what they're looking for, particularly in the United States. But if you want just a job—what about a job outside the U.S? Candidates ought to be scarcer, and employers might be less choosy about whom they would hire—you know, for a position which career candidates might feel are undesirable—for a third world country, for example."

"That's a good idea. But—I don't think I'd like to leave the country."

"You don't?"

"I haven't the heart for rugged duty, like that."

The Ruins at Uxmal

"You'd better have a heart for something. Look," she said, kindling some enthusiasm, "a change to a foreign environment—some place where your living and your surroundings would be entirely different—would be best to get you over this tragedy. Kind of bury yourself for a couple of years. And pick a small, unknown company—avoid the big boys. You minored in Spanish at Columbia—were pretty good at languages—weren't you? I think you could land a job fairly easily in some firm looking for men like that—in Central America."

"Oh, what the devil am I to do in a foreign country? I'm damned if I want to go off to some place—like in Central America—all of a sudden. Have you lost your marbles?"

"I think it'll be a damned good way for us to recover. It'll give us totally new perspective—a complete change. It's what we need. You'll be fit to resume a new life after that."

"Well, maybe. But I suppose you're right—we do have to get away. But..."

His attitude made her flare. She rose to her feet.

"You don't have a point in your favor..." She broke off and ruminated a moment. "Central America...Spanish is pretty easy to learn—at least in an elementary way. Maybe I could also get some kind of a job—maybe?" She thought further. "And a couple of years away from here would, of course, be a good thing for me, too. Like you I'm about finished off. I have no real enthusiasm to return to school. So what you say deserves some thought."

"I feel it's the right thing."

"Well, let's see what our parents think of the idea."

But, as she lay in bed that night, her depression recurred strongly. Doubt still plagued her. "Do you think you're capable of standing up to a trip out of the country?" she then asked Kirke.

All he said was, "I think so."

At that she nearly felt beaten. She asked herself, what kind of a man had she married? And was she about ready to break? But then the thought that she could have children of her own comforted her. And she realized she was not ready for suicide. She then resolved, for better or worse, to carry on—after all, what other option was there—really?

Chapter 11

The next night, before dinner, Sally advised Kirke to wait until the possible results of the trial had been discussed with all their parents before asking their opinions on the subject of a job for him in the Caribbean area. She felt that a favorable decision would be most probable at that time. When the question was raised, although not surprised at the reaction of his mother, who, immediately flabbergasted, began objecting passionately, she was highly pleased by the statement his father made.

"Considering the type of relief necessary for you two, I would think that after the trial, if its judgment is what we hope for, your idea is not at all unreasonable. Kirke, you aren't—and won't be—for a year or two in any shape to resume the grind at law school, and I think that a billet in which you worked at a routine job for awhile—preferably far away from here—would be the best thing for you. People take ocean trips for the same reason you want to go to the Caribbean—to get their minds off their troubles by getting away from it all. You might even find you liked business better than law, and if you're successful, you'd have a chance to make more money. And you wouldn't have any language difficulty because you minored in Spanish at college."

"I agree with you completely," said Sally. "Get away from it all. What has happened is almost too much to live with."

"Also," continued the doctor, "you know from what was said at dinner last night that Bob Johnson thinks the penalty against you will not be too severe because you, Sally, and your parents requested leniency. The charge will probably be for negligent homicide—you might get off with just a fine and a suspended sentence. You might not even be put on probation."

"And that, of course, would free me to leave the country," said Kirke.

"I don't see how you could be held."

"Now how can you say that?" excitedly interjected Helen Moore. "Leave the country! My Heavens, at this point these two children need all the help they can get—and who but us can really give it to them? They should stay here—at home with us!"

"For about a month that will certainly be necessary," agreed Dr. Moore. "But being kids they're pretty tough, and that need will pass in not too long a time. The important thing after that first stage is to get them occupied doing something completely novel—to get their minds off the immediate past—and an overseas job—a site in Mexico, for example—would be excellent to do just that."

"Well," said Mrs. Parks to Sally, "what are you going to do.?"

"Learn what little Spanish I can in six months and then look for some job I can fit into,"

"Well, you're pretty brave," said Mrs. Parks, "but most women would feel differently about the case of you two, and I think Helen is right. Mexico, you know, is a relatively primitive country, and who knows what kinds of shortcomings you might have to put up with—are you in any shape to face them? I think the best thing, along with Helen, is for you to stay right here—for quite awhile."

"Mother, don't worry," said Sally. "We'll be allright. We're not salt or sugar and won't melt when a little rain falls. After all, we're not going outside civilization, and a job in a foreign country will open up some new interests which will undoubtedly help us. I feel that to go is the right thing."

"I agree with you," said Jim Parks, "provided that you're in good shape when you leave."

The Ruins at Uxmal

"However," said Kirke, "as Dad said, what we do all depends on the outcome of the trial. We'll know what that is in another five weeks. After that, there's nothing but mooning about the past and sinking into the dumps if we stay here—the past will be too much with us for me to function well. Both Sally and I need something really different to pick us up."

"Yes," said Jim Parks, "after you've gotten over the blow."

"Well," said Mrs. Moore, "being a woman I still don't agree, but if you really feel it would be best for you, go ahead—and good luck—although," she added, "it may be lot different—and more difficult—than you think."

"Now that we've allayed all your fears..." said Sally smiling, and then addressed her father. "The next thing is to get a job. Look here, Dad, do you remember that man—oh, what's his name—who was in the congregation when you had your ministry back in Topeka who does business in Mexico?"

"Could I contact him and ask about the possibility of a job for Kirke down there?" asked her father rhetorically. "Yes, dear, I could. Roy Bainbridge was one the staunchest members of my church, and I'm sure he'd be more than willing to help."

"What is his business in?" inquired Kirke.

"He owns and operates a small soft drink bottling business—Crystal Cola is the name of the stuff. He thinks he can cut in to the peripheral business big outfits have established in the smaller towns in Yucatan. In Yucatan, for reasons really unknown to me, he thinks there isn't much profit for big business—-the Indian populations are too sparse or too poor, I guess, for them."

"It sounds just like what I want," responded Kirke enthusiastically. "Yucatan, I imagine, would be very interesting, and it certainly would be different."

"But, as Pat has said, it would be a much more primitive life," countered his mother. "However," she then added, feeling forced to acquiesce, "you're both young and can rough it. But be careful of what you eat and drink—raw vegetables and fruit without skin." She shook her head. "And always drink bottled water. I don't want either of you coming down with an attack of amoebic dysentery. And last but not least," she concluded, "even brush your teeth with it."

"We'll take all precautions," said Sally, as everybody laughed.

"Well," said Jim Parks, "since everything but the outcome of the trial has been settled, we'll just have to wait for that, and, then, if everything is ok, I'll write Roy Bainbridge and make inquiries."

"It certainly is nice of you to help us in this way," said Sally. "My thanks."

"Mine too," added Kirke.

"And also mine," said Dr. Moore. "Lets hope that everything works out."

He glanced towards the door. "I guess we'd better be going."

"It's not much to oblige you," said Jim Parks, also rising to shake Dr. Moore's hand. He then helped Mrs. Moore into her coat and opened the door for his guests' departure.

Chapter 12

At the end of the week, Sally decided to locate some luggage in the attic of her parents' home in preparation for the expected trip to Mexico. But as she lifted a heavy box, while rummaging, she suddenly felt a slight pain in her chest. "Guess I just pulled a muscle," she thought and continued with her task. But the pain lasted, even after she had finished and descended to the living room to join her husband for a mid-morning coffee break. He agreed with her diagnosis, however, so she decided to dismiss it. But she still continued, nevertheless, to suffer from the pain for another week until it was replaced by a queer sensation at the base of her spine.

The change occurred while she was dressing, and it seemed as if her spine had suddenly been transformed into what felt like a series of little ripples rising from just above her buttocks and progressing upwards to the nape of her neck, as if a pebble had been tossed into a pool of water.

"I think I ought to see your father," she then remarked to Kirke.

Acompanied by him she went to see Dr. Moore the day after. After the usual greeting, Sally retired to the inner office with the doctor who, after inquiring when the symptoms had first appeared, gave her a thorough physical examination.

"Can't find anything wrong—yet," he announced, going to the medicine cabinet. He took out a bottle of pills, gave her one and indicated a small room containing a couch and told her to lie down until he came back.

When he did, Kirke was with him. Dr. Moore then held a small flashlight close to her eyes and peered intently into them.

"Well," she said as he finished, "what's the verdict?".

"There's nothing to worry about, my dear. You're going to be perfectly allright."

"That's not what I asked, Doc," growled Sally. "What the devil is wrong with me?"

"I assure you, you have nothing whatever wrong with you," he replied.

"What about these freakish symptoms I have—they're from something, aren't they?"

"In time, they'll disappear. Strictly temporary."

"What were you doing giving me that pill and then looking into my eyes with a flashlight?"

"My dear, I was just making a little observation."

"That tells me a lot."

"Your eyes are a window to certain aspects of your nervous system. I was merely checking to see if all is in order."

"And?"

"It is."

"Then why do I have these symptoms?"

"As I said before—a temporary condition. It will eventually clear up. Don't worry about it."

"Is that all you have to say?"

"Yes—for now. I'll see you in two weeks. After the trial. You'd do better to think about that than this. It's nothing, I assure you."

"You're sure I'm going to be perfectly allright?"

"Yes."

As Sally and Kirke left Dr. Moore's office, Sally felt that the doctor had hardly been frank with her, but she liked him

The Ruins at Uxmal

personally, knew his reputation and trusted him implicitly. He had told her not to worry, and she was not going to. And that was that.

But from that time to the day of the trial she had increasing cause to worry. She became acutely aware that her husband needed bolstering for the ordeal. He was becoming very nervous, much inclined to expect the worst and to fall into a blue funk. She desperately tried to think of ways to raise his feelings, but all she could really do was offer words of comfort.

"Please try not to worry. Whatever penalty you get will probably be minor," she exhorted him, attempting to imbue her words with the most intense compassion. "We're all praying for you."

But in spite of her earnest attempts, his depression was unrelieved. She became disgusted first with him and then with herself. She felt guilty because she had contempt mixed with pity for him. In spite of herself, she thought his attitude was, to some degree, unjustified. Then she wondered, am I normal having the feelings I do? —I seem to be so dispassionate. Then she considered her husband's act. What had he done? Because of his carelessness, he had caused the death of her sister and now, when he would probably only face the slightest penalty for it, was behaving as if he were going to be given a life term. And she was married to him! She could only say God! And that he had also delayed their future! All that could be said for him was that his act was not deliberate, and by the highest ethics of civilized society he deserved mercy and forgiveness. But why shouldn't these ethics be questioned—after all, Eileen had been her sister? Somehow or other, they just didn't seem to fit the occasion. But then she said to herself: No! She was this man's wife, and it was her duty to stand by him. And stand up for him. But however she reasoned she could not repress the feeling that the ethics of the Devil were more justified than the ethics she had just been considering and were wrestling with them for control over her.

On the day of the trial, Kirke, Sally and their families met Johnson on the courthouse steps. As they went inside, Sally noted that it looked as if they were entering prison.

The walls of the lobby were of gray stone, the interior doors to the courtoom were of enormous size and of oak stained dark so that they appeared to be the entryway to a dungeon. The courtroom itself, however, was a pleasant contrast: cheery, with light brown wooden tables, chairs with green coverings and bright sunlight which flooded in through French windows.

The jury, the two witnesses and the district attorney were already seated, awaiting only the arrival of the judge and the parties to the trial. No one else was present for the proceedings.

When all had assembled, a bailiff entered and announced, "All rise," then when the judge entered the courtroom, looked about him, drew a deep breath and continued in stentorian tones, "The court is now in session, the Honorable William Fuller presiding. Be seated."

As the order and protocol of the trial unfolded, Sally followed it very attentively. When it came Johnson's turn to rebut the charge made against Kirke by the district attorney, he first called the bearded man. After the man took the seat in the witness stand, Johnson posed the question: "Sir, can you state anything to refute the charge that the accident was caused by careless driving?"

The witness emphatically replied, "Sir, that night rain had been falling, and anyone could have inadvertantly skidded off the road."

Then Johnson called the bearded man's wife to the stand. Again he asked the same question. She made an even more dramatic reply. "What my husband said is true," she said, "and there are also some sudden curves in that area. We almost had an accident ourselves."

The district attorney seemed greatly impressed. When he came again before the bench, he reflected for a few moments, then apparently feeling that the weight of his evidence was insufficient, said, even kindly, "In consideration of the testimony of these two witnesses, I will not press for conviction on the charge of manslaughter, but only for negligent homicide."

Tremendous relief overwhelmed Sally. Then she felt even more relieved as Robert Johnson spoke again. He forcefully re-stressed the fact that it was only just possible that Kirke's driving was the basic fault and emphasized again that slippery road conditions might have been the major factor. Then he called her to the stand and had her make an appeal to the emotions of the jury. She repeated what he had previously requested at the arraignment.

"Neither I nor my family are vindictively inclined. We all realize that it was just a terrible accident, and our hope and plea is that you will grant the utmost leniency to the defendant."

After she had come down from the witness chair, she elatedly watched as Johnson made an equally strong plea in which he reiterated what had already been said, plus an additional entreaty for release from probation.

"In view of the fact that the evidence of careless driving is only problematical and in light of the further fact that neither the plaintiff or her family is inclined to be vindictive, pleading, instead, that the defendant be granted the utmost leniency, I would request that you give those factors the fullest consideration before making your decision in this case. Furthermore, as the defendant's future chances of gaining employment in the immediate future are dependent on being free from a probationary status, I would also request that you give consideration to that fact so that you would feel that a recommendation for freedom from any restriction which that status would entail would be in order."

Jeremy S. Wood

After Johnson had concluded his statement, the judge rapped with his gavel on the bench before him and announced, "The court will now be in recess. You will be informed when the verdict is to be read." After that the bailiff rose and announced, "All rise"; the judge left and was followed from the room by all the others to await the outcome of the trial.

During the hour before dinner that night at the home of her parents, the strain on Kirke of waiting became very evident to Sally, as all he could do was pace the floor. Finally, he looked at Johnson and asked, "Do you think we'll get what we're hoping for?"

"You can never predict a jury," replied Johnson calmly.

The next day Sally took a call from the courthouse at eight o'clock in the morning telling them to report to the courthouse by ten. After Sally had passed on the news to the rest of the family, they all hurried there, then filed anxiously into the courtroom. After they had assembled the judge said to the jury foreman, "Have you reached a verdict?"

After the affirmative answer, he said, "Hand your verdict to the clerk."

The clerk looked at the verdict, then handed it to the judge.

"Mr. Moore, please rise," said the judge.

Kirke rose to his feet.

The judge nodded and rapped with his gavel on the bench.

"Mr. Kirke Moore, the courts finds you guilty of negligent homicide. However, as leniency has been recommended, your sentence shall be a fine of one thousand dollars and a sentence of one year in jail, suspended, and with no obligation of probation."

Sally and the others all heaved a collective sigh of relief, and as Sally warmly kissed Kirke, his face broke into a big smile. Then she wrapped her arm around him as the bailiff announced

The Ruins at Uxmal

the end of the courtroom session. At least that part of their problem was over.

Two weeks later Sally and Kirke received good news from her father. He told them Roy Bainbridge had answered his inquiry favorably. He had written, saying that upon his recommendation, provided Kirke was approved after an interview in the New York office, he would accept him as a representative of his firm doing business at a branch located in the city of Merida, Yucatan. He said he badlly needed a man who was an American who could speak and write both English and Spanish to fill a position to handle shipping orders, and that young Americans who were willing to go as far away from civilized American life as the interior of Mexico were hard to find, indeed. He also extended his congratulations to Kirke and Sally for their hardihood together with a list of instructions to Kirke, telling him when and to whom to report in the New York office two weeks later.

After the interview, Sally learned from Kirke that it had gone well. He said he had all the qualifications for the job except experience, but as the company badly needed a man like him and as Bainbridge, knowing Jim Parks would not send him one he thought might not work out, had strongly recommended him for the position, it was more or less of a formality. Following this good news, after a two day trip to Ithaca to clean out their apartment, Kirke and Sally spent the next six weeks getting ready for their journey south. After shopping for all their required gear, getting their passports and inoculations against disease and their airline tickets to the capital of Yucatan, Merida, via Mexico City, only the result of their last visit to Dr. Moore could possibly worry them. As the queer sensation in her spine was still with her, Sally was a bit apprehensive, but, as the doctor greeted her, the warm smile on his face tended to dispel her fears.

Again she took a little pill. Then Dr. Moore looked into her eyes, beamed and said, "You're making a nice recovery."

"From what, Doctor?"

Dr. Moore then sat down in a chair alongside her couch, beckoned to Kirke to come in from the other office and for the first time spoke frankly.

"The strain of what you've been under—the shock of the auto crash and the anxiety of waiting for the trial has created a slight disruption of your nervous system."

"It has? Is it serious?"

"Not if you follow prescribed instructions."

"For how long?"

"I'm afraid permanently."

"My God, you mean—for life?"

The doctor sat back and folded his hands before addressing her.

"Believe me, I wouldn't have told you outright, like this, except for the fact that you're going away—-and I think it's better for you to know than to remain ignorant. It's bad medicine, however, because of the upsetting effect it has on the patient but under the circumstances what could I do?" He paused. "Yes, it's for life. But, as your case is not at all bad, you're just going to have to take a mild medication. That's all."

"What will it do to me?"

"Just prevent you from becoming too excited and overwrought about anything."

"You mean a tranquilizer?"

"Yes, a very mild one."

"What's the term used to describe my condition?"

"Neuro-circulatory aesthenia. Not much is known about it. Without getting too medical, your nervous system functions by electrical impulses transmitted through what are called synapses at the tips of your nerves. Something—we don't know what—has interfered with the proper transmission of your electrical impulses between the synapses. This malfunction is caused, as I said before, by an excessive strain on the nervous system."

"I see. So I am to be permanently incapacitated?"

"Not seriously. You'll be able to function quite normally—just so long as you don't work too hard or too long at any thing. Pace yourself—that's all you have to do—and you'll be perfectly allright."

"No high pressure work, therefore?"

"Right. That's out for you. Even working at a routine job might be too much for you. It would cause that back trouble you now have—which will eventually clear up in a few months—to recur, and we must prevent that."

"What you're telling me is that there's no chance of a complete recovery."

"That is correct. Nerves do not come back—that's one of the big medical mysteries. But really, live right, and you'll never even know you have it."

"Well, what about this journey to Mexico?"

"You'll be allright. I'll give you a notification which you can give to a doctor down there, and he'll take over. You'll probably need to check in once or twice with him, stay on your medication and forget it."

"I see."

To her he then nodded his head.

She smiled. "Bye doc,"

He laughed in return. "I see you're inclined to be flip. That's a good attitude to have. Run along, now, and be happy."

But that night, in their room, the shock of her incapacitation hit her. She fell into a depression.

"What more has to happen to sink us?" she wailed. "All our hopes for the kind of life we want have been shattered. First, the accident, then that terrible trial and now this! —a permanent physical disability. All I can say is, enough is enough!"

"Honey, through it all, you've been magnificent. Don't give up—not now!"

At his words, she at first felt comforted, but then anger welled up in her. "Here I am," she cried, "tied to and dependent on a man whose suitability as a husband I'm beginning to doubt. Damn it, I don't know what to do—especially with you!"

"Oh Honey, the strain you've been under has broken you."

"Believe me, I've about had it! Damn it, I think I want a divorce!"

"Divorce? Oh, no, Honey, don't do that! Please give me another chance. Please!"

"I suppose I should give you a break," she said, as his plea roused her pity, "After all, the accident really wasn't your fault. Nothing deliberate about it. Furthermore," she said more logically, "since my parents are of moderate means and can give us nothing and yours—what with this trip to Mexico—are witholding all money until they see whether our marriage turns out—and I can't work..." And then her pride told her the real answer. "I guess we've made our bed," she said, "and now we must lie in it."

Chapter 13

Sally counted the days until they left for Mexico a month later. Exerting great will, she made a determined effort to put the past out of her mind and was abetted in this effort by an unusual experience at the International Airport in Mexico City, where she and Kirke had to change flights for the trip to Merida, capital of Yucatan, five hundred miles further south.

Some Americans joined them as they boarded their plane; Kirke ignored them, preferring to read a newspaper, but Sally, realizing from the way they congregated that they were a tour and hoping to cull information about Mexico, introduced herself to one of them seated next to her. This person responded affably by saying she was Mrs. Elizabeth Collins from Mexico City and director of the tour.

Even though she was busy with clerical and interpersonal duties, Mrs. Collins seemed willing to talk so Sally drew her out. She soon learned that the group was going to climb the Mayan ruins at various sites throughout Yucatan—the very place she and Kirke were going—in order to study the culture of the race from the extant remains to be found in those structures. Mrs. Collins also told her that she was an American woman who had lived in Mexico for many years, was an Associate Curator for the National Anthropological Museum in Mexico City and also served as a tour director for several of the Travel/Study programs of the Hathaway Tour Association of Memphis, Tennessee. She also impressed Sally by her manner and appearance: outgoing, very animated—having, apparently, a high energy level—and because she was handling three operations at once, undoubtedly a capable executive. Sally noted incidentally that she was very attractive, having unlined, youthful features in spite of being white-haired—a few yellow streaks through it indicated that she was once blonde—and her trim figure signified an age of no more than fifty-five.

"You're just the person I want to ask about life in Yucatan," said Sally. "My husband is going to a job down there, in Merida, to represent an American firm which sells and distributes soft drinks to the towns throughout that area."

"Well, I can tell you right off, it's going to be hot in summer—100 degee weather, at least," rejoined her new acquaintance. "It's in the tropics, of course, and even in winter, it's terribly warm. But live there long enough, and you'll get used to it."

Then replying to Sally's further questioning, Mrs. Collins told her that in Merida she would probably have to get accustomed to living in more modest, although surprisingly clean, surroundings, with little of the efficiency and few of the comforts of home and that the material things she would use would be about thirty years out of date by U. S. standards.

"For example," she continued, "you'll undoubtedly have trouble from time to time with the plumbing—it's not up to what is done in the U. S. The water will not always be hot—it'll be lukewarm. Be sure, also, to get adequate lighting where you live—that's not always good. It's things like that you have to put up with."

"Well, I'm young and can stand the inconvenience," Sally replied, then thought, after what I've been through. "From what you say," she resumed, "I can see that I'll have to get used to a primitive life. But one hurdle I won't have to jump very high for is actually getting a house. The business back home has arranged to have us directed to what's available by the company down here. And, of course, they've given us a housing allowance."

"You won't have any trouble. You can probably get a fairly adequate little house. It'll have a patio, of course, and shuttered windows, although it might front flush with the street."

The Ruins at Uxmal

"I won't mind the location of the house. But I'd like a fountain."

"Well, if you're willing to pay a higher price you might get your fountain."

"What's there to do in Merida?"

"Not much in the way of night-life, although its population is five hundred thousand. There are, however, lots of shops where you can buy native goods real cheap—especially leather and gold and silver filigree work—and then there's also some fine beaches."

"Anything more, locally?" asked Sally.

"Well, of course, one thing every foreigner does is visit the Mayan ruins at various sites in Yucatan. A couple which are near you are those at Uxmal and Chichen Itza. And there are others, and those farther south on the peninsula are not more than a weekend away."

"I see. Now, can you tell me something about the native customs?"

Mrs. Collins laughed. "Too much to explain. You'll have to pick it up on your own. But one thing—hire a cook to prepare your food—it'll be done native, of course—and give her your 'gasto'—that's the allowance for the day—to do shopping because if you try it before you know the score, the merchants'll cheat the devil out of you. You see, in Mexico we haggle, and you'd better be prepared or else you'll get taken."

"Well I can see where she will be necesary."

"Wages are very low," said Mrs. Collins conclusively. She then rose. "I have to collect some papers from my entourage. You will excuse me now."

"You've been so kind. Do you stop regularly in Merida?" She summoned her nerve. "I'd like to see you again and learn more about Yucatan."

"Why, yes—yes, you may. We stop there for a few hours on every journey. Tell you what—when I come through there in another six months, why don't I look you up and see how you're doing. You seem to be very nice, and I'd be interested in helping young Americans living in Mexico. We could have lunch together."

"You're wonderful. You'll be able to get my address from the company branch—it's called Amer-Mexco, and the supervisor is Senor Ernesto Gutierrez.'"

"I'll be seeing you, then."

When Kirke and Sally arrived at the Hotel Casa Del Balam at 9:30 p.m., Sally looked it over while Kirke checked in. The place, although appearing to date from about nineteen-ten was unusually attractive, having the striking feature of a central courtyard. This particularity was, she thought, considered desirable by the owners, undoubtedly because Mexican architectural style always has a patio interior. However, later that night she and Kirke learned of the impracticality of the yard which became very evident during a severe tropical rainstorm which splattered on to the rugs running along its sides and lowered the temperature by about fifteen degrees throughout the hotel. They were, however, far more overwhelmed by the court's uniqueness than by its infeasibility, and Sally even welcomed it, with relief, as a beginning of their great adventure.

Their rooms were equally old-fashioned and quite comfortable, and Sally checked and saw that everything they needed was adequately provided for, especially two treated bottles of water for protection against intestinal disorders. "Now

The Ruins at Uxmal

this precaution is really foreign," said Kirke, with a laugh. "However, we've heard about Montezuma's revenge."

"Here, brush your teeth with some of this," said Sally handing him a bottle, "and let's retire early, so you'll be fresh for your meeting with your boss tomorrow."

While Kirke made inquires the next day about the wherabouts of 14 Calle Street 13, the locale of the company office, where he had an appointment at 1 p.m., Sally consulted a street map of Merida as she wished they could do some exploring before that time. After finding out that the office was only a few blocks away, Sally said, "Now for our first real taste of Mexico, to see, explore and eventually to use."

"You know," she then remarked, "I'm more interested in exploring than in contacting the company today. This new country is so exciting to me."

As they did so she found the heat to be up to Mrs. Collins' predictions, but in her initial view of Merida she found it exceedingly interesting. However, "As this map is bum, try your Spanish out," she said to Kirke. Kirke smiled and did so. Although his Castillian Spanish caused a few smiles among the Mexicans he talked to, or rather the Yucatecas, as he found they preferred to be called, he had no difficulty in ascertaining the directions needed to explore some sights. Both Sally and he were favorably impressed by their friendliness and also, in an adverse sense, by the architecture of the city—the fading whitewash of the buildings on its sidestreets in combination with the haphazard arrangement of garish yellow, white and pink structures along the main streets gave it the appearance of a middle class slum in New York. The traffic, they noted sardonically, was also very typical of New York—fast moving and disregardful of pedestrians. But the appearance of the people! All were, of course, dark-skinned and seemed Indian, and the clothing many of them wore—the women in white blouses and black skirts, either trimmed with red or yellow flowers, the men in pleated shirts worn beltless over the pants—certainly suggested Mexico to them. However, also quite prevalent was khaki.

"Interesting," said Sally. Then, "See what you'll be dealing with."

The first sight she wished to see was a twin-spired cathedral on the zocalo, or town square. After they arrived, they were impressed by the air of fervent devotion evident among the townspeople attending the hourly Masses; the great influence of the Catholic church was most apparent here among unsophisticated masses. Sally also noticed an unusual feature of this church; where the cross was placed at the center of the nave, a figure of the Christ was affixed to it. Not characteristic of Protestant churches, at least in the states, she thought, but I guess they do it here to impress Christ deeply into the minds of these simple people. Then she led the way to the Governor's Palace on the northeast side of the square. This building was quite ornate with a large reception room with huge wall paintings the size of frescoes depicting scenes from several uprisings of the Maya against the central government in the nineteenth century. One showed a Maya being tortured with red-hot irons, which caused Sally to reflect on the cruelty of life, in general.

But the most interesting sight by far to them was the market, fifteen minutes away by bus. It was a large building, like a mall, but looked as if it was out of the eighteenth century. The aisles were narrow, and the stalls containing wares were like those at a small circus—jerry-built with no metal or glass coverings at all. But it was clean, and the vegetables looked good, and the meat smelled fresh—Sally judged it must have been just killed; there was nothing putrid about it at all. And she noted the place was crowded with the real John Q. Public of Yucatan. Previously, aside from the casual inquiries they had made in the street, they had only encountered the employees at the Mexican International Airport and the hotel, people who had been educated, who spoke a broken brand of English and who wore American style clothing, but here, right before their eyes, in the tumultuous uproar going on around them, was the Yucatecan average—the real McCoy. Most of them were women—peasants, campesinos who had come from the country, bringing their wares of vegetables, meats and other produce to the market for sale. "This is the kind one meets away from the big city, the country folk, the people of the soil," Kirke remarked, and Sally nodded agreement. These peasant women were quite friendly—with neatly combed hair, almond eyes and dark brown skin—and more than willing to talk and do business with them. At one pew Kirke was offered a live goose for sale, at another a gobbling turkey.

And clean! Before coming to Mexico, Sally had heard much talk about "dirty Mexicans," but her experience this morning utterly belied it. Without exception the people she saw—all Indians—at that market were impeccably clean. In addition to having their hair neatly combed, their faces and hands were washed, the clothes they wore was absolutely spotless and the legs of those who did not wear stockings were also clean. She was rapidly forming some very vivid first impressions of Mexico, at least Yucatan, and of the Yucatecas, and was beginining to like what she saw very much.

"Your public," said Sally to Kirke, as he nodded.

When it was eleven forty-five she proposed having lunch. Just a few blocks from the market they came upon a tastefully designed "merendero," featuring black iron grill work, characteristic of many buildings in Merida, along its second story balcony. After being seated, they enjoyed examing the menu for items prepared in the Mexican style of cuisine. Sally ordered chili con carne, and Kirke contented himself with a "rost beef" sandwich prepared with a dressing which was totally unfamiliar to him. They began to feel native. Following that as it was close to the time of Kirke's appointment at the company, they left the restaurant and proceeded by bus to its locale.

"From what I understood from the guy who interviewed me in New York," said Kirke, "there's nothing glamorous about this post. The company's very small and what they have down here now is just a small branch. But they hope to expand, of course."

When they came to the building it was certainly not very prepossessing, being just a small office shanty with yellow adobe walls, a worn tar paper roof and one doorway framing a dirty black and white puppy. But as they approached, the pup rose to meet them, wagging his tail.

"See, he's friendly," said Sally. "Now are you ready for your adventure?" Kirke nodded.

They entered a small room with an open doorway leading to an even smaller inner office. In it, a short, stocky, mustachioed man of Mexican extraction was seated behind a desk, smoking a cigar; guessing they were Americans from their dress, he rose to greet them, smiling broadly.

"Welcome," he said in fluent English, but tinged by an accent, "I'm Ernesto Gutierrez."

"How do you do, Senor Gutierrez" said Kirke, shaking his proffered hand. He was then a little startled by what followed—a warm embrace, then two hearty shoulder slaps. But he kept his poise.

"I'm Kirke Moore, freshly arrived from the states and ready to go to work," he managed "and this is my wife, Sally. I hope I haven't violated protocol in bringing her with me, but we thought she could get information about housing from you and start looking around this afternoon while you explained my duties to me. Sort of kill two birds with one stone."

Senor Gutierrez nodded. "I'm honored to meet you," he said, bowing. "You have a good idea. She can see them after two. After siesta. And how was your trip down?"

The Ruins at Uxmal

"Most interesting," said Kirke, "especially for my wife, who talked to a woman about Yucatan." Then he added, "And since I wasn't to report in until after lunch, we took a stroll around Merida this morning. That was really fascinating."

"For your sake, I'm taking my siesta at two o'clock, today," said Senor Gutierrez, with a laugh. "But it's nice you are prepared to start getting settled this very day. Please be seated and tell me something about yourselves. You can make it short."

"Of course."

After detailing a bit about their past lives, but dealing principally with his educational background, Kirke raised the practical problem of getting them settled. In discussing this topic, Senor Gutierrez gave lengthy, detailed directions to two available real estate agencies which would be open and one of which he had personal knowledge of and, therefore, knew to be reliable. "You see," he explained, "we have no housing facilities of our own, being, up to now, only a one-man office operation employing nine truck drivers." Then he added that in renting a place in Mexico, one did not make any demands. One took what was offered or left it alone. After hearing this about them, Sally left Kirke with Senor Gutierrez to discuss business while she went to the one Senor Gutierrez had said was open and reliable to see about renting a home.

The man at the agency, a Senor Martinez, was excellent, speaking good English, being most cooperative in showing her two houses for rent and keeping his prices in line with what Senor Gutierrez had said was reasonable for the area. She took him to be thoroughly honest and, being anxious to get settled, chose the second home which impressed her the most favorably. It was just a modest yellow adobe house, square-built, with one bedroom, a bathroom, sparse cheap furniture, only fair lighting and a small kitchen, but it did have exactly what Mrs. Collins had told her she would find—a patio with a garden, shuttered windows, a front flush with the street and also—a fulfillment of her additional wish—a fountain. After taking it she said that she and her husband hoped to move in within two days, and that, if it suited the Senor, they would come to his office later that afternoon to sign the lease which was to be for a year. Senor Martinez signified his assent to her plans, by nodding, smiling and saying, "Bueno," and "Muy bien," several times.

After they had bade good-bye to Senor Gutierrez, Sally showed Kirke her choice, saying it was only what they could afford. Kirke approved her judgment, and then both, after paying the necessary visit to Senor Martinez, retired to the hotel to discuss their future.

"I guess reality is setting in, after seeing that house," said Kirke.

"Don't complain," admonished his wife, "We're going to like it here—I've made up my mind to that—make ourselves like it, if we have to."

"You're right," said Kirke. "And, after all, my job has raised my enthusiasm a great deal. Senor Gutierrez told me I was going to be a lot more than a clerk. He has also slated me to be a contact man with the institutions in which we're going to try to install cola machines. I'm going to see a lot of Yucatan. And he said he wouldn't mind at all if you cared to string along. How do you like that?"

"Not bad. I'd long since decided we were going to make every effort to discover this country, and this looks like an easy way to do it."

"You see, during about two weeks of the month, I'll be at the office taking care of invoices, overseeing the shipment of the cola to the businesses which have ordered them, and the rest of the time I'll be out drumming up new business. I'll be both a clerk and a salesman.'"

"That means more variety in your work. And, in the long run, if you do well, it'll mean more money." She paused.

The Ruins at Uxmal

"And now for a big question. How do you like your boss?"

"He impresses me as being ok, at first meeting, although his approach was a little startling, However, I didn't mind that."

"That's because he's a real Mexican," said Sally. "With them a greeting like that is customary, You see, with a name like Gutierrez, he undoubtedly has Spanish blood, although his features show the maternal side of his parentage—that is Indian. He's a real mestizo."

"A mestizo?"

"A person with both Spanish and Indian blood, Silly."

"Uh-huh. Well?"

"As you know I'm a bookworm. In the month before we came here, I read a bit about both the Maya—that's the pure blooded Indian we'll find around here—and the Mexican of mixed Spanish and Indian parentage—the mestizo. The mestizo predominates throughout Mexico."

"Well, I wonder what kind of a guy he really is?"

"The book says," chirped Sally, feeling quite professorial, "that Mexicans are meditative and philosophical; they are discreet, evasive and distrustful. I think it'll be awhile before you get on a first name basis with him."

"You do? It didn't seem like it to me."

"His approach was a sign of mutual reassurance, not friendship."

"It was? Why?"

"Well, according to the book, it was their defeat by the Spanish that inculcated a sense of inferiority in the native Indians. That, you see, was inherited by the mestizos, and resulted in a racism which, today, despises the pure Indians and has a special respect for whites."

"And?"

"It leads to self-denigration—and insecurity. This is hidden behind machismo and bravado behavior."

"What you're saying is that this guy, Gutierrez, may feel inferior to me, even though he's boss. So he's really distant."

"Exactly. So tread on eggs when you're with him. It'll pay off. Don't mind his ceremoniousness. It's natural for him, and you'd better understand it. Work well with him. It's important to our future. Remember!"

"I'll be careful."

"However, once he accepts you, he'll become very warm and affectionate towards you. He'll probably invite us to his home. And that'll be nice." She paused again, then continued.

"Did you meet the other men?"

"Yes. They seem ok. I'll travel with them on the trucks. But I'm responsible only to Senor Gutierrez."

"When do you start work?"

"Three days from now, at ten in the morning—Gutierrez has to get my instructions prepared. We'll have tomorrow to get settled. Then the next day I go out in the afternoon on a two-day trip to the town of Valladolid. Gutierrez said we could spend a couple of hours seeing the ruins at Chichen Itza, which is only twenty miles from Valladolid. He recommended a place in Piste, the site of Chichen Itza, where we could stay overnight and also to take our swim suits for it'll have a pool. He said the hostels the drivers bunk up in wouldn't be suitable for us."

"Say, he doesn't seem like a bad fellow, at all."

"I agree. Now let's hit the hay and rise early tomorrow. We have a lot to do."

The Ruins at Uxmal

But lying in bed her thoughts turned away from her preoccupation with the moment and dwelt moodily on the tragedy they had left behind them. She became depressed. "I really wonder what the long term future holds for us?" she asked Kirke.

He comforted her. "We're going to return to a happy life in the states. Now be good and cheer up."

Yes, she then thought, we're going to do that. We're going to dismiss the terrible tragedy that has happened to us. And now we're going to take advantage of the opportunity to right our ship and also, for what useful knowledge it might yield, to study the fascinating past of an ancient people.

Chapter 14

After Kirke and Sally spent the next day getting settled in their new home—cleaning it, unpacking and arranging their clothes, interviewing and choosing from several job applicants (all of whom had seen them moving in and wished to work for the "gringoes"), they were ready for their adventure.

The succeeding morning Sally rose very early to greet Maria, who was to be their cook and maid of all work. After packing their clothes and instructing her in her duties, Sally gave her the "gasto" for the purchase of some food, locked all the closet doors containing their other clothes—their only real valuables—and the key to the front door and told her they would be back tomorrow evening. And then, after Kirke was ready, they were off, about nine-thirty, to the office of Amer-Mexico to receive final instructions from Senor Gutierrez and be on their way to Chichen Itza and Valladolid.

"You will go to Piste, the site of Chichen Itza, this afternoon when most everybody is at siesta," said Senor Gutierrez. "It's about ninety miles away. You can stop there overnight, before seeing the ruins and doing business the following morning. Go to the Mision Hacienda Chichen Itza; it's very nice."

"That'll be swell," said Sally, inwardly wondering how Kirke would do selling.

"Then," continued Senor Gutierrez, "in doing business next day with the manager—a Senor Garcia—of a pottery factory and Senor Gonzalez, who grows henequin and is an old friend, say that their commission for the use of their places as distribution outlets are higher than those offered by the major supplier in this area. That's your best selling point. It'll be a good trip for you, breaking you in on the job and also allowing you to satisfy your

The Ruins at Uxmal

curiosity about our ancient civilization down here. Sort of," he added with a smile, "killing two birds with one stone."

"Will do," said Kirke cheerily.

"But before you leave, let's do the necessary paperwork for the trip. And it would be well for you, Senora Moore, to learn these procedures also, since you seem to want to be a willing assistant to your husband, and, for that matter, he might need a little help away from the office." He grinned broadly.

After completing the preparatory work and then meeting Pedro, the truck driver, Sally and Kirke got into the vehicle and began the trip. Of interest to them as they traveled was the landscape, conspicuous for its ugliness, quite unlike anything either of them had ever seen in the United States. It was worse than a desert. Level as a board, with just a thick forest of scraggy, dry looking trees of even height, faded pale green color and exceedingly monotonous to look at; punctuated only so often by fields of purplish, spiny shrubs which Pedro told them was hennequin, also called sisal, and which was the chief product of Yucatan.

"This is the first feature of Yucatan I really dislike, said Kirke, surveying the dreary landscape.

"Get used to it," said Sally, with a touch of irritation at having her enjoyment of novelty interrupted. "We'll be living for the next year or two in such surroundings."

"I suppose so," agreed Kirke.

Midway through their journey, their truck passed a group of children picking their way through a pile of garbage by the roadside. It was the first sign of poverty Sally and Kirke had seen and caused her to remark, "Even in our slums in the states, they don't do that."

Jeremy S. Wood

"True," agreed Kirke. "This country is really poor, way below the material way of life we have back home. Aren't we fortunate to be living there?"

In four hours they came to the town of Piste and proceeded to the Mision Hacienda Chichen Itza, located close to the ruins. Sally and Kirke noted that its being "built-in" to its natural surroundings and its architectural style, quite different from U. S. hostels, made it uniquely attractive. Spreading out in a horseshoe shape from the central check-in office and restaurant were individual stone cottages with thatched roofs, arranged around a pool and tucked away among tropical trees. Sally noted the presence of a small palm outside her bathroom window, nestled in a forest of other growth. Nature was very close; she felt it and liked it. I think I'm going to enjoy the next year or two in Mexico, she concluded.

After changing into swimming suits for a plunge before dinner, they noted the profusion of tropical plants and small palms as they walked along the cobbled walks leading to both the pool and the central building. And the water was fine, just about eighty degrees, the way they liked it. This recreation and, afterwards, the dinner, consisting of "pork chucs," tacos and, "as usual, refried beans," noted Kirke, put them in the mood to sally forth to see the ruins and to complete the business part of their excursion the next day.

They rose early the next morning and took a bus to the ruins. After they got out at the grounds, they stood and gazed, transfixed by a huge structure—the El Castillo, a four stairway pyramid, supporting a flat-topped temple, about four hundred yards away across a grassy square.

"We're not dressed to clamber up that thing this morning," said Sally. "Furthermore, we probably don't have time, as we want to see a lot of other buildings. It certainly is big, isn't it?"

The Ruins at Uxmal

"Ninety feet from the ground to the top, according to Senor Gutierrez," said Kirke.

After refusing a guide, they walked the distance to the foot of the pyramid.

"Well, from the book I learned it has nine terraces, with four doorways into the temple," said Sally. "One of the doorways—I guess it's the main one—is divided by two feathered serpent columns. I suppose they worshipped a lot of animals, among other things."

"We'll have to read up on these guys."

"As I said, I've got the book, but I've only gotten into it partway."

"We'll have plenty of time to get into it. I wonder what they used that building for?"

"It was associated with their religious beliefs, One of the functions—it was the principal one—that they used it for was sacrifice. They'd take some prisoner of war up there, cut his heart out and then kick the body downstairs."

"Nice custom."

"Sacrifice was an important part of their religious belief. And the religious belief was the most important thing in their lives. The gods they worshipped—Sun, Moon and many, many others—controlled their destiny; hence they were both revered and feared, principally the latter. The ritual of sacrifice must have represented a religious culmination of some sort, and the temple was, I suppose, the most important building in the entire city."

"Speaking of religious sacrifice, remember, we had the Spanish Inquisition going on at the same time in Europe so we could hardly consider this more primitive."

"True. Now let me tell you a little about their history. They were an Indian race which crossed the Bering Strait and settled in most of Yucatan about fifteen hundred B.C. Then came the Spanish conquest—that was by Cortes—in the sixteenth century. According to the book, they were a highly civilized race numbering, I believe, about fifteen million people at the peak of their era."

"There were other races of Indians down there, weren't there?"

"Yes, many. They lived throughout Mexico and Central America both before and after the Maya—the Aztecs in Mexico, for example—but the Maya were the most cultured. They were a big, widespread civilization, and they had cities, quite large, for the time in which they were built."

"What was the average population?"

"Don't know, but the biggest was Tikal, with a total of ninety-two thousand. And all of these cities, I believe, had temples—plenty of 'em—erected to various deities like the Serpent God, the Sun God, also ball courts and other public buildings like royal tombs. These were adorned with inscriptions, heiroglyphic writing, art work, etcetera, etcetera from which archaeologists today construct the history of their civilization. All these buildings were associated with religion.

My won't we become sophisticated, after seeing all these ruins?" she then queried humorously.

"Indeed we will," said Kirke, winking at her. "And you'll be able to lord it over all your friends at those grand soirees you figure on throwing when we get all set up—eh?"

"Yes, we certainly will," said Sally. Then she thought more seriously—travel certainly is one way to become truly cosmopolitan—also just what she needed for her life.

After scrutinizing the edifice closely and marveling at how the Maya had learned to construct such an architecturally well planned building—indicative of the importance attached to it—with its technically perfect 45 degree angle steps, its symmetrical, comely form and, also, to perform the more mundane climb up those steps which looked terribly steep, Sally and Kirke proceeded next to the main ball court.

"According to the book, they had thirteen of these courts," said Sally, "and each had a religious significance. In fact, the entire layout of the city, from the mightiest temples to the smallest houses formed one big cosmogram, that is, a symbolic representation of the Maya universe."

The playing alley of the ball court was longer than a football field, about as wide and was enclosed lengthwise by two high stone walls.

"Those walls were for the spectators to watch from, I presume?" inquired Kirke half-humorously. The vertical sides each had a stone ring, set midway in each.

"The object of the game," said Sally, "was to drive a large rubber ball through one of the rings, using only the elbow, wrist or hip."

"They had rubber?"

"Yes. The Spanish discovered it when they saw them using it."

"The game had a humorous side," continued Sally. "When the ball was driven, rarely, through the ring, the spectators had to forfeit all their clothing and jewelry to the player who did it"

They then proceeded to examine the relief sculptures along the basal terrace of the ball court's walls which depicted a gruesome outcome: an apparently victorious player with a knife in one hand and the head of his vanquished opponent in the other. "It was a ritual re-enactment of warfare—that's what the book says—"said Sally—"culminating in the religious sacrifice of captives—to some god, of course. What a bloody routine. Awful."

They left the ball court and decided next on the Temple of the Warriors, passing on the way a tzompantli, a sculpture depicting racks of human skulls impaled on poles, grim, peering visages, presumably sacrificial victims.

In the temple they saw a sculpture of a chacmool, one of the Maya deities, mural paintings of captives, their bodies painted in black and white stripes and a painting of a coastal village. On two sides were colonnaded halls through which people had to pass to reach the summit of the temple and which may have served as council meeting places.

"Quite a layout—this building," said Kirke. "You know, as I knew nothing about the Maya or any other Indian tribe, I just thought they were a bunch of primitive jokers who lived in thatched huts and took scalps. But seeing these ruins—and Chichen Itza is only one of many Mayan cities throughout Yucatan—what a revelation!"

"You bet," chimed in Sally. "And, as you know, I never heard of these people either before I started reading. This whole civilization has nothing to do with our cultural heritage. But boy, does it make an impression. Think of it as great. It's just not as widespread as ours."

Yes, she thought to herself; here was this great culture, spanning over two thousand years, a highly organized, highly civilized society, in spite of its sacrificial ritual—a theocracy, that is ruled by an elite few, utterly different from democracy—a society she felt she must learn much more about. It was so different from the culture back home; intrigued by it she again felt an urge to question all her old ethical standards.

They then walked to the site of the Caracol, the astronomical observatory, and went inside and saw the alignments of the

The Ruins at Uxmal

upper windows, built so as to show the setting of the moon along its southern and northern declinations and the setting of the sun along its vernal equinox, thereby indicating the considerable astronomical knowledge of the Maya.

"They also had an accurate calendar and a heiroglyphic system of writing," said Sally.

"They really were tremendously civilized. They had many books, but the Spanish, wishing to obliterate their pagan civilization, destroyed practically all of them. Only a few remain."

They continued their tour by examining the sacred well of sacrifice, which was an oval shaped cavity with a water level sixty feet below ground level into which victims were thrown as sacrifices to the watery underworld. Then Kirke looked at his watch.

"Time to be going, hon; Pedro is probably waiting for us back at the hacienda."

Reflecting a moment, Sally thought, I wonder how much this will affect me? Then, these people were certainly as intelligent and as civilized, by their standards, as we are by ours. The moral relativism implicit in that idea struck her most forcibly then and again raised the question of the absolute validty of her own standards. She thought again, I wonder just how much this will affect me? Then, "Ok, hon, let's pick 'em up and lay 'em down."

On the drive of twenty miles to Valladolid they came upon a small band of natives, all gaily caparisoned, most on foot but some on horseback, pulling a woman in a makeshift carriage holding a cross in her hand.

"That is a parade of the Virgin of Guadaloupe," said Pedro, by way of explanation.

"All people turn to her with their prayers."

"A method of supplication? They beseech her? They ask her help?" Sally asked Kirke who interrogated Pedro. Pedro nodded.

"Just like we saw in the church in Merida," said Kirke. "The influence of Cathlolicism in this country is extensive and profound." Then to Pedro. " Catholicism is influential, eh?"

"Yes," agreed Pedro. "Most Mexicans—oh, 95 percent are Catholics."

In an hour they came to the quaint town of Valladolid. From a distance it appeared to be provincial to Sally and Kirke, but larger than they had thought. Pedro nodded his head. "Forty thousand live here," he said to Kirke. "Second largest in Yucatan."

Their first stop was on the outskirts at the hennequin plantation, Belle la Vista, owned by Senor Gutierrez's friend, Senor Hector Gonzalez. They drove up a cobble-stoned driveway, lined with pepper trees and lush gardens on each side of the hacienda, which Sally guessed was a combination of home and business office. Senor Gonzalez met them at the gateway. Kirke's first prospect, thought Sally.

"Buenos dias, Senor Moore. Buenos dias, Senora Moore," he said genially. "My old amigo in Merida has already told me of your coming." He followed this by greeting Kirke with a handshake, then the customary embrace—"ah—an abrazo," said Kirke—and finally bowing low to Sally.

Sally noted that Senor Gonzalez was about seventy, had silver hair and mustache and reminded her of a character actor she had seen in reruns of old movies back in the states—Frank Morgan.

"I will have my son show you my place, Senora," said Senor Gonzalez, "while you, Senor, can talk your business with me."

As they entered the hacienda, they were met by a tall, slim, dark skinned young man in his late twenties, with black hair and eyes, but what was most apparent to Sally was his manly bearing, his air of command.

"My son, Emilio," began Senor Gonzalez, then, after the introductions had been completed, "Emilio, do me the kindness of showing Senora Moore around while I and Senor Moore have a little discussion." Emilio bowed low again to Sally and said, somewhat stiffly, "This way, Senora."

Gentlemanly manners, too, thought Sally, what one would expect from the son of the owner of a hacienda. As if he were of the Spanish nobility. She was quite impressed with him.

As he took her outside, Sally remarked on how he and his father spoke English.

"Oh, my father needs it for business as he also grows chocolate which he ships direct to the U. S. Me, I went to the University of Texas. I know your customs well. And language."

"Like them?"

"Quite a bit. Ours are a bit too rigorous." Then he continued.

"A lot of educated Mexican businessmen speak English. It's a necessity for export trade."

She nodded, then took a look around. She was surprised by the physical structure of the hacienda. It was a big edifice, consisting of two separate low buildings of one story with only a large courtyard between them. Antiquated machinery stood about the rear of the building. It was certainly obsolete by U. S. standards, she thought, but it still must be quite serviceable here. Then, looking to the very rear of the back area she saw a primitive stone swimming pool with two huge bath houses with large towel racks visible through their open doors. The pool, about twenty feet square, was filled with fish.

"Piranhas," said Emilio. " Rare fish—imported. Man-eaters. The family likes eating them."

Then "I will show you a little of the interior of our home," he said. After they had re-entered, he led her into a sparsely furnished dining room, a long living room and indicated, with one hand, a spacious adjoining office. But what really surprised Sally was another room in the building entirely given over, apparently, for the purpose of worship—it contained an altar positioned under a large cross.

"My father is a very devout man," said Emilio, by way of explanation.

"I can certainly understand that," said Sally. "Are you also religious?"

"I am, but not as much as my father. I break the rules, if they displease me."

"What does your mother say to that?"

"My father rules in this house."

"An old Spanish custom, eh?" Then, "What do you do?"

"I am an agronomist. I am attached to to the governmental office in Mexico City. I am down here for a year, doing some field work at the site of Chichen Itza for the National Museum of Anthropology in Mexico City. They're interested in the farming methods of the ancient Maya and rely on us for help in that area."

"You are! Why then, you may know Mrs. Elizabeth Collins. I met her on the plane coming down here. She was very nice."

"Indeed I have a slight acquaintanceship with Senora Collins. She is a general assistant to the research staff at the Museum."

"We arranged to have lunch together when she came through here again in about six months. I want to ask her a lot more about Mexico and Yucatan."

"You will find her as informative about this country as she will be about my work. She is my immediate supervisor and frequently accompanies me to my home here."

"Really!" Then Sally turned to other topics.

"Your father has quite a spread here, doesn't he?"

"Yes, he does. And when he dies, I, as the eldest in the family, will inherit most of it." He smiled in apparent satisfaction. "Now, let me show you some cacao. We also grow a small amount of that for local sale." He took her outside again.

A number of workmen were tossing cacao pods into a large cart. Emilio took a pod from the cart, broke it open and handed the bean inside to Sally. "Try it," he said.

To Sally the taste was quite nice, although different from the chocolate one gets in a store back in the states.

"You can have a box of cookies, made from them, when you leave."

"My thanks."

He nodded. "I would imagine your husband has talked with my father now. Shall we go back?"

As they drove off, Kirke turned to her, jubilant.

"Things went very well," he said. "He not only was very nice; he gave me a good deal."

"How many cases of cola did you sell him?"

"Thirty-five. And two vending machines."

"That's not bad for the first try. I think he has only about forty men working for him. It's not a big operation."

"Most of my customers will be about that size or smaller. That's why we have the edge on big boys. Our operating costs are so low we can appeal to a smaller market and still make a profit. And retain them by paying them a higher commission."

"And what is yours?"

"I'm worth 350 bucks right now. My commission was 10 percent. Not bad for a start."

"That is allright. Selling is a good way to make money, if there's a market."

"And meeting the old boy was quite nice. I didn't have to put the screws to him. So it's all ok so far. Now what were your impressions of Junior? And how did you like the hacienda?"

"Emilio is ok. As for the hacienda, it's hardly up-to-date by any standard you can think of. But Emilio agreed with me when I said his father had quite a spread. He also said that he would inherit most of it when his dad dies. He impressed me as rather looking forward to inheriting it"

"Well, you can't blame him for that. Someday he'll be all fixed up. Hope we'll be in a similar position someday."

Their second, and final, stop was at a pottery plant, near the center of town.

"Suppose I just sit in the car and wait for you," said Sally. "Pedro can visit a local watering hole for an hour before you come back."

Left alone, she reminisced for the second time since they had come to Mexico. She thought gosh, so much has happened—it has all been so new and exciting. The trip certainly was having the desired effect: it was creating such a novel experience that it had only occurred once to her to look back. Now, for the second time, the effect of her sister's death struck her. It was a tremendous loss, a very great loss, but, very surprisingly, that loss was being rapidly replaced by her new life. And new life it certainly was. These fresh, vivid experiences were rapidly forming a new complex which was transforming her. The beginnings of a strong feeling that the past was over and that there was no use thinking about it except as being a prologue to the present overwhelmed her.

As for Kirke, he seemed, like her, to be recovering, being curious and extremely excited about his new occupation here in Yucatan. Yes, she figured, this experience was what was right for them at this time in their lives.

In a very short while Kirke returned from his second foray, but this time he was wearing a somewhat crestfallen look. He was a little subdued as he got into the truck.

"I'm glad Pedro hasn't returned. This last one I've got to talk about, and it isn't good."

"Well, that's what I'm here for."

He then blurted out, "The old son-of-a-gun in there hardly gave me a chance to open my mouth. As soon as I said I was a representative from Crystal Cola, an American firm, he threw up a hand to shut me up and said, 'Chinga los Americanos.' If you don't know what that means, ask Gutierrez. Apparently, he's had bad dealings with foreigners before and has sworn off 'em."

"Take it in stride," immediately advised Sally. "You can't win 'em all."

"I know," said Kirke. "But I'm not inclined to take a lot of abuse." He sat back in his seat, looking very morose and glowered.

Sally looked sharply at him, then thought again what kind of a guy have I really married? I thought I was marrying a fighter and doer. Then she ejaculated, "Man, you've got to have more guts than that. You've got to have stick-to-itiveness to make it as a salesman. You just can't walk away from a situation like this and make a go of it." Kirke said nothing.

She felt quite disgusted, then thought, well, we'll see if he'll recover. If he does show fight, fine. If he doesn't, she thought mournfully, we're in real trouble. Right now, however, there's nothing to be said in the mood he's in. Just wait for Pedro.

Chapter 15

That night at dinner, feeling a bit nervous about their future, she talked further with her husband about it.

"Look, how you may feel about this job has nothing to do with how you go about it. Our whole future is at stake down here. You can't let your pride or your delicate feelings interfere with your effectiveness. You've got to make good. What happened today occurs, in one form or another, to any salesman. They have to take a lot of guff and button their lip when it happens—and keep their eye on the goal—to sell these people the product you represent."

"Yeah, I know. But when some guy tells me to go fly a kite, the way that guy did today, it really galls me."

"Forget it. The hallmark of a good salesman is persistence. He must keep coming back in spite of setbacks like that."

"Well, I can do that—I think—at least, for awhile. But another thing bothers me. What I should do when a situation arises in which I have to angle my shots—you know, distort my pitch slightly, say something I can't really verify, like exaggerating the profit I think a customer will make by coming with us? Salesmen, you know, have to do that sort of thing sometimes to make their quota. How good I'll be at telling those lies—I don't know."

She figured it was time to give him a good talking to.

"You should have thought of that before you took this job. Anyway, wait until that happens before you start worrying about it. You may not have to do it at all. This business is not what is called 'one shot selling.' That's where salesman can get brutal and get away with it, even if, in so doing, they alienate their customers. After all, they'll never see 'em again. But with you it's repeat business all the way. So, in order to retain your good relationships, I would imagine you'd probably have to be pretty straight with them. You probably won't have to twist too many arms. I think you'll be allright. Just concentrate on your presentations, and you'll do well because you're a fluent talker."

"I guess you're right," he said. He grinned and held up a finger. "The price of wisdom is above rubies."

"Furthermore, dear, think of our future. One of the reasons I married you was because you looked to me like a pretty good prospect to do well—both materially and socially. And that prospect has by no means disappeared from my thinking. I want it badly, and if you do ok down here, you can not only get over the past—I have to admit I've only thought of it twice since I've been here—but that future will be open sesame for us. In a couple of years we'll have a bit of change, gotten over the past and can either return to law school or continue in this business if you like it better—we'll be on our way. You can rise in business as well as law. Think of that, not about folding up on this opportunity."

"Well, I have to admit you do have a point."

For the next month his work proceeded smoothly. Her own spirits lifted considerably after this initial period of worry, and she felt happy and optimistic. But then a dramatic change occurred. One morning she awoke to the realization that she might be pregnant!

She was utterly floored "My God," she said to herself, "at this time, what a complication in our lives." Kirke, however, was overjoyed.

"Oh, hell, don't tell me that," he exclaimed when she raised the question of financial instability. Then, giving further vent to his feelings, "Darling—my congratulations! Boy, am I proud of you!"

"Oh, Sweet, I understand your happiness," she replied warmly. "Of course I want children, but right now? You haven't proved yourself on this job, really, and..."

"I'll murder it!" he cried emphatically. "Why not? There's nothing to hinder. We'll be allright. I'm so looking forward to being a father. I'm young, hard working, in good health. And you are, too, basically, so what's the problem? Don't worry."

She was cheered by his attitude. He then arranged to take the next day off to accompany her to her doctor. The doctor confirmed her suspicion. Kirke was so greatly pleased by this confirmation that he proclaimed that he would be the finest father that ever was. This statement made her very happy—she felt the new situation would further stimulate him to do well on his job. So it might be all for the better. And things were still going their way. He was, so far, getting along fine both with Senor Gutierrez, from whom he earned a couple of compliments, and the other men on the job. And she herself had managed the problems of domestic life quite well. Maria had proved no problem, as she was a mature woman and had no conflicting personal interest. So all things considered, everything was jake.

Chapter 16

This period of tranquility lasted for another month. She looked forward to exploring more Mayan ruins with her husband on those weekends, before her child came, when she was free from household duties and to seeing Mrs. Collins in four months. Next year seemed jubilant.

One morning on the way home from an errand to town, she thought she'd stop off at Amer-Mex and take her husband out to lunch. As she approached the office, she saw a woman emerging from its doorway. Her appearance was so striking it transfixed her. The perfect oval of her face framed a full, pouting mouth and insolently flashing eyes, and her long black hair had an attractive width of grey running through it. She was very tall and, though amply proportioned, extremely well built with full erect breasts, and her waist had a youthful trimness which revealed her approximate age which Sally estimated at about twenty-five. The most enticing feature about her, however, was the undulating sway she gave to her hips as she walked.

As Sally passed her on the steps, she took note of the fullness of her plump thighs evident under her skirt.

Knowing her husband's previous proclivity for women, she became a bit suspicious. Although, like most men, he never mentioned the women in his past, since his marriage he had been quite frank with her about all matters, including any chance meeting with other women. But he had made no mention of this one. Why? Well, if this was her first visit to the office...

She decided to find out. Over lunch she asked, "Do you know that attractive woman I saw coming out of the office today?"

"Oh, sure," he replied offhandedly, "she's Consuelo Lopez. Works at the library. They sent her over here with information we needed on local population shifts. You know, we're going to expand our operations in various areas."

"Just as a messenger, eh?"

"No. She's speaks beautiful English and is a library professional. She was very helpful in interpreting these government documents as they're quite technical."

"She's also quite pretty, isn't she?"

He smiled. "Yes, indeed," then laughed. "Why, if if weren't married—."

Quietly, "And is she a senorita?"

He grinned. "Yes."

Her jealousy flared. "And will she come back for repeat business?"

"Probably. She's been here a couple of times, so far, but why do you ask?"

"Oh, nothing. But I just wondered why you hadn't mentioned seeing her to me."

"Because, even though she's well-educated, she's not of our social class."

"Oh," she said, thinking to herself, you're lying, Kirke. Although you've mostly hung about with girls in our own class, socially, I know you for one of the least class conscious men alive. You took your liberal education seriously. You were active in community work in college. And your family has no prejudice. You'd very likely be interested in socializing with her. And talking to me about it. And then there's the out-of-character behaviour—not mentioning the fact that you've met her. There's something fishy.

She decided to drop the topic, and the rest of the luncheon hour passed amicably. But when he returned to work she decided she'd satisfy her curiosity. She'd stop by the library and have another look at this number.

Continuing her walk home she came to the library and stood for a moment admiring its beauty. The building, located a block from the zocalo, together with the nearby Governor's Palace was built in Colonial Baroque style, of adobe and stone with an arch forming an oval entryway. It was suggestive of the town's past. A meticulously mowed lawn encircled the building and extended to the main street. This street ran in a beeline through the business district until it reached the outskirts of the city.

The library interior she found equally pleasing. It was divided into two sections. One, the central building, housed the main literature collection; the other, an annex, held more specialized material, the music and art books and government documents. It was in this section, she thought, that she would find Senorita Lopez. Just inside the entrance which opened into the reading room was an oak and mahogany circulation desk; over in the left rear corner was a well-stocked reference section. On the side opposite and in a gracefully curving balcony were the bookshelves. The rest of the room was open except for some handsome exhibit cases and numerous lounge chairs. The rear wall was glass paneled and opened into a patio with a fountain in the center. The room was sunlit through broad windows and emanated an air of comfort, repose and study.

At the main desk in the annex she saw the woman she was looking for. On second glance, Senorita Lopez confirmed her previous estimate: dressed in a simple white dress, she was a knockout. And her nameplate confirmed Kirke's statement: she was a professional librarian. She was obviously no dummy. Now let's ascertain how personable she is, thought Sally.

Walking up to her she introduced herself as the wife of Kirke Moore. Senorita Lopez responded with a flashing smile and a warm reply. "Oh, yes, Mr. Moore—he is a delightful person. I so enjoy him. So interesting to talk to. I'm so glad to meet his wife."

After conversing for a few minutes about the kind of work she did—the Senorita was the documents librarian—Sally left with the strong impression that she knew her p's and q's and was exactly the type of person Kirke would be attracted to. And the upsetting thought that if she were unscrupulous she would constitute a definite threat to many a happy marriage lodged in the back of her mind. She thought she might have something to worry about.

Although the evening chats they had about his work had many references to the documents Senorita Lopez brought to him from the library, Kirke made only brief and, so it seemed to her, guarded references to her personally. He never elaborated about his relationship with her, a feature most uncharacteristic of him, for she had always found him quite open and frank with her. Her suspicion deepened; she knew that seven out of ten men would engage in promiscuity if the time and circumstances were propitious, and her husband had been a bit of a gay blade in his college years.

About two weeks later she made another trip to the office, this time to deliver some invoices her husband had brought home the previous night and had forgotten to take with him that morning. No one, however, was in the office. Sally wondered where her husband and Senor Gutierrez were. Then, deciding to leave, outside the office, in the parking area reserved for the trucks, she ran into Pedro, the driver who had accompanied them on that first memorable trip to Chichen Itza. She decided to see if he could understand her elementary Spanish to answer a couple of simple questions.

"Donde esta Senor Moore?" she asked him.

"No esta aqui," responded Pedro.

"Not here? Entonces donde?"

"Es en Ticul con Senorita Lopez."

"Ticul? Y con Senor Gutierrez?"

Pedro shook his head.

"Gracias, Pedro," she said in a steely tone, and with a great effort exerted all her self-control, turned on her heel and walked off, inwardly in sudden tumult. What was he doing in Ticul with that Lopez woman?

She knew he was cool enough to have an artful answer prepared for any direct question. She resolved to handle the situation by being calm and calculating herself. By subtle questioning she felt she could find out a good deal about this Lopez girl.

"How was your work today?" she asked him at dinner.

"Quite pleasant. Went to Ticul—you know, that's a small town near Uxmal—another big Maya center. Ticul is the pottery center of Yucatan, and I wanted to make contact with a number of businesses over there."

"Did you go over with anybody?"

"I went without a driver, as I felt I knew the route ok."

"And how was the trip?"

"I made quite a few contacts and did good business selling."

Knowing that he had not told her everything, she waited patiently.

After hesitating a moment, he resumed.

"I also took Consuelo Lopez. She wanted to make a survey of some sort connected with her population work, so I didn't mind her coming along. She was good company."

"I'll bet. I met her at the library a few weeks ago, and she told me you were most interesting to talk to."

"That's nice to hear. I find her also quite charming."

"Tell me more about her, will you?"

"Well, she's not originally from this area. She's from Mexico City. She was an only child, of parents now deceased. She was educated at the city university and after a few years of work with the government statistical office, thought library work would offer a fine career so she became a librarian. She worked in the city library in Mexico City for a couple of years, then transferred down here and has been employed locally ever since."

"Brains, beauty and education all wrapped up in one."

"Pretty much so. She's a delight to work with. Also, she's interested in the arts—books and music—and has not only the capacity to discharge difficult work but also the taste to appreciate the niceties of life. She's really ok."

"Did you really feel it necessary to take her to Ticul with you?"

"Just a favor."

Sally flushed.

"There are other means of transportation—aren't there?"

"Well, yes. But I felt our way was more convenient."

"H-m-m-m."

"I just know Consuelo in a business way."

Yes, she thought inwardly, that's why you were only too happy to take her with you on your trip to Ticul. She felt apprehensive. Her husband had been a bit too enthusiastic in his appraisal of the Senorita to suit her.

At home the next day she was very upset, as further thoughts disturbed her. What would her situation be if her marriage were disrupted? She was pregnant. On what or whom could she rely for financial support? Only her parents, and they had little to spare. And they were more than twenty-five hundred miles away, and they expected her to look after herself. Ordinarily she could do that, but now, she thought again, what could she do, being both pregnant and with a physical disability which, slight though it was, would effectively prevent her from working? What could she do? Nothing. She was dependent on her husband, financially.

And what about him? She felt disillusioned. He had not been the man she thought he was during his trial and now seemed to be displaying further lack of character by showing a somewhat more than casual interest in another woman. Was she only getting her just reward for snagging her husband the way she had? Then she thought that in her case, she was going to learn the hard way what Kirke's mother had cautioned—"Marry in haste, repent at leisure."

Chapter 17

For the following month Sally bided her time, awaiting developments. She saw that as Maria was doing an excellent job at the household duties and as Spanish was no longer interesting, there were only minor things to do. She then realized that she had neglected her bird feeder which she had installed on a tree in the center of her patio, so she made a mental note to secure some food for it the next day. Also, she caught up on some loose ends—she wrote a number of letters to old friends back home and listed a few supplies which were in arrears. But still, during her mid-morning coffee break, she wondered what her future would be.

During this period she thought again about the worth of her husband. She had become more aware of her slow estrangement from him since the death of her sister. In spite of her earnest attempts, she had never forgiven him for the accident. Even though he would be the father of her child, she had nursed an antipathy towards him which together with the possibility that he was now becoming disinterested in her had augmented it to the point of contempt. But nevertheless, she then reasoned, he was her husband and still felt bound to him by the bonds of pride and passion.

But recently he had made her even more dissatisfied. His work had begun to entail working more closely with Consuelo Lopez. Since the city government, being anxious to develop good relations with American firms, had given the library carte blanche permission to assist them, he felt perfectly free to make use of her talent. A good deal of reference work on population statistics in connection with increasing sales was necessary, and reports on the results had to be made and filed away. In these respects Consuelo Lopez was invaluable to him as a technical assistant. He was seeing far too much of that library worker to suit her.

It didn't help matters either as he spoke to her enthusiastically about how Consuelo was helping him. He said he found the cataloguing of reports very challenging indeed.

"Many of them are quite long. They average forty-five pages and have to be carefully perused before assigning subject headings because they are very complicated. However, it's very gratifying to me to review how we're handling the affairs of our customers. And, boy, is Consuelo a big help in showing me the ins and outs of working with the filing system and assigning the index numbers."

"I'm sure she's very useful," said Sally halfheartedly.

After he had worked with Consuelo for about a month, Sally felt he became even more inconsiderate. He aroused her ire by taking Consuelo out frequently for lunch.

"But after all," he explained to mollify her when she questioned the need, "when you see a girl regularly, three days a week, it would be ill-mannered of me if I didn't ask her to lunch now and then. I know you're broad-minded enough to be tolerant of that."

"Oh, I suppose I am," she replied matter-of-factly. "It's customary in business, after all."

Then, in the fifth month of their stay in Mexico an incident occurred which made her, for the first time, deeply suspect that her husband was being unfaithful to her.

On the tenth of the month, she called the office to express her appreciation and acceptance of an invitation Senior Gutierrez had extended to her and Kirke to attend a party the following night at his residence. It was to be a big formal party including many of their customers and future prospects, and Gutierrez said he wanted Kirke there to meet them. To Sally this indicated the

The Ruins at Uxmal

increasing importance of Kirke in the plans of the company. Possibly he might become a long term employee—that wouldn't be so bad, with a royal future for them back in the states. She, of course, felt it was absolutely necessary for them to accept.

"Buenos dias, Senor," she said as he answered. "You are so nice to invite Kirke and me to your party. We certainly accept your invitation most happily. Now—," and she laughed, "what time is it customary to show up for a Mexican party, anyway?"

"Oh, eight-thirty would be just fine. We Mexicans eat late in the evening and then get gay afterwards."

"Fine. We'll look forward to it. Kirke, as you know, will be due back from Sayil this evening, and he'll be delighted to learn of it."

"Kirke? Back this evening? Why, no, Senora. He arrived back this afternoon and left early, around two o'clock. He said he was going to see Consuelo Lopez about some business at the library."

"He is?" she exclaimed, greatly startled. "Why he didn't mention..." but then, recovering, broke off and, "Well, thank you—he's back so I don't have to worry about him on the road."

She hung up the phone and reflected—hard! Then, making up her mind, she called the library, her suspicion mounting. "Yo deseo hablar con Senor Moore."

"Senor Moore no es aqui. El salio con Senorita Lopez." Utterly furious, Sally hung up!

So—he was spending the afternoon with Consuelo, not in the library, not at the office—and probably not to discuss business! And he had previously told her he would be away on a two day trip to Sayil and expected to be home not before the evening of the second day—today!

"I wouldn't doubt but that they're meeting in her apartment," she surmised with suppressed fury. Even though she was with child, he was probably philandering!

Nevertheless, she restrained her wrath when he showed up about six o'clock that evening. She knew a lot was at stake at the party tomorrow night at Gutierrez's and was aware that their lives had to be on an even keel until it was over. Furthermore, she realized again she was dependent on her husband for financial support and could think of no solution to that problem. She decided that self-contrtol was better than an outburst; she had better shut up, at least for the moment, and make no scene.

She continued in this frame of mind up to the time to dress for the party the next evening. She hardly spoke to her husband when he returned home from work. However, as he had just completed a big contract with a local hennequin-growing company, he was too exuberant to notice her indifference. He just said a brief hello and retired to the bathroom to bathe and dress.

In the bedroom, Sally thought of how hard she had worked to make their marriage a success. She had borne the tragic death of her sister with reasonable fortitude, had bolstered her husband in his times of weakness and had been instrumental in keeping their lives headed in the right direction after they had come to Mexico. She spent quite a bit of time reviewing that and felt he had a lot to thank her for.

She saw that Kirke had completed dressing and was surveying himself before the full length mirror in the bathroom. Carefully he straightened his maroon bow tie, brushed a few specks of lint off of his evening clothes and adjusted his cummerbund. Then, having at his age a perfect figure, he patted his flat stomach and paused for just a moment to only caress her at her dressing table before marching into the front room, fully prepared to enjoy the evening.

The Ruins at Uxmal

His perfunctory action only roused her resentment. She continued to wonder if her suspicion that her marriage was going awry was correct.

She undressed and got into the shower, relishing the hot, needlelike drops of water on her body. Afterwards, she took a long look at her figure in the bathroom mirror. Her breasts and arms were full and firm, and there was no trace of a bulge around her middle. Not too many tamales, she reflected. Her legs were perfect, and her body showed the bloom of youth. I don't see what that Lopez dish has on me, she thought.

She donned a terry cloth robe and seated herself at her dressing table. Carefully, she brushed her hair glossy and sleek and then examined her skin which was absolutely clear—no blemishes of any kind. Her regular features gave her a perfect profile. She was good looking and knew it.

She finished her toilette and began dressing. From a gigantic wardrobe closet she selected the outfit she had worn the night of the accident—it was her best—the white organdy dress with a pink satin sash and white pumps with roses across the toes and took a pair of the sheerest silk stockings from a crudely paneled credenza. But as she dressed, her only thought was, oh, if only I could be happy.

But she was terribly worried. She considered Kirke's attitude. Recently he had become rather testy, berating her when she had mislaid his bathrobe or failed to put the shoeshine kit back in its proper place in the bathroom cabinet. Did this indicate that he was becoming sick of her? It had not been usual with him to fly off the handle that way. It was quite different from the consideration he had shown her before they were married.

Then she thought of Consuelo Lopez. It was infuriating how Kirke had first met her. A business contact through the library, further developments as the need for her in his work grew, one thing had led to another, and now he was infatuated with her. It was not unlike Kirke to be forward in meeting women; she knew he liked them, but was he capable of infidelity? Was he not only a weak sister—as evidenced by his wilting on his second sale—was he also an immoralist? So much for her judgement: she just didn't know.

Would it be like Kirke to divorce her? Or was he the type to be discreet? Again she didn't know. If his attraction to that slut was only on the animal level, once his fling was over she hoped he would deftly discard her and return to her. She felt he knew she was too valuable to lose.

Kirke was probably capable of operating subtly; he was intelligent and worldly and, therefore, could likely be crafty and devious. But because he had always been straightforward in his dealings with her, she was only the more deeply hurt by his double dealing.

She knew she had been, as a devoted and loving wife, a great asset to him. In spite of feeling somewhat dispassionate, she had been strongly supportive in his travail both after the accident and with the law; she had offered no real objections to his wanting to come to Mexico and had adapted well to the life here, having been fully capable of running their home and catering to his every whim, from purchasing his favorite brand of Mexican cigarette to his choice of Mexican beer. She reasoned that she had a right to be proud of herself, although, what with this ongoing affair, all that she had done seemed unimportant now. She felt that she had suddenly become, for Kirke, simply an article of display; she would be useful for going with him to company parties, for entertaining clients and also something to satisfy his vanity by showing her off. Yes, he had changed from being the attentive lover she had first known, the one who regarded her as not only the stable linchpin of their lives, but also his cynosure, the center of his universe. She felt that even in the short time they had been married, she had failed to become his sensual companion-in-arms; she had not fulfilled her womanhood with him. She was like a flower which had withered prematurely on the branch. It was these thoughts that were with her as they left to walk to the party.

Chapter 18

When they arrived at the home of Senor Gutierrez, Sally took note of its looks as they waited to be admitted at the front door. She was quite surprised; it was much larger and more elaborate than what she envisioned the manager of a small branch for a U.S. company in a foreign country would have. Its size was 1/3 as big as a hacienda, and it was built in Colonial Baroque style. Unusual for a house in Merida, it sat back from the street. Its walls were of whitewashed plaster, and its single doorway was of vertical planks. On one side of this door, near the corner of the house was a loggia. Sally presumed the interior of the house would be laid out in corridors surrounding a patio and contained in these sides would be the various rooms. One of the larger rooms, undoubtedly located near the front, Sally also thought, would probably serve as a reception room. The white color of the house blended with red shutters, almost tall enough to reach to the coping. A red-shingled roof completed the picture.

"Gutierrez must have money," said Sally, amazed.

"He's been with the company for some years, and they pay well," answered Kirke. "After all, the price for a native good enough to supervise an expanding operation must be pretty high as they're hard to come by. Secondly, he was in the army, fairly high up, and the opportunity for it to become well off by colluding with whatever governmental administration is in power is legendary. Furthermore, he's a sharp businessman, and I imagine he's well invested. By any standard, especially Mexican, he's undoubtedly well to do."

"Some fellow, eh? Well, why the devil would he want to work—especially for our firm?"

The Ruins at Uxmal

"I think he's as ambitious as the deuce, wants to become a local big shot—politically—and hopes to use this position to reach that goal."

The door opened, and a servant greeted them.

"Buenas noches, Senor, Senora," she said, smiling and curtseying.

She held the door open for them and indicated the way down a hall, furnished with small, ornate tables. As they stepped down into the reception room, Sally noticed at the farther end a huge fireplace and a handmade breakfront containing many objets d'art. Also, hanging on the walls were portraits of the Senor, in military uniform, an older woman and a young man and woman.

"That's the family, I guess," said Kirke. "The other three are probably his wife and children."

To the left was a small couch, done in blue and gold-braided textured fabric. On the right were four blue velvet chairs. By the fireplace was a blue and beige oversize divan. Just inside the doorway to Kirke's left stood a tall wall clock and to the right a Chinese red writing desk made of hand-painted wood with a large mirror hanging over it. In a far corner stood a brazier. Three brass lamps stood on three small mahogany tables with matching chairs, situated about the room.

"Buenas noches, mis amigos," said Senor Gutierrez from the landing, extending his hands and then advancing into the room. "My home is your home." Such a gallant greeting, thought Sally. She couldn't help noticing how youthful and handsome he looked, with unlined features, carefully trimmed grey mustache, full head of hair and springy step. I'll bet, she thought, that as a single man he was quite a hand with the ladies.

"My, you have a most attractive place, Senor," said Kirke.

"You have, indeed, Senor," added Sally. "And I'm amazed at its size. If it were on a larger plot, it would be an estate."

"Yes, it would," replied the Senor. "But as it is, it serves very well to entertain my guests. Later on, I'll show you around, if you like. Now shall we join the others?" He indicated the large wooden door leading to the patio. As they went outside numerous couples were strolling about or standing at serving tables—Sally presumed it was a buffet—or seated at other tables arranged about the patio, eating.

Senor Gutierrez led the way to a small group of men, standing by themselves, a short distance from the people who were seated. Among them was Senor Gonzalez and his son, Emilio.

"You know Hector and Emilio," he said to Kirke and Sally. "But, Kirke, I want you to meet the others. They're among the most important hennequin growers in the area."

After making the introductions, he left Kirke with them and taking Sally by the arm withdrew a short distance. "It's wise to leave him alone with them," said the Senor. "They'll get to know each other better that way." He turned to her. "Now let us talk."

"Didn't I see portraits of your wife and children in the reception room?" asked Sally, curious. "Where are they? I'd like to meet them."

The Senor sighed. "My wife is not here. She is very ill with a deadly illness—cancer—and is confined to the hospital. She is only expected to live a few weeks. My daughter? She is away in Mexico City. She teaches school there. My son—he died several years ago from malaria."

"Oh, I'm sorry to hear such news about your wife and son. I hope her passing will be peaceful."

"We have been married for many years. I cannot bear the thought of being alone. So, after a decent interval, I will probably remarry."

"That is wise. Put the past behind you."

"You are right. But now let's talk of more pleasant things."

"Yes, of course." He's not one to dwell on his unhappiness, Sally thought. Then, "First, let me tell you Kirke so enjoyed Senor Gonzalez when he made his sale to him. It got us off to a fine start. And I certainly liked his son, Emilio. We had quite a chat while Kirke was talking to his father.

"Emilio is a fine young man."

"I don't know much about his official position, only that he's an agronomist who works for the government."

"Well, as he's the son of a well-to-do and well-connected family," said Senor Gutierrez, "it wouldn't surprise me if he rose pretty high, not only in government circles, but also in the upper class of society in Mexico City."

"He said he was interested in inheriting his father's business."

"Oh, he could hire someone to run it for him while he would live the good life in Mexico City. There's not too much for a young man to do in Merida, or in all of Yucatan for that matter."

"Well, I've heard, of course, that Mexico City is a magnet which draws."

"True. It does, in spite of seemingly insoluble problems. Its location is in an earthquake zone, it is surrounded by volcanoes, it sits in soft subsoil and is far from water, food and energy supplies."

"Why would people flock there, then?"

"Because the country's economic strategy in the nineteen forties forced them to do so."

"Could you explain—a little."

"Very well. Resources were poured into industry, commerce and urban construction. Schools were nearby, and health services were accessible. Many jobs were there—and not much anywhere else. And with that came chaotic growth."

"I always thought Mexico City was a great place to live."

"It still is. But uncontrolled growth will ruin it. You wouldn't mind living there now, however, and probably even for the next twenty years."

"Tell me more about Emilio."

The Senor laughed and then his eyes twinkled. "My you're curious."

"I have reasons for being interested in the family—my husband's work."

The Senor assumed an impish look. "Oh, really? Come now—aren't you really thinking of romance?" He threw back his head and chuckled. "Are you, by chance, interested in Emilio? —his prospects, from what I know, seem to be excellent."

"Oh, Senor, you are an old scamp. Assuming that I would make a play for Emilio. I've only met him once."

"Oh, does that stop you?"

"Yes." She laughed and blushed.

The Senor laughed with her. "I see you understand my sense of humor."

Sally looked for a rejoinder.

"Well," she said, "if I ever tire of my husband, I'll keep Emilio in mind."

"You could do worse. You're young, of course, pretty and winsome—that's enough to attract any man, including me, even though I'm twenty years older than you."

"Well now, Senor, I promise I won't count you out. After all, you're quite handsome, and, of course, you have money."

"And that last is very important, isn't it, my dear?" The Senor bowed. "Now you must excuse me. I have to circulate among my guests. But before I go, let me introduce you to a young associate of your husband's. Her name is Consuelo Lopez. I invited her tonight so she could help him by charming his clients."

"I've met Senorita Lopez before," said Sally, flushing. Then, feeling an urge to size her up further, "Why don't I just, as they say in America, sashay over and chat with her?"

"As you wish," said Senor Gutierrez. "Now I must go."

After Gutierrez had left, Sally could not find Consuelo anywhere in the patio. And where the devil is Kirke? she then asked herself, not seeing him mixing with the guests. Well, she then thought, why don't I just look around for him?

She opened a door from the patio into a dimly lit room in a wing of the house and then suddenly stopped. On the farther side, standing outside an open window, illuminated by the light from the room she saw Consuelo, speaking very animatedly to her husband, her arm around his neck, gently stroking. Sally became tense with anger. Cautiously edging up to the window, she listened—very carefully.

"Mio caro," Consuelo was saying, then in English, "My dear. What do you care about her? Since we've met, both of us have known the happiness we've both longed for. You know that your wife isn't for you although I understand your feelings about the oncoming birth of your child. You feel you have to stay married to her for its sake. But I can put up with that—I'm a girl from Mexico City, and I have the ideas of a modern Mexican city girl."

"What do you mean?"

Sally needed no further information. She had learned at market a few derogations of "modern Mexican city girls"—

independent, fast living and "on the take," some of them anyway.

"I mean that I'm not like most girls from the country. I'm a city girl, can maintain myself as I have an income of my own, and I've been educated out of the customs of the peasantry."

"Now I think I understand you," said Kirke. He grasped her tightly in his arms and kissed her passionately. Kirke, you swine, muttered Sally under her breath.

"I have no objection to becoming your 'la querida,'—how do you call it, your inamorata, your mistress?"

"You're willing to settle for that?"

Sally just managed to restrain an outburst.

"Of course. In this country it is quite customary for a man to have a 'casa chica,' a 'segundo frente,' as we say down here. No stigma attaches to it. Furthermore, what you call feminism in your country has just started in a few of the large cities in Mexico—particularly Mexico City—and, as I have just told you, I am from there."

"Well—in spite of the custom of your country, your forwardness surprises me."

"Have you any objections?"

"'Well—," he released her, hesitated a moment, scratched his head, laughed and then, "No." Again he grasped her and embraced her passionately. "You're the most dynamic woman I've ever met. I'm crazy about you."

"Good!" she said in a tone of firm conviction and then smiled winningly at him. "I'm so glad you feel that way."

He patted her affectionately.

"Well, I'll have to see if I can work it out. Although extramarital situations occur everywhere, they're a bit more ticklish in

The Ruins at Uxmal

the states—they're not really acceptable, and my wife...It'll be a new experience for me." Then he kissed her again. Sally clenched her fists. "Now we'd better be getting back. Gutierrez will be wondering where I am and what I've been doing." He took her by the arm and escorted her along the outside path which led to a patio entry.

For several minutes Sally just stood, pent-up with fury. Finally she felt she had to sit down, exhausted by her experience. She paced slowly to the door, went out into the patio, picked out a chair and seated herself, apparently composed, but still inwardly furious. For several more minutes she sat in this agitated state until a hand gently touched her shoulder, interrupting her mood. Senor Gutierrez stood by her, smiling.

"Why do you look so peturbed, Senora?" he asked. "Tonight you should be gay."

She realized the necessity for a front. "Oh, I'm angry because I was unable to locate my husband or Senorita Lopez and was wondering where I should look."

"They're somewhere about—don't worry about them," advised the Senor. "Now I was wondering if I could show you the rest of my house, since my official duties as greeter have, for the moment, been discharged, and you are available. You remember, I offered to take you around—I like to do that to my friends."

"I'd be delighted, Senor," said Sally, anxiously seizing upon something to do.

The Senor conducted her through some remaining rooms of the house—another reception room, the dining room, a living room, the bedrooms, his office containing a desk with a hand-tooled border, before arriving at the last—the library.

"Let us sit down and talk," he said, "I've got something to say to you." He escorted her into the room and sat down in a leather lounge chair.

"You do? Well, I imagine you're very well equipped to do it," said Sally, now in control of herself, taking another chair and looking at the sets of Thackeray, Balzac, Stendhal and Cervantes together with other fiction, philosophy and history lining the walls around the room and drawing the obvious conclusion that the Senor was a very cultivated man. "I would imagine from these," she said indicating the books with her hand, "that you are a graduate of the University of Mexico?"

The Senor shook his head. "No, I went to military school in France—to St. Cyr. But I took a few courses in literature at the Sorbonne before embarking on a military career here at home. But I was retired because of a slight disability."

"But it's obvious you're still active."

"Yes. I hope to achieve something politically, and this job I hold with the company is one avenue to it."

"Kirke told me as much."

"Yes, a regional post—of importance—in the government of the province of Yucatan would be a nice way to live out the rest of my life. After all, I'm only forty-two and hardly ready to retire. It would give me a position of power and prominence, both politically and socially, and the prestige which goes with it. And also considerable emolument."

"From what you've just said, you would be leading both an important and gay life—even in Yucatan, which you spoke so disparagingly about as a place of social activity."

"Oh, one can find much to do on the level of a regional governor," said Gutierrez knowingly.

"You're set to fly pretty high."

The Senor nodded and said, smiling, "And I think my chances are pretty good. After all, I was fortunate enough to be associated with the government, politically, when I was in the army—and that's an important connection—and I have done considerable work of an administrative nature. I also have a splendid education—which is also important."

"Well, I hope Fortune smiles on you," said Sally, judging the Senor as both an ambitious and impressive person, "Now, you said you wanted to tell me something."

The Senor took a cigar from his breast pocket and very slowly removed the wrapper before putting it in his mouth. Then he deliberately pulled a lighter from his pocket, lit the cigar, sat back in his chair and looked about the room, carefully considering what he had to say.

"I hope you will realize that what I am saying will be for your benefit—yours and Kirke's," he began. "In the long run, it is my hope that it will be, although what I have to tell you may, at first, be somewhat upsetting."

Although a slight tremor of fear stirred her, Sally appreciated his tact. But what could he be referring to? Everything, so far as she knew, was going well at the office; Kirke had expressed no concern to her. Anxiously she waited for the Senor to continue.

"I'm speaking this way because of what I have gathered about you, that is, about your character. In talking to you when I first met you, and, right now, you impress me as a strong woman, and as you know how to handle yourself, you probably have considerable influence over your husband."

"Well, I hoped I had," said Sally sardonically. The Senor ignored it.

"What I have to say concerns him. When I first met you two, I thought fortune had smiled on me. Here you were—two fine young Americans, intelligent, well educated, ambitious and ready for anything. The man seemed ideal for work; his wife—ah! —a beauty who also looked like a true helpmeet in the typical American tradition—" he smiled and puffed on his cigar—"not like the stereotype we have down here." .

He is gracious although he has something unpleasant to disclose, she thought.

"Now this matter is of concern to you because it is about Kirke's work. I don't mean to worry you, but I have to tell you for the good of both of you. I was very pleased with Kirke's work, at first—but now, to speak frankly, I'm not. He has been very inattentive to the details of his job recently—he's been making too many errors; something seems to be spoiling his concentration. I was wondering if there might be trouble at home. May I ask, is there, and, if so, can you correct it?"

Sally was taken aback.

"Have you mentioned this to Kirke?" she then asked anxiously.

"No. Not yet. I thought you could express it to him more tactfully than I and hoped that would suffice."

Sally thought of Consuelo Lopez. It must be because of her; she must be distracting him. That devil! Should I tell Senor Gutierrez about her? Could he stop Kirke from seeing her? Or should she handle it herself? No, she decided, the first way would be best, if possible. It would avoid a ruckus at home which she must avoid—she almost cursed as she realized once again she was dependent on her husband.

"Senor," she said, "I think I know the reason for Kirke's falling down on his job. Now what I have to say embarrasses me greatly, but..." She paused.

The Senor raised his eyebrows. "It does?"

"Yes." She hesitated a moment, then plunged in. "It's about this girl, Consuelo Lopez. I know my husband has become interested—a bit too interested—for his own good—in her."

"Senorita Lopez has been helping him in his work."

The Ruins at Uxmal

"Perhaps a bit too much, Senor. Kirke praised her to the skies, but I thought, even at first, she might be more than just a business asset. And," she said viciously, "as is has turned out, she's an aggressive vixen—I found this out for sure just this evening." She threw out her hands before continuing. "I have to tell you bluntly because I don't know how else to do it. And," she concluded, "may I ask your help?" The Senor nodded.

"I heard them in the garden outside the patio, he accepting her offer to become his mistress."

The Senor looked at his hands, then, "I understand. But how can I—what do you want me to do?"

"You might tell Kirke his work is falling off, his job is threatened and that it would be advisable for him to concentrate on it and not on anything else."

The Senor thought for a moment, then nodded. "I can do that," he concluded. "But why do you ask for help from me regarding a domestic matter?"

"I'm asking you to do this—you see, Senor, I feel that you would have more influence on Kirke than I, at present."

"I see" He nodded his head and rose to his feet. "I will speak to Kirke about the importance of discharging his job. I can do that, but, of course, I can go no further."

"I understand, Senor. And thank you so much."

"I am sorry for you that your life is becoming so complicated."

"It's even more complicated than you think. I'm pregnant."

"That is too bad. Very, very bad. Again, allow me to say I'm sorry."

"That's the way I've been hit. Now, it's getting late, and Kirke will be looking for me, I'm sure." The Senor nodded, rose to his feet to escort her back to the patio, taking her arm as he did so.

But a surprise awaited Sally when she re-entered the patio, looking for her husband.

"Senora," said Emilio, addressing her from a table by the door. "Where have you been? I have been looking all over for you. I wanted to meet the lady I found so charming when I met her at my father's a few months ago."

Although hardly in the mood to be flattered, Sally welcomed the distraction.

"Senora, con mucho gusto," he then remarked, getting up and bowing. Sally, considered his manner—it was gallant; then, she thought a trifle defiantly, why not enjoy another man for the moment. She then delayed her search for Kirke for a few minutes, exchanging pleasantries with Emilio. Finally, she said, a little impatiently, "I have to go now. But I've enjoyed speaking with you."

"It causes me to regret that our talk was so brief." he replied warmly. "Perhaps we can continue it some other time."

"Well, why not?" replied Sally assertively. "Remember my invitation to lunch with Elizabeth Collins? When I hear from her, I'll contact you at your father's address, and you can join us."

"That would give me the greatest pleasure," said Emilio, "Now Kirke is approaching so I know you must go. Adios, Senora, until we meet again."

"Adios, Senor Gonzalez." She nodded to Kirke as he came up, then led him away towards the door, saying only curtly that she had become ill and that it was impossible for them to stay.

Chapter 19

Having decided not to say anything to Kirke about his extra-marital affair, Sally occupied herself by watching for any telltale sign which might indicate that he had given up Consuelo.

An apparent indication of this appeared when he told her he was seeing less of her at the office. Sally thought Gutierrez's warning was working. However, as time passed, she realized it had not availed. Kirke simply got around this limitation by seeing Consuelo in the evenings. Always for these visitations he had the usual excuse—the pressure of work, saying that Gutuerrez had told him to devote more time to the preparation of his sales pitches and that this change had entailed the late meetings with Consuelo at the library. He had asked her not to call him, telling her that his time at the library was limited by its hour of closing. She figured that he was becoming more like the typical Mexican husband—openly carrying on in a fashion accepted by Mexican mores and became even more contemptuous of him.

She was distracted from thinking about this, however, when her mother wrote and told her that her father was sick and might have to enter a convalescent home—money would then be short. Should she return home now? No! —wait! This would only add her problems to her mother's, which were very bad—then she received a telephone call from Elizabeth Collins to make an appointment for lunch. The ring reminded her of the time she had been in Mexico—six months, and all she was experiencing flashed through her mind. Feeling burdened by its drama, she mentioned that a great deal had happened to her.

"Not trouble, I hope?" said Elizabeth.

"Oh, nothing to bother you with," said Sally, recovering her aplomb. "I think I can handle it."

"Well, if I can be of any help..." said Elizabeth. "You're a young person and may need a bit of advice." She laughed. "You appeal to my motherly instincts."

Sally dropped her guard a little. "I may take you up on that."

"Well, of course, I don't mean to meddle, but I am available. For now, however, how's your husband doing on his job?"

"Just fine."

"Good. And where would you like to have lunch?"

"I remember a lovely place where Kirke and I stopped on our first day in Merida. It's up the main street of town, about two blocks from the Hotel Casa del Balam."

"I know the place. What say I meet you there at twelve o'clock tomorrow?".

"That'll be fine. See you then." She hung up the phone, then remembering her promise to Emilio, picked up the receiver and put through a call to the residence of Senor Hector Gonzalez.

Elizabeth was already seated at a table in the patio when she arrived. She was beautifully dressed in a black and white print dress, her white hair falling to cheek level, her eyes alertly observing the movement of the crowd, and as Sally approached, a warm smile crossed her features. Her usual vivacity and charm, thought Sally.

After a drink, Sally relaxed completely. In response to Elizabeth's friendly inquiries, she said yes, she and Kirke were having a wonderful time, Kirke was getting along very well with his boss, the house was fine, the maid had turned out to be a gem and Kirke had taken her on a trip to Chichen Itza where they had seen the Mayan ruins and were planning more. Mexico was proving to be a busy and interesting experience. Throughout her recital Elizabeth Collins listened attentively, offering now and

The Ruins at Uxmal

then helpful comments on how to manage things better and some interesting observations about Mexico, especially the Mayan ruins Then Sally turned to more intimate talk.

"You know," she said, "even though I scarcely know you, both from your knowledge of the world—which is obvious—and from the sympathy with which you've listened to me, I feel so friendly that I 'd like to have a heart-to-heart talk with you. You're so damn nice—I really want to. Do you mind if I open up a bit and tell you something personal?"

Mrs. Colliins smiled. "No, of course not. Feel free to do so. I'm a sympathetic listener."

Sally leaned forward, gesticulating as she spoke.

"It's about Kirke. I really can't think of a sophisticated approach so I might as well barge ahead. Although I've already talked this over with Senor Gutierrez, Kirke's boss, I don't think it has done much good. I need some advice, and I feel you're the one to whom I should talk because you're the only American woman at hand and a friend."

"Well, I'll be glad to help, if I can. What's on your mind?"

"When we came down here, we were fleeing from a tragic incident back home. My sister had just been killled in an auto wreck, and Kirke was inadvertantly responsible for it"

"Really!" said Elizabeth, astonished. "How terrible!" Then, most compassionately, "You've been though quite a lot for a youngster." Sally nodded.

"We had to put it behind us so we figured we could do it by working a couple of years at some job far away from Long Island—where we're from. As I said before, things went well, at least, at first."

"Go on," said Mrs. Collins.

"About the only thing which complicated matters then, however, was that I became pregnant. But Kirke was delighted so, in spite of the additional responsibility, I imagined things would still be ok."

"Uh-huh."

"Trouble, however, has cropped up in the last two months. And," she hung her head and looked disgusted, "it's serious."

"What is it?"

Sally hesitated and then blurted it out. "Kirke seems to have gotten interested in another woman."

"No! I am surprised! I would have thought the prospect of having a child would drive all such thoughts from his mind."

"You'd think so, wouldn't you? But that isn't the case. He's just flipped his lid. Gone nuts over some local belle."

"Oh, I'm sorry to hear it. And you're so far away from home."

"That is one bad feature—but the blow to my pride is much worse. After all, we haven't been married very long. I'm pretty badly shaken up with nobody to turn to."

"I can appreciate how you feel—I really can. Speaking frankly, I had a similar experience a number of years ago. And I too was with child."

"Furthermore, in addition to that, all the dreams I had for our future have been blown sky high."

"Well, I can see that they would be."

"All our ambitions for Kirke to have a brilliant career and for us to rise socially in the New York world of society have been destroyed. All because Kirke has lost his head over this woman."

"Know much about her?"

"Her name is Consuelo Lopez. She's a local librarian. Kirke met her when he had to dig up information he needed for his job."

"Do you think he'll get over her?"

"I don't know. But even if he did, would I want him back? I doubt it. I've been pretty badly bruised by this thing."

She waited while Elizabeth finished her drink, then continued.

"And furthermore, she's a pretty formidable rival. She's beautiful, smart and knows her oats. She's talked herself into being his mistress and will probably take him away from me entirely."

"It's quite possible she would try that. Kirke is an American; she probably thinks he has money, and she might want to go to the states, preferably as the wife of a 'rico Americano.' Nowadays a lot of Mexican girls from Mexico City want to, as they're lured by the more unrestricted style of living for women in the states."

"I really don't know what to do."

"You're not going to fight with her about this?"

"No. I am pretty disgusted with Kirke, not so much with her. But to be frank, maybe I'm reaping my just reward. Of course, being only twenty-two, I was nuts about Kirke, at first, but, essentially, I married him for his prospects—that predominated."

"But you really did care deeply about your marriage?"

"Oh yes—there was, of course, an element of physical attraction and his personality—romance—but that has all faded what with his infidelity, and now I'm concerned only with my practical situation. As I said before, I'm pregnant, and I also have a slight physical disability which prevents me from working."

"Well, you could divorce him. Even if you can't work, there is alimony And as the one who was injured, you'll be given custody of the child."

"Yes. I could count on that."

"How does he feel about the child?"

"He's looking forward very much to becoming a father."

"Well, he probably won't divorce you because of that," said Mrs. Collins thoughtfully, "Not at first, anyway. But even though it may be complicated..."

"Divorce looks like the way out," finished Sally.

"Be comforted by the fact that Consuelo Lopez may not have shown her real hand to your husband. She may be using him for her own benefit—exclusively. He may be sowing the seeds of his own misfortune by getting mixed up with her. And there are worse things that could happen to you. So don't take life so hard. You're young, and you'll survive. What you have to think about is your immediate problem." She leaned across the table and patted Sally's hand.

"You're so right. It's such a relief to talk to you."

"Now, from what I'm going to say, don't think I'm cynical. It's just realistic, practical advice. As I said before, I'm a divorcee—and damn happy to be free of men. I don't dislike 'em, but I prefer my freedom. It's not so bad to be free. But with a child and in your state, you need a man—at least to talk to, if nothing else. It'll buck you up. And, furthermore, think of this: if you're in the mood to take on another, why don't you look around? I know that's a daring thing for some people to do, but it's justifiable for a young woman in the position you're in—on the outs with your husband—and I think it's most practicable for you. You're pretty and charming. I think you could do allright in using your wiles to snare some man."

The Ruins at Uxmal

"Well, that's interesting. But you make it sound so cold-blooded."

"It's done every day—cold-bloodedly or not."

"I'm rather startled. But what you say may be a good idea, as I still want romance, and I'm not really sour on men. I suppose it's inevitable. But right now? In a foreign country? And with a foreigner?"

"Mexicans are no worse than anybody else. You might like their charm—they have that."

"H-m-m-m." Sally smiled.

"Tell me—do you know anyone?"

"Only Senor Gutierrez, Kirke's boss, Senor Hector Gonzalez and Emilio, his son, who is joining us this afternoon. When we visited his father's hacienda, he told me he knew you so I felt free to invite him. He was charming."

"Yes, he is. And he's also quite handsome, don't you think?"

"Yes."

"Could you go for him?"

Sally laughed. "I know he's well set up, with excellent prospects careerwise and financially." She then thought, my father is sick, money is short at home. Marriage?

"Well, now, look here—although I don't know the reason why, it seems to me that Emilio is unhappily married. We became friendly during our work together, and, once, he passed some cynical comments about marriage. I bet he's on the outs with his wife."

"He did?"

"Yes. And his attitude was consistent over the week I was with him—very morose. From the way he acted, it looked as if his gripe was of long standing."

"Are you saying that Emilio's marriage may go on the rocks?"

"That's what I'm presuming—exactly that."

"A prospect for me, then, is what you're implying, are you not?"

"It seems as though he might be ideal for you. If you like him, you might pay him some attention And, as you say, he's joining us for lunch. You could look him over then."

"Well, I hadn't figured myself as a home wrecker."

"What have you to lose?"

"Nothing, I suppose, except that my life would become even more complicated than it now is. I might be biting off more than I could chew."

"Nothing risked, nothing gained. But, of course, there are risks. You would be taking on a different culture in marrying a Mexican man. But I know Emilio. He's charming and, in spite of his present difficulty, impresses me as potentially a good family man. I don't think you'd be troubled by a problem with a mistress, if you remain desirable to him—even in Mexico."

"You know, you might have a good idea."

"Let me emphasize what I said before. Emilio is of good family, moneyed, and life in Mexico as the wife of a local financial and social baron might be ok. Think about it."

"What you say is intriguing." Far better then burdening her mother at home.

"Your child will be taken care of, you'd probably give Emilio heirs—and you'd lead quite a nice life. You'd have entree to the best society both here and in Mexico City and plenty of money. Think about it. Opportunities like that are hard to come by—most anywhere."

The Ruins at Uxmal

The waiter arrived, and they ordered a second drink while waiting for Emilio. Elizabeth continued talking enthusiastically about life in Mexico, saying that if Sally liked the tropical atmosphere, was able to either live in or visit Mexico City and if she liked bathing on Mexican beaches, she wouldn't have anything to complain of. Sally tried to pay attention to her talk, but her thoughts were far more about the very interesting idea Mrs. Collins had proposed. However, these were soon interrupted by the arrival of Emilio.

She saw him when he arrived at the gateway of the patio, looking about for their table. She studied him carefully. Her previous appraisal proved correct. He was quite manly looking, tall for a Mexican, with carefully cut black hair, and he was wearing a white linen suit which hung loosely on his spare frame. When he saw them, he smiled broadly and waved his hand in greeting as he strode over to their table.

After drinks, he said, "Let me order for you." He picked up the menu and beckoned to the waiter.

As the meal progressed, he became quite talkative, addressing both of them in the florid style of a Mexican gentleman and inquiring about their personal activities. He was especially interested in Sally, repeatedly turning the talk to her.

"What have you been doing, since you're not working? I presume you're not sitting around the house all day—to use an American expression."

"I haven't gotten around as much as I expected," Sally replied, "although I have been on one trip to the Mayan ruins at Chichen Itza. I'm very much interested in exploring them further."

"You should be thoroughly rounded in your researches" he replied, "You should not only see the ruins, but also explore a typical up-to-date Mayan village, as well. There is one near me, only a few miles from Valladolid."

"I'd love to go there," said Sally.

"Senora Moore, would you give me the pleasure of taking a lovely lady like you together with your husband there on a visit?"

Sally smiled, appreciating his gallantry.

"You're very kind," she replied, "but at present I'm limited. As you can see, I'm pregnant. I'm due in two weeks."

"I understand." replied Emilio with a laugh. "But the village is very unusual to see because it is so primitive. You will see how the Indian population in Yucatan live. Now let me repeat— I'm not easily put off—why don' t you let me take you and your husband there sometime? —when you are ready, of course. I can explain its features to you—they are most unusual."

"I noticed that they do have some unusual characteristics," said Sally. "One of the most striking is their cleanliness. I saw that when I looked at them on the street in Merida—and in the market as well. They, the street and the market were so clean."

"Yucatecan Indians are clean," said Elizabeth. "They bathe every day."

"Yes," added Emilio, "and their homes are just as clean. Now would you really like to see the village, Senora Sally?"

"Emilio, I'd be delighted. And so would my husband. He sometimes has the weekend off, and we could go then—after," she concluded with a slight blush, "I've had my baby."

"Very well. As I'm down in that area a good deal, when I get some time free I'll contact you and make arrangements. I know a family in the native settlement we can visit."

"That'll be swell," said Sally, feeling grateful for his thoughtfulness. She concluded he was, indeed, charming. Nice for a starting appraisal, if only that.

"We shall go then. Now, I have an appointment. You will excuse me." He rose to his feet, bowed and strode gracefully from the table.

Chapter 20

Two weeks later she was delighted with the birth of her son. Kirke was also overjoyed. He was the typical nervous father in the delivery room at the hospital and afterwards displayed such solicitude for her welfare that Sally, almost forgetting that he was mixed up with Consuelo Lopez, thought optimistically about a possible rebirth of his affection for her. But then he went so far as to say one evening that Consuelo had extended her congratulations to both of them. How clever of her, being so decent, to get in even better with Kirke!, Sally thought. This move tended to kill all hope of a reconciliation. Sally was forcibly reminded that he hadn't given up Consuelo, and she resolved to think seriously about Elizabeth Collin's suggestion.

A month later Emilio's call came. Sally answered and again his manner was charming. Gallant, effusive, possibly a bit too much so, but always formal and very respectful. He had set the time for the excursion on Saturday, and with a marked interest Sally accepted for both herself and her husband.

Leaving baby Bill in the capable hands of Maria, they journeyed to the village in about two hours in Emilio's automobile. As they entered through a low gate, Emilio pointed to a statue whose significance greatly intrigued Sally.

"That statue is a native spirit called a 'balam,' which watches to keep evil away from the householders," he said. "Native traditions are more important to these Indians than Christian."

Yes, thought Sally, the Christian are so foreign to them. And, she thought further, to learn about them from such a guide. From this comment—he's undoubtedly well informed. Emilio then began speaking of the area.

The Ruins at Uxmal

"See the houses of white-washed walls, see the thatched roofs, see the women in spotless white hupils—you know, their blouses—edged with colorful embroidery. Pretty isn't it? This village is a picture of native tranquility—" Sally nodded, thinking he's going to do his best—"It is very different from the Maya past."

Yes, this will really be good, thought Sally. Emilio continued.

"When the Spanish and later the Mexican government began to rule the native Indians, they really resisted. Even today they hang on to many of their pre-Hispanic customs—this, in spite of the political control of the government."

"Just how successful were they in doing that?" asked Kirke. Sally thought again, this is really going to be interesting and felt a surge of admiration for Emilio.

"Fairly so. The Maya have changed many foreign elements to fit their own culture—which they inherited from the pre-Conquest era. You will see this as I show you around."

"In what way have they retained their native customs?" asked Sally.

Emilio really warmed to his task. Speaking enthusiastically, waving his hands in most expressive fashion he spoke in a manner which impressed Sally as resembling that of a campground evangelist.

"The biggest difference is in their religous rituals. Although there is a layman who knows the Catholic prayers and their use at baptism, weddings and funerals, there is one—and he is the native shaman—who possesses far greater powers and influence. He's a sort of all-knowing person—he plays an important role in the agricultural rituals of rural life. By divination and prophecy, using his crystals, he tells the future."

Pagan rites, thought Sally—yes, she ruminated further, always connected with religion which was most important.

They came to a set of three huts, arranged in a triangular pattern. These huts were behind a low wall, about twenty-five feet in diameter and connected by narrow wooden walkways. The first one they entered had dirt floors and walls of branches tied together, but was as clean as the home of Sally's parents. Sally was amazed. She also noted that a woman who was seated behind a weaving loom had not a thread of her hair out of place as she greeted them with a broad smile.

"Buenos dias, Senora," said Emilio to the woman. Then, cordially speaking Spanish and indicating them with his hand, he introduced Kirke and Sally to her. The woman smiled again. He has perfect manners, thought Sally, just like at the hacienda.

The household furnishings were primitive. A basin but no sinks or running water. A crude rack for holding utensils stood in one corner. In another section of the one large room were several hammocks.

"Hammocks?" said Sally questioningly. "Don't tell me they had them."

"These hammocks are not native," said Emilio, impressing Sally by his immediate responsiveness. "Mats were used in ancient times."

Then they went outside and walked down a walkway to another hut. In it there was an old motorcycle. "Rather out of place, but attesting to the intrusion of the consumer lifestyle of the mestizo," said Emilio.

"I expected to find a BMW," wisecracked Kirke.

In the rear of the yard was a baby pig in a sty, and ducks and turkeys were walking about the yard. Yes, it was all very primitive, thought Sally, but all very clean. No filth of any kind, no stale food, no garbage visible, no flies, no rats or mice, no

The Ruins at Uxmal

animal excrement. Just like we saw in the streets of Merida. All the talk I heard about 'dirty Mexicans,' before I came down may be true in other parts of Mexico, but not among these Yucatecan Indians—that's for sure. They are one clean race of people!

She commented on this. "Such cleanliness, in spite of the fact that they live in such hovels."

"Their cleanliness is a sign of their native culture," said Emilio, ever attentive to her. "To be clean is to be good inwardly—it is a sign of pride. It was associated with their religion." Then he spoke climactically, in most dramatic fashion.

"The ancient native world—you understand, of course, a supernatural belief—is always present to the Maya. Look at that old woman preparing those stacks of tortillas—bean smeared—and broth made from fowls—those are sacred foods. They aren't eaten in ordinary life—they're offered to the various gods." He waved his hands expressively. "You see, what underlies the ceremonies is the idea that 'what man wins from nature, he takes from the gods.' The gods are asked for favors, and they are repaid through prayers and rituals. The best known to you was sacrifice, which included prisoners of war, sometimes others, children as well as animals."

And their beliefs shaped their totally dissimilar morality, thought Sally, but in comparison with western civilization it could not be said to be more cruel. Possibly, in some respects, it might even have been better. Was she outgrowing her old morality? But that sacrificial ritual—she shuddered.

However, she thought further, this info is certainly interesting. And you'd think this lecture was being given by a college professor. Although he's an agronomist, he knows a lot about these Maya. I'll bet he's most competent at whatever he does. Yeah, this guy is quite a fellow. In comparison, Kirke impressed her as rather drab.

"But the Spanish rule was pretty oppressive, wasn't it?" asked Kirke. "I'm surprised how these native traditions have been retained."

"But they were. However, when the Spanish came in the sixteenth and seventeenth centuries, they transferred the Indians into villages and towns—utterly unconcerned with their needs—they could be better controlled and converted to Christianity there. These new settlements were laid out on the pattern you can see. Look around, as I tell you about it."

Sally and Kirke surveyed part of the village from a vantage point in the yard. It was laid out in a grid plan, with rectilinear streets, a central plaza, a church and a small store visible.

"I don't suppose this layout was any better, was it? " asked Sally.

"No, just for a different purpose," replied Emilio. "The ancient villages were organized around centers, and these centers served various purposes—like ceremonies, gatherings, ball games, other public functions and, of course, temples—all centered in their religion. The Spanish had other ideas." He threw back his head and laughed.

"To continue with my lecture, my most attentive audience," Emilio continued, —Sally reflected, even though he seems tremendously knowledgeable, he's not at all stuffy—my type of a guy. I wish Kirke had a temperament like I think he has. Then she thought further, how would this guy be as a father? —then she picked up Emilio again.

"...this settlement plan is still to be seen throughout all the Maya areas. There is a building housing the Ayuntamiento, that is, the civil government run by a mestizo overlord, called a ladino. See it there."

"What else did the Spanish do to disrupt this native life?" asked Sally.

The Ruins at Uxmal

"They transformed everything—yes, everything—by imposing an economic order: Iron and steel tools were imported, cattle, pigs and chicken replaced game in the diet. Citrus trees and watermelons, sugarcane and coffee were also raised. And alcohol—this latter is very detrimental to the Indian population." a principal agent of acculturation, wasn't it?" asked Sally again anxious to show her interest and to impress Emilio by questioning him.

"Yes."

"But the culture of the Maya," continued Emilio, "and other tribes as well is still prevalent. It is greatly expressed through their art. As Americans, I imagine your are most familiar with that—Indian jewelry and weaving, but also, of course, the work of great artists like Diego Rivera—he was Indian. You can see it in Mexico City."

"I know that David Alfaro Sequiros also painted about the Indians," said Kirke.

"Yes," said Emilio. "We are proud of our Indian past, but ashamed of our Indian present. Our Indian past, great; our Indian present..." He shrugged.

"How sad," thought Sally.

"Government buildings are covered with murals and sculptures praising the heroism of the Aztecs, while museums house the jewelry—which is exquisite—pottery and artifacts found in pre-Hispanic ruins. The Indians themselves, however, remain a conquered race, victims of the worst poverty and discrimination to be found in Mexico today." He shrugged again and sighed. "Now let us leave and go to lunch, after I say good-bye to the Senora."

They left the village and journeyed to Valladolid, an hour away. They went into a very unpretentious little restaurant, which, although in the same category as a fast food restaurant in the states, was still furnished with white table cloths and had waiters. In addition, there was a small stage at one end of the room.

Midway through their meal, entertainment began. Four people—two boys and two girls, all about sixteen—performed native dances, the most notable feature of which was a rapid drumming with their feet to the rhythm of fast Mexican music. Sally saw no orchestra and concluded that the music was piped in. At the conclusion, the girls pushed the boys over as a form of exit; then they appeared at the other end of the room and, while still dancing, wound striped paper ribbons around a pole. Sally wondered if the pole and dances were carryovers from some Indian rite. They certainly didn't appear Christian in origin. But to her the important fact was that it was the real thing—genuine native Indian entertainment in a provincial Mexican town. She was delighted. This really did make her aware of differences in ethics.

As the meal progressed, Emilio relaxed and began talking expansively of his personal life.

"I spend about 50 percent of my time in Mexico City," he said. "The rest of the time I spend down here. I expect to be in Yucatan part time for quite a number of years."

"But when you inherit your father's estate, you will be a rich land baron, and then how much time will you spend in Mexico City?" asked Sally.

Emilio smiled. "Quite a bit. It's a great town, and I require some city life to stay young and healthy."

"Is there anything unique about Mexico City which would differentiate it from other citiies?"

"It is unique from cities in other countries, but not in so much as what differentiates it from the rest of Mexico. Mexico City—ah! —is the country's entertainment, cultural and religious capital. It's great! And in another twenty or thirty years, it'll be the industrial, financial and commercial center as well." He

The Ruins at Uxmal

paused, then," But those last features are definitely a mixed blessing, as it leads to overdevelopment. You see, the city site is not suited for that because of natural handicaps. But museums, theaters and concert halls are always crowded, there are intellectual elites, and the humanity of the city is always there. In it a person can have a wonderful time."

"Sounds like a nice place to visit, if not to live," said Sally,.

"It is that unquestionably. But"—and he nodded for emphasis—"there is a dedication to family life and leisure, a preference for a slow pace of life which keeps its body and soul alive—and which makes it a worthwhile place to live."

He paused to look directly at her, seeming to take note of her beauty. Sally felt flattered.

"You would like it. Especially Chapultepec Park. There, everybody goes on Sundays, usually in family groups, bringing food and drink for picnics—but then, there are young couples, teenage maids, children by themselves, looking for partners."

"Just like Central Park in New York back home," said Kirke, a trifle wearily. Sally looked sharply at him; was he getting bored? Or was he a little jealous of Emilio? She hoped she hadn't betrayed her feelings. "I really don't think it's as much as what you say," he finished.

"Are you going to give up being an agronomist when you take over your father's estate?" asked Sally, ignoring Kirke's remark.

"Yes. I can retire from government work at an early age, around forty, I suppose, and run my father's hacienda. That is, if his plans for growing products other than hennequin work out."

"What do you mean, if his plans work out?" Was he stable? she anxiously asked herself.

"The war, you see, has led to the invention of synthetic fabrics which is ruining the world-wide market for hennequin—

or sisal, as it is more commonly known. So, in spite of a modest government subsidy, my father is faced with the prospect of losing everything he has."

"That will certainly affect you."

"I may end up being an agronomist permanently. I'll have to see what happens. But my father is a resourceful man and is very fond of money. He'll think of something." Relieved, Sally sat back and observed.

She couldn't help noticing the contrast between Emilio and Kirke. As Emilio continued talking, he leaned back and concentrated his gaze on her, speaking deliberately for dramatic effect, in clearly enunciated speech and sufficiently loud to hold her attention. He was very interested in being interesting, and Sally found this characteristic personally appealing because she felt he was definitely speaking to her. She responded by paying rapt attention. Kirke, however, from his remark seemed to be paying heed more out of politeness than anything else; she felt he was bored or angry and resented him for it. Whereas Emilio was concerned to be gallant and charming, Kirke was indifferent, even inconsiderate—and not only to Emilio but also to her—in the recent past—she reflected in a sudden flush of anger. Yes, she thought, Emilio was quite charming, and she wished to find out more about him personally.

"Tell me," she went on, "as Mrs. Collins told me you were married, how did you meet your wife? Is she a local girl or a belle from Mexico City?"

"She is from a fine old family in Mexico City. I married four years ago."

The kind of romance one reads about in story books, thought Sally. Then to see his reaction, she inquired further, "Any children?"

He shrugged his shoulders and said, with a touch of regret, "No."

"Oh, I'm sorry to hear that. But four years is not very long. Have hope—you're the type to have many children."

"I like to think so." He lowered his gaze and morosely looked at his hands on the table.

"But on the other hand, one can have a happy marriage without children."

He shrugged. "If I weren't so family-oriented, I might have an illegitimate child, like many other men, and make him my heir. My wife..." He shrugged his shoulders and looked despondent. "I really want one."

Conversation lagged for a moment, and Sally felt that she had pushed any inquiry she wanted to make as far as she could at the present time. Therefore, she raised the topic of what places to go and see in the area—heard again that the local beaches were delightful places for foreigners to spend a weekend—and then deftly concluded by thanking Emilio for the excursion and suggested that as it was well into the afternoon, she was getting tired and wouldn't mind returning to Merida for dinner.

Jeremy S. Wood

Chapter 21

As Sally and Kirke arrived home, she realized that Emilio was charming, moneyed and a gentleman. I could really go for him, she thought. And I think from his manner today, I could assume that if I made myself at hand, he might be interested—he obviously has been disappointed in his wife because she hasn't given him an heir. And as for your life with Kirke—it had started out so happily with such glorious hopes for your future, but now it had all gone to smash! —at least, with him. But, she then reflected, she was not through yet. Emilio's really nice. Also, he hasn't become involved with anyone else yet, and, boy—she became almost breathless as she thought—with a child do I need a husband! But then—do I really dare? However, looking back, as a last resort couldn't I really live at home? But again looking ahead and ignoring her caution—why not? You have nothing to lose! And from what Elizabeth said—the opportunity is probably there! But! —you must first get rid of your present joker—for what he has done, he must go! —and then make yourself available. She thought of her possible rosy future. Her child would be well taken care of—by a family nurse, and she would have time to enjoy herself at other activities. Yes—you want the whole hog, not just the position of mistress, second fiddle to some babe in the family entourage. You want the money, position and freedom which comes from being the spouse of a prominent Mexican gentleman. Yes—the probability seemed to definitely be there!

That very night she decided to act. As her husband made himself a scotch and water and settled into an easy chair to enjoy himself before going to bed, she observed him through the bedroom door. Then, just for a moment, she hesitated, wondering if his conscience might be troubling him. The thought of their happy first months again occurred to her. Could he

The Ruins at Uxmal

possibly be thinking of repenting, writing off Consuelo Lopez and returning to a proper life with his wife? Could he be thinking of discarding his routine of meeting Consuelo a couple of evenings a week at the library? Had he reached the conclusion that a foreign girl was not the type that could carry off being the second Mrs. Kirke Moore? Wouldn't fit in very well in the circles in which he hoped to move. But no! She didn't want him. She was not prepared to accept a straying husband; she was angry through and through and wished only to get rid of him. He had shown himself to be feckless. It was time to act! Her pride welled up and with it rage; suddenly she was no longer coolly calculating; she became ferocious!

"Kirke," she called, "come in here!"

Startled by her strident tone, he looked, then rose. "Yes, I'm coming." He entered the bedroom, irritated at having his leisure interrupted. "What the devil do you want?"

He looked threatening. But she began coolly. "You remember the night of Gutierrez's party, three weeks ago?"

"Yes. What.about it?"

"I was wondering," she said, rising from the bed, "where you were most of the night? You left me alone."

"Oh, hell, honey, I didn't mean to. You know I had to meet those guys Emilio wanted me to glad hand."

"You hardly spent the whole evening with them! " she snapped. "Afterwards, what did you do—you flitted off like some damn bird."

He threw out his hands. "What the deuce has gotten into you tonight? I thought you had a swell time at that party and..."

"Just answer me! Why did you fly off the way you did?"

"Oh, Consuelo Lopez—surprisingly she was there—trotted up after the meeting and collared me for a minute or two. She wanted to show me a few pictures she discovered that Senor Gutierrez had in one of the rooms. So what could I do? I had to be nice to her."

"Oh wasn't it just great that she was there? I'll bet you enjoyed that."

"So what if I did? Is it improper to speak to another woman? And, for that matter, where did you go? I just stepped outside with Consuelo for a few minutes, and when I returned you were nowhere around."

"Senor Gutierrez was showing me the house," she exclaimed. Then very sharply. "Of course, I had nothing else to do."

He ignored her sarcasm.

"Well, why didn't you wait for me before you did that? I would have enjoyed it"

"Oh, since you were enjoying yourself with Senorita Lopez, wouldn't it have been most inopportune for me to intrude? Consider it fortunate that I wasn't aware she was with you."

"Oh, come on! Stop being sarcastic. From this demonstration, I'd think you're jealous."

"Don't I have reason to be?"

"No."

It was time to lay it on the line.

"Kirke, I'm mad enough to keep fired up for an hour. Now a sensible woman, I suppose, ought to keep quiet and not mention this, just accept it in stride as one of those things men do, but I've gotten so damn riled up I'm going to damn well let go!"

"What the hell is wrong with you? Just because I spend a few minutes with another woman at a party..."

The Ruins at Uxmal

"It's hardly just that." Then she demanded very angrily, "Where have you really been spending your evenings with Consuelo Lopez, anyway?"

"You know damn well where—at the library."

"Is that so? And were you, by chance, discussing cataloguing problems when you were looking at Senor Gutierrez's art collection that night?"

"Say, look here..."

"Look is the right word. Especially when I looked at you and her."

"You what?"

"In the little patch of garden outside the open window I looked through and not only saw but heard what you two said to each other!"

At that, Kirke could only look at her—very warily.

"And how did she address you?" she suddenly shouted. "Oh, let me think—how did it begin? 'Mio caro'—such an endearing term! —my beloved!" Suddenly, with all her strength, she struck him across the face. "'I heard every word and saw every action! —you swine!"

Startled, he retreated two steps, then brazened it out.

"Well, damn you, since you know, what are you going to do about it."

"Do about it?" she screamed at him. "Do about it? Plenty, you low-level louse! You contemptible piker! You aren't worth a damn, not now—to me, and later, I'll bet, to that slut you're camping out with! Ha! When she gets through with you, you'll be even more sorry than broke. She'll leave you flat, after taking you for every cent you've got."

"Shut up and—"

"Don't tell me to shut up! Look at how I've been repaid for my efforts at being a good wife. A man, for whom I've done everything, takes every gesture of affection I make and treats them with cynical contempt, who apparently regards all sentiment and trust with a sneer and who has treated the bond of marriage with scorn."

"Go to hell!"

"I've seen this affair developing after I looked that tramp up at the library. I sized her up as an operator of the first water, an article who could really be dangerous if she met up with a playboy like you."

"Who are you to cast stones at me?" he cried, thororoughly enraged. "Don't tell me you weren't attracted to that caballero, Emilio, this afternoon. I saw you hanging on his every word, making goo-goo eyes at him all the time. And don't say he didn't respond. I have two eyes and..."

She had had enough. "Damn you, take this!" She picked up a decanter from an end table and hurled it at him.

He dodged it and then came at her. Hauling off, he knocked her flat across the bed and on to the floor. It was a savage blow which almost caused her to lose consciousness. The next thing she recalled was him sitting on top of her and beating her furiously about the head and neck. She screamed at him to stop, but he did so only when he was exhausted. Then he dragged her to her feet and stood, just looking at her. Wild with rage she shrieked, "Get out of here, you dog! I never want to see you again."

"Suit yourself," he shot back venemously. He turned, got his suitcase from the closet, opened the credenza drawer, put in a shirt and socks and, while she still just stood, left through the front door. Sally, utterly racked, then threw herself on the bed. After an hour, she got into it and turned out the light, but spent the night, just tossing sleeplessly—and thinking.

The Ruins at Uxmal

A momentous question troubled her. Nothing had worked out satisfactorily. Her problems had culminated. She recounted them. First there was the accident, then the decision, apparently wrong—to leave home and come to Mexico, then the inception of her disability and now a broken marriage! Was Fate conspiring against her? It seemed to be that—Chance was giving her a bum deal.

And now she was left with only two choices—a return to home to be a burden which she was very doubtful her parents could carry or snaring Emilio, if it were at all possible, and trying to build a new life for herself here in Mexico. Then she thought of the third possiblity—living on alimony. But with a child—and the way she was used to living? It would be like living in poverty! It would be most unsatisfactory! The better way, by far, would be to find out if Emilio was interested in her.

The next morning, after waking, she put on her robe and looked at herself in the mirror—her right eye was blackened, and her body was covered with a bruise which extended from her collarbone to her left breast. She looked in no condition to go anywhere. But her mind was made up even more fully than the last night—she would certainly locate a lawyer through Emilio to see about a divorce.

Chapter 22

After disguising her eye under a heavy application of powder, she sent Maria off on a trip to the market, then prepared a simple breakfast and telephoned Emilio at the Departamento de Agricultura in the Palacio del Gobierno, the city hall of Merida. She detailed her plan to him, feeling no compunction to be circumspect.

"Emilio, can you recommend a good lawyer? I have had to make an important decision—a very drastic one—which may surprise you. To put it on the table, my husband and I have broken up, and I have decided upon a divorce."

"You have? My God, at the village you seemed so serene."

"Your observation was correct—I'm pretty good at concealing my feelings—I have a great deal of pride—but your assumption was dead wrong. Kirke has done me a great injustice which I in no way deserved, and I am fed up with him. So I am calling you to see about a lawyer."

Emilio became most solicitous.

"Senora," he said, "I am most sorry to hear of it. Believe me, I can sympathize because I have an idea how you feel doing this."

"You do?"

"Yes. To be frank, I have thought, of late, of doing the same thing myself."

"You have? Why—what on earth for?"

"I sort of mentioned it to you at the village two days ago. It has to do with not having an heir. My wife has been barren so far, and I—you see, it's very important for a Mexican man to

The Ruins at Uxmal

have a child which will carry his name. So I am quite dissatisifed with my wife."

"It's very surprising that you should feel so deeply about it that you'd think of divorce," said Sally politely, but thinking, how fortuitous for me. "But let me say I'm very sorry for you."

"In Mexico, motherhood is a very important thing."

"I see. Well, by your own lights, you have reason for wanting a divorce."

"Yes."

"So you can have some understanding of my case. Now can you recommend a good lawyer to whom I can go?"

"With pleasure, Senora," he answered. "The man you should see is an old friend of mine, a Senor Jose Mendoza. He is a lawyer who speaks English and who would be most simpatico towards you. His address is 24 Merida Street 15."

"How nice of you to do this for me."

"It is a pleasure. But tell me—where is Kirke?"

"I don't know. After a brutal fight last night, he left. For all I know he's bunking up at the apartment of his mistress—that's what caused the trouble between us—another woman."

"I see. Who is she?"

"Some worker from the library. When Kirke needed some information, he consulted her. That's how they got acquainted. Name of Consuelo Lopez."

"Consuelo Lopez? A librarian? My God! She was the recent mistress of my father!"

"Of your father? Well, I'll be damned! This is a surprise—ha! —especially for Kirke. She certainly gets around."

"Apparently."

"I think Kirke may be biting off more than he can chew, getting mixed up with that number. I'll bet she's tough. But I am not concerned with her. So let's not talk about her now."

"Very well. Nothing more shall I say."

"Fine—but now to get back to what we were discussing. How can I repay your kindness?"

"I can suggest a way. It's a bit soon, possibly, to say it, but you are so attractive and will soon be available—socially—I want to beat everyone else out for your company."

"Flatterer. But you really do want to see me, eh?"

"Allow me the privilege I'm asking for. You see, I, in spite of being married, am quite lonely and am looking for companionship."

"Oh, Emilio, I don't know. I'm pretty upset right now...oh, give me a few days, at least."

"I understand, Senora. Perhaps in a week?"

"I would be delighted then. But, you know, it's dangerous to be seen with another man when you're in the middle of a divorce, at least in the United States. Legal complications can arise."

"I don't see how they could arise if we met in a public place. Your husband couldn't accuse us of anything then."

"Well, that's true, I suppose."

"Why don't we meet for lunch, then, say next Tuesday?"

"That'll be nice." They then arranged to meet for lunch at the same cafe where Sally had lunched with Elizabeth.

The next thing she did was call the office of Senor Mendoza to ask for an appointment and secured one for ten days later.

Then she wrote a long letter to her parents telling them the bad news and asking them to send her what they could afford. Then she lay down, worn out from the strain of last night, but was almost immediately interrupted by the ringing of the phone. It was Kirke.

"I want to see you."

"Listen, you low-level piker—I can't think of anything bad enough to call you—go to the devil! What do you want, anyway? I'm through with you, and I'm going to see a lawyer about a divorce."

"Oh, you are, eh? Well, I expected it. And it's ok by me. I don't want a reconciliation.

But I still want to see you, and since you're going to see a lawyer soon, tonight would be quite suitable."

"About precisely what?" she asked irritably.

"It's better to discuss it in person."

"Our child?"

"Yes."

"Oh."

She knew his love for Bill was very deep, deeper she admitted candidly than hers—she knew her trait of dispassion was most unusual and realized she was inherently unsentimental. Nevertheless, what would make Kirke think she would ever give Bill up? Put him under his bad influence? As a mother, she realized she had a strong parental duty to fulfill, and she was one who fulfilled obligations. The devil with talking to Kirke about it. "If you're thinking about getting custody of him, that'll be settled in court," she said firmly.

"I want to offer you a deal for him. Without going to court."

"The answer is no sale."

Jeremy S. Wood

"Really? Well—maybe. But after you hear me out, you might change your mind."

"Well—allright, if you insist. I'll see you tonight—around seven."

After the call she lay down on the bed and fell into deep reflection. It was understandable that he would want Bill. No one could have been a more loving father. Too bad he couldn't have been as devoted a husband—he owed her that for what she had done for him. But he was in for a scrap if he demanded the child. There was about as much chance of her placing him under his bad influence as a snowball has of surviving in Hell. She would fight him tooth and nail to retain possession.

She rose from her bed and looked at Bill. He was asleep. Maria had put him in his crib before leaving for the market that morning, and he never looked cuter.

When Kirke arrived, he was most businesslike. Characteristically, he went straight to the point of why he had come.

"There's no point in shilly-shallying around," he said. "I want Bill, and I'm prepared to offer you a nice deal for him so as to avoid a nasty custody hassle in court."

"From that I assume you think you'll lose the custody battle?" she replied sarcastically. He made no answer. "You're apparently aware that I, as the injured party, might have some claim on him."

"I don't know about that," he said belligerently. "I'll be able to provide for him far better than you ever will on alimony."

"Oh, will you? I don't suppose, my dear, the fact that you are an adulterer will have any influence on the judge, would it? You louse! That fact, I imagine, will weigh pretty heavily with him "

The Ruins at Uxmal

"I'll admit that's true and that's why I want to talk about a deal. I know you're interested in Bill's welfare, first of all, and that should be enough to persuade you to let me have him."

"Oh, would it?"

"After all, I can provide him not only with better parental supervision—there'll be two of us—but also a much better physical environment in which to grow up. Now consider the importance of that—you're a decent woman, and you have the best interest of your child at heart. You'd want him to have the best, wouldn't you? You, of course, will have visitation rights."

"Stop it. You're just entertaining yourself."

"Am I? Also, let me ask you, frankly, that what with your other overwhelming interest in getting to the top—of something or other—probably anything—would you be willing, honestly, to give that up in order to raise your child? Wouldn't you get fed up—being the kind of woman you are—with all the mundane details of caring for an infant? You're not basically the home, mother and apple pie type—in spite of having a child. Think of that and think of Bill. Now you know I wouldn't be that way."

"You think so?"

"Am I not more affectionate and sentimental than you? That, of course, doesn't mean at all that you don't love Bill. Not at all. But be honest and admit the problems you'll face, will you? Last but not least, I know you value money—as you know it comes with prestige—very highly, and I can, at least, get you started on that way."

"A nice pitch!" she said sarcastically. "Well, now, what are you leading up to?"

"Look, I'm pretty sure my father will advance—"

"To tempt me with that!" she cried, exploding in fury. "Money! You scurvy bum! Listen, I'm in no mood to listen to you! I'm in the mood to shout!" She launched into a tirade.

"So you want your child, eh? Well, you won't get him! So you want a divorce! Well, you will get that! Let's just go over the reasons why! Take up with some broad! Walk out on your wife! —after beating her up! And, of course, shelve your conscience—if you have any! And, last but not least, take your child with you—simply pay off your wife. And getting a divorce is so easy in Mexico. S-o-o why not? Isn't that just cushy for you?"

"I don't want to get into another quarrel. Now look, I'm damn sorry for what I did last night. It isn't customary for me to hit women..."

"You can still be a revolving so-and-so and not do it," she shot back. "But you, you did go one better..."

"I'd appreciate it if you'd not replay the fight we had. Now look, as you're entitled to alimony, you'll get that."

"And I'll take as much as I can get," she shot back savagely. "I have ample reason to."

"Plus what I will offer you for custody of Bill."

"I'm going to keep Bill."

"Look, Sally, can' t we be sensible about Bill?"

"Not much."

"Why not? I can offer him much more, eventually, than you can—in the condition you'll be in—a divorced woman. And please try to see the other side with Consuelo. I couldn't help it. It just happened Can't you understand? We've had a loveless marriage—I knew it as soon as we came to Mexico, after having gotten over the accident. I know now that you made a hell of a play for me, and I fell for it."

"What d'you mean? I loved you, at first! Furthermore, you went into it with your eyes open! It's me who's gotten short changed."

The Ruins at Uxmal

"There's something called romantic love—I have it for Consuelo Lopez, and she has it for me—I knew it from the very moment I met her—and which you and I—or at least I—never had. And I don't really believe you ever had it either. You just latched on to me because I was the best prospect you knew to give you everything you really wanted—money and social position. That, I think, means more to you than anything else!"

"What nonsense! " cried Sally, "I'm not that cold. It's just you blaming me for everything! After we were hitched, I put everything I could into making this marriage work—stood by you during the accident, took care of you by suggesting Mexico, advised you when you felt discouraged about your job—and what do I get for it?"

"Stop acting the outraged wife! My God, you've got a vindictive streak. Can't you see the other side—at least for a minute! Why don't you calm down and try growing up for once! I didn't plan to step out on you. I just met Consuelo Lopez and realized suddenly that she was the one for me. It just happened—all of a sudden—like that." He threw out his hands in exasperation.

"Oh, sudden true love for you—eh? How touching!"

"Look, a loveless marriage is nothing to stay in, at least as far as I'm concerned. Oh, if only you had shown me some real warmth and affection; if only you , just once, had sidled up to me, taken my hands in yours, buried your nose in my breast, emitted a cute little squeak, possibly a chuckle—so that I would have known that you had some feeling for me—but no, all you ever did was make decisions and issue commands. I want a woman—with womanly qualities, and Consuelo has them to a degree unimaginable—and you don't—that's why I fell for her!"

She fired back. "Who else was there to make the necessary decisions? Who handled all the details of arranging to get you into a fine job, who handled the details of getting us a suitable home down here, who handled all the details of running a home in a foreign country—I don't believe you could have done it on your own. Whether you know it or not, you've been well taken care of—by me. You even got discouraged when you were repulsed on your second sale. It was me who rallied you. You lack the guts to stand on your own two feet. I was optimistic, mostly, looking to the future, and we had it all until you turned out to be such a piker. I lost respect for you when you started looking at another woman, and now with this offer I've lost all affection for you entirely. I've become disgusted and contemptuous."

"Ok, you've got it off your chest that we're estranged."

"That's the word for it allright. It takes two to make a marriage, and I don't plan on being part of this one any longer—any more than you do. Hell, I wouldn't take you back if you came crawling in here on your hands and knees."

"So, it isn't going to happen. Very well. There's no point in bringing it up. I' ve met the kind of a girl I've always dreamed about..."

"Is that so?" snapped Sally. "Well, you might be interested in hearing something about your girlfriend that I'm sure she hasn't told you."

"What?"

"Simply that you haven't been the only man in her life, brief though it has been."

Kirke simply stared at her. Sally carried on. "She was the former mistress of Senor Hector Gonzalez!"

Kirke was stopped for a full three seconds, then pointedly asked, "And how the hell do you know that?"

"I learned it today from Emilio. He told me about her when I telephoned him to get the name of a lawyer to whom I could go for a divorce. Apparently your girlfriend has been around."

"Well, even if she has been, she's my woman now."

"Just for now, I would presume."

"She loves me and..."

"Oh, I'm sure she knows exactly what to say to please her new—er—shall I say, lover boy? But from any woman's viewpoint, she's playing you for all she can get out of you; after she's taken you, she'll leave you flat."

"I don't know about that. It seems to me she's pretty fine..."

"Ha!"

"Oh, shut up! You're a fine one to cast stones, considering what I think your plans for the future are."

"I should tell you. I don't have to."

"I suppose I don't have to be told. You'll probably make a play for Emilio. He's available, undoubtedly has everything you really want, and go-getter that you are...maybe my offer of money was pointless."

"To confess my aims—that's a possibility, which, however, I'll do legitimately—if at all."

"If you can land him. But I sensed your attitude pretty thoroughly when we toured that Mayan village."

She shrugged her shoulders. "So what if I do like him?"

" Are you going to seduce Emilio and destroy his marriage?"

"It's none of your business."

"You wouldn't stop at anything."

"Listen, you joker, let me tell you I've learned a few things about living since I've been here with you. Watching your antics has about cured me of the old-fashioned game of being the wronged wife—who just stands around wringing her hands while her husband goes on his merry way. Furthermore, seeing those

Mayan ruins has also caused me to think that outside life in the United States, things are done differently. I assume you've also learned that—in your own way.

I'm through being the nice girl who has been taken advantage of. What I'm going to do will serve my own interests solely—being married to you has cured me of all altruism. I know what I want, and I'm going to get it. If Emilio wants out from his wife—and from his conversation during the village tour you know as well as I that he may be in the mood for a change—well, I'm right in line to benefit. As you say, he has everything I want. And I'll make him a good wife—and spend all my time forgetting about you!"

"I can see that's about the size of it. But let me say this—really think about this—your plan for romancing Emilio might not turn out and then you'll have regrets about turning down my offer. And you can be sure of it; your future with Emilio is problematical. Don't count on it."

"I prefer to play for Emilio. And ignore you. There's no strings attached to that."

"I want the boy."

"Not a chance."

"For fifty thousand dollars. I can get it from my father."

"Still no sale."

"I know damn well you're hell bent for a position and prestige—you may get it if you snare Emilio. But if you don't, or even if you do, it might be well for you to have a nest egg of your own. You may need money, and fifty thousand will go a long way in Mexico."

"Oh, you've got everything figured out, eh? Well, this is final. I'm hanging on to Bill. You can take your offer and stuff it up your nose."

The Ruins at Uxmal

"Think—I'll be able to give him a fine home and a good education. Alimony won't do for him what I'll be able to do."

"How do you know your future will be so rosy?"

"No problem. I've already settled into my job and with Consuelo at my side I'm going to have a fine career with the company—go to the states in a year or two and..."

Go to the states? Would he become a deadbeat and send her no alimony? It was very possible. How could she—thousands of miles away from him and with a marathon of red tape to go through—make him pay? Furthermore, that could be done only if Mexican law applied in another country. Plus the expense of doing it. It would be impossible. She might be left with nothing at all. God! Play then for Emilio—for all you're worth! It's either that or home. Barely able to contain her anxiety, she, nevertheless, called on all her will power and brazened it out.

"Hell, wait until she leaves. She'll take most of what you've got. She's too clever—and experienced—by far for you my dear ex-to-be."

"Let's drop Consuelo. Now, what are you going to do, if the Emilio deal doesn't work out?"

"Stay right here, after the divorce, and live on alimony—and keep my child, of course, if the courts give me custody. Or, maybe, go back to the states—in time," she thought grimly, "if I have to."

"And live with your parents?"

"Until I remarry. If I do."

"You'll hook some other guy—on the way up or already there."

"Life as the wife of a financial baron would be allright—anywhere."

"Money and position are so important to you."

She shrugged her shoulders. She then wished to end the turmoil. "If you've got anything more to say, let's have it."

"No." Then, rather desperately. "I'll up the ante—say to one hundred thousand."

"No."

"Very well. See you in court."

When Emilio showed up the following day, she was even more impressed by his qualities than in their previous meetings. After she had told him about the brutal way Kirke had treated her and his insulting offer about Bill, he expressed his warmest condolences, and she felt even more romantically inclined towards him. She urgently wished to find out more about his domestic situation.

"You know," she said, "I felt strongly drawn to you on the village trip, and I was sorry for you. You implied that you had trouble at home. Although I don't wish to intrude, as a friend, I'd like to help you if I could. Possibly, as a woman, I could give you a little advice—if I may?"

"Go ahead."

She was direct. "Tell me—apart from having an heir, is there anything else wrong with your marriage?"

"My wife is hardly the obedient servant she's supposed to be. She's a shrew."

"That doesn't make for much happiness, does it?"

"No. My domestic life is a wreck. I wish I could get rid of her. She's not worth a damn."

"Why don't you?"

"My father doesn't like the idea. Old miser that he is, it's his interest in the money she brings into the family—her background is wealthy. If she flew off, she would take most of it with her as it's in her name. My father wouldn't like to lose that, even if he has plenty left."

"You have some problems. But still you could survive—even if you were divorced. Wouldn't you inherit the rest of his estate?"

"Maybe—maybe not." He shrugged. "Oh, I could divorce her, but I would be flying in the face of my father's disapproval, and that takes more gumption than I usually have. Down here, the father's rule is the law. And as he considers the maintenance of the family very important, I might even lose an additional gift from him—a lot of money—five hundred thousand dollars."

"That much? Whew! But still, you can defy him, if you really want to."

"Yes. I can, but the gift...that would be coming soon, not on my father's death."

"I can see why you would be unwilling for five hundred thousand."

"True." Then, "I would have to have a most compelling reason to defy him. And at present—," he looked downcast, but then studied her closely, —"well—" he hesitated, "there is one-" again he hesitated, "an overwhelming reason."

"What?" inquired Sally, blushing slightly.

Emilio sighed, then took a deep breath, thinking deeply. Then he sat very upright, put his hands on the table and learned forward, speaking very earnestly.

"Something has turned up."

She eyed him demurely, waiting.

"You."

"Oh, Emilio!" She grasped his hands.

"Darling, I've—damn it, I've just made up my mind. I am a fool romantic. Just seeing and talking to you—ever so briefly. To me is life anything without love? Here I meet a girl who is just right for me, she seems to be interested so then—," he threw out his hands, —"why not? Isn't she worth the loss? But damn! —so much money! But—," and his excitement increased, "you are a girl who I am sure would favorably impress my father! Honestly, knowing you—really, truly, I'm sure he wouldn't oppose—he knows I am not happy with Carlotta—in spite of the money loss involved. I would then get my gift. And even the estate—also"

"And I could provide you with children."

"Of course. It is most important to me. Now, will you marry me?"

Sally blushed. "You're really saying it, Emilio!" Then she thought, she would really be cared for—after all her disability...and the domestic situation back home. He was the opportunity she had hoped for. But she still hesitated—the risk—terrific! —even in spite of her native impetuosity. Even for all that money! Wasn't it better to play it safe—go home? Was it too soon? Maybe. Then she temporized. "Let me think about your proposal for a few days," she said. "Although I have no objections to being the wife of a wealthy Mexican social lion, I do need a bit of time to consider it." Then she patted his hand. "You've restored my faith in men. I think you're terrific."

He looked at her gratefully. "If you accept, you'll make me very happy." Then he changed the subject. "I will bring up the subject of divorce with my father. Tell me, when are you going to see Senor Jose?"

"In three days. And that'll keep me occupied."

"Yes, your divorce will occupy you for awhile. But afterwards, when you are free from your entanglement, I would, of course, see you—very regularly.

"You're charming."

The Ruins at Uxmal

"Tell you what we could do. After you are free, how would you like to go swimming at the beach at Akumal? A diving club of which I'm a member has a place there. The beach is nice, the sand, surprisingly enough, doesn't cling to you, and the water is quite warm. You'd like it."

"That sounds like real fun. I'll take you up on it."

"In the meantime, let's keep in touch. Call me up, and tell me how you're doing."

"Will do. Now, I'll run along now and prepare myself to see Senor Mendoza."

Chapter 23

When she met Senor Mendoza in his office, he lived up to Emilio's recommendation. He was a short, fat, jovial individual with a cordial manner. Sally judged he was, as in Emilio's comment, most "simpatico" and immediately felt perfectly at ease with him. As she talked, she felt quite calm in stating the reason for the divorce, which would be uncontested. He replied that there would be no difficulty in securing alimony as she was the wronged person and was dependent on her husband for financial support.

"We just have to file some papers regarding that and division of property before the first hearing," he said complacently. "The second, at which time the judge will attempt to reconcile you, will be about fifteen days later. It will be a mere formality."

For a brief period they talked about the amount of alimony she could expect and division of property. As the amount of alimony was meager and the division of property equal, she expected no difficulty with Kirke. But then she raised the question which was troubling her.

"My husband wants custody of my child. He said that he could provide for it far better than I could, and I am worried that he might be right. Is there anything I could do to insure that I would get custody?"

"The court will probably award custody of the child to you as you are the wronged person. However, to make it as certain as we can that the decision will be in your favor..." He paused, looked closely at her, and then asked, "How honest are you, Senora?"

"How honest am I? What kind of a question is that?"

"It would be wise to be a little, as you Americans say, 'shady.'"

"What do you mean?"

"I mean that your chances of gaining that favorable decision would be considerably improved by a slight gratuity to the judge."

"You mean a bribe?"

Senor Mendoza nodded his head and continued.

"Here the courts are quite corrupt, and bribery is—er—quite necessary in order to secure the—ah—right decision."

"My gosh, you have to resort to bribery in a divorce case?"

"That is the way things are done down here, Senora Moore."

"Why, I've never done anything like that in my life."

Senor Mendoza shrugged his shoulders.

Well, thought Sally, what a proposition! She hesitated before replying, but then conscience made up her mind. I simply must have custody of my child. She then summoned up her gumption and asked, "How is it arranged?"

Senor Mendoza leaned back in his chair.

"It's simple. Just give the money to me, and I'll see that he gets it."

"What if the judge should be honest?"

"Don't worry about that. Bribery is so customary, he would be surprised if it were not tried."

"Won't my husband have the same option?"

"As the wronged person the judge will probably award you custody. But the gratuity would make it more certain. It would be wise, however, to make it sufficiently large."

"How much should I offer the judge?"

"I think that 300 pesos would be adequate."

"Very well. I can scrape that much together. And I'll do it."

Senor Mendoza nodded.

"I guess that's all, then," said Sally.

Senor Mendoza shoved a paper at her. "Here, sign this. It's necessary paper work for the first hearing, which will be held in about two weeks. I'll contact you a day or two before." He rose to signify that their meeting was over. Sally shook his hand. The Senor bowed. "Now let me say I have enjoyed meeting you," he said, "and give my regards to Emilio."

But as she was still worried about the possibility of losing baby Bill, she had to relieve her mind and decided to talk it over with Emilio. Consequently, she called him from her residence that evening. He was most willing to see her and consequently a second date for lunch was arranged for the following day at the restaurant.

Emilio was very comforting.

"As Mendoza said, Bill, I imagine, would be placed in your custody," he said, reaching across the table and patting her hand. "The court would probably compel Kirke to pay child support for him."

"Oh, I hope you're right," said Sally.

"Everything is set up for the hearing?"

"I gave Senor Mendoza all the details yesterday."

"Then all you have to do is wait to hear from him."

"But there's something else that bothers me. Kirke said he might be returning to the states in a year or so. That raises the

The Ruins at Uxmal

definite possibility of his welshing on my alimony payments because they'd be hard to collect, I imagine, in the United States.

Emilio laughed. "It looks as though your best option is me."

She smiled. "Well, now, that is a comfort—your availability!" She patted his hand and smiled. "However, now I must go. But I'm looking forward to that date at Akumal."

They rose and made their way toward the patio entrance. But who should Sally see, sitting at a table near the door, watching them with a morose stare, but her husband. He's just watching, thought Sally, trying, I'll bet, to get something on me. Boy, isn't he vindictive! Thank God, this is a public place. Her fears about being watched had been justified.

Chapter 24

In the two weeks preceding the first hearing, Sally gave some time to thinking about herself, considering the changes she had undergone since she had come to Mexico. Although not particularly given to introspection, she knew that several major transformations had occurred. In the first place, she had proven she could handle herself in trying circumstances—and in a foreign country. She was handling the difficult circumstances of her private life satisfactorily and had adapted well to existence in Mexico. She had not buckled under the strain of having a broken marriage and was making a nervy attempt to come out of it smelling like a rose. She was competent. In dealing with those circumstances, however, she knew she had become more knowing and worldly, but still had not degenerated into complete cynicism: she had retained a modicum of idealism, a throwback to the way she had been raised. But she had, however, become less trusting—that was probably good—and she had been compelled to abrogate her standard of absolute honesty in order to retain her child. She had also discovered that she had more than self-confidence; she had a lot of courage. To think of marrying so soon after a divorce—and doing it with a foreigner. Well, why not? —some people might think she was foolhardy, but the opportunity wouldn't last forever so—damn it, take a chance and strike while the iron was hot. Nothing risked, nothing gained, as Mrs. Collins had said. She had found that she could be a tough cookie but then, reflecting further, asked herself was she really so hell for leather? But last—and importantly—there was the problem of the possible loss of alimony.

So, thinking favorably of life in Mexico, she calmly awaited the day of the trial.

On that sunshiny morning Emilio accompanied her from her home to the courthouse, where Senor Mendoza met them.

The Ruins at Uxmal

"I think the trial will be more or less perfunctory," said the lawyer on the front steps. "Our questions and answers," he said addressing Sally, "will be related to the judge through an interpreter. The same procedures will apply to Kirke. Now, let us go inside."

They entered into a small courtroom, sat down and awaited the arrival of the others.

Kirke, with his lawyer, accompanied by Consuelo appeared almost immediately. There was no jury. In a few minutes a bailiff entered, announced the arrival of Judge Luis Obregon, who, after casually glancing around, seated himself at the bench. The bailiff then announced in Spanish that the court was in session.

The judge, speaking Spanish, made a preliminary statement in which he addressed the lawyers—Sally, understanding a few words, gathered that all papers for the uncontested divorce were in proper order and had been filed—and then rapped with his gavel and uttered a command to Kirke's lawyer, mentioning Kirke's name. Kirke's lawyer indicated to him that he should take the witness chair.

The lawyer, looking very confident, then drew Kirke out, addressing the question of who was to get custody of Bill. He induced Kirke to say that he was financially reliable, had the potential to provide Bill with a good home environment and make the assertion that his violent behaviour was simply because he had been provoked to the point of unendurability by Sally.

"She got so angry, she picked up a decanter and threw it at me!" Kirke said dramatically. "Could I be blamed for hitting her?"

After the lawyer finished, Sally felt he had done too good a job. She leaned forward, terribly nervous about the outcome and addressed a question to Senor Mendoza.

"What do you think?"

The Senor looked at her and just smiled.

Then, "How did the judge react to the gratuity?"

The Senor patted her arm to quiet her. "Don't worry," he said. "He behaved as expected."

The Senor was then asked if he wished to cross-examine Kirke.

"No, Your Honor," he replied.

He then took full advantage of the opportunity to have Sally present her side of the case. He was brief. His questions asking Sally to show the brutality of Kirke's attack and to emphasize that this action showed an immature, imflammatory and brutal temperament were most trenchant. Then, to make his argument as compelling as possible he asked Sally to state as fully as she could the chief reason why she should be given custody of Bill. She rose to the occasion.

"More important than the fact that my husband is the guilty party, the adulterer, is the ultimate consequence of his act, namely, the bad influence that a person of such character would have on my child. I, therefore, beseech you, your Honor, to grant me custody of the boy."

The judge nodded his head and after Kirke's lawyer had declined to cross-examine her, motioned to her to step down. With her heart beating wildly from trepidation, Sally descended from the witness chair to await the outcome of the trial.

Leaving baby Bill in the care of Maria, Sally then passed the ensuing fifteen days with Emilio, as he had taken his vacation leave to be with her. At his suggestion, they patronized the few restaurants and clubs in the city, but Sally still spent most of the time talking worriedly about the possible adverse outcome of the trial. Emilio wisely refrained from pressing his suit, only telling her that her concern would soon be replaced by the joy of being

The Ruins at Uxmal

courted and to try not to worry in the mean time. He was quite confident that the decision would be favorable.

Finally Sally was summoned back to court to her final confrontation with Kirke. After a perfunctory attempt by the judge to establish grounds for reconciliation between them failed, he rapped with his gavel on the bench, cleared his throat and announced, "The court finds both pleas of the plaintiff in this case to be justified. Therefore, she will receive her divorce and custody of the child, plus alimony of 500 pesos per month, for her expenses, including child support. Visitation rights for the defendant are granted for every Saturday."

He rapped with his gavel again, rose to his feet and left. Then, as the bailiff announced that the court was adjourned, Senor Mendoza also rose, smiled and pointed to the exit.

Weak from excitement, but overjoyed by the result of the hearing, Sally happily left the courtroom on the arm of Emilio.

Chapter 25

When they came to the doorway of her home, Emilio took her by the shoulders.

"Darling," he said. "I can't wait to see you. What say we go to the beach this Saturday? The weather is so perfect. We can spend the day and the night there and then drive over and see a most interesting grotto, the Cenote Dzitnup, near Valladolid on Sunday."

"That'll be just fine, dear."

Early Saturday morning, after she had dressed, there was an intense tropical rainstorm. Sally called Emilio to suggest going to a restaurant for lunch followed by an afternoon at her home, but he told her that such storms did not last and thought it would be over in an hour. Anxious to go to the beach, she gaily accepted his prediction. If true, the rest of the day would be clear, and the beach was more romantic. Then, pleasing her, the day became idyllic, with an intensely warm sun, a clear blue sky and just moderate humidity for Yucatan. She retired to the patio to enjoy it and while there also considered her appearance. In her white cotton dress and brown and white sport pumps. she felt perfectly dressed for the occasion.

Then reflecting on her future, she felt quite confident that, in spite of what Kirke had said about her, she had plenty of what it took to attract most men. Being well-proportioned, full in the thighs, bosom and buttocks, with an enticing fold of flesh under her jaw, a finely modeled nose, keen blue eyes, and most intriguing of all, reddish brown hair which curled in ringlets over her forehead and which always caused men to call her "cute," she figured she'd do allright physically with Emilio. As for her personality she had what she needed to run an aristocratic household. Mexican men looked for women who were, first of all, good mothers and, after that, good home managers. As she had the discipline to execute those requisites, she could keep mistresses at arm's length. What's more, Emilio felt she had lots of charm—so much for Kirke!

At 10 a.m., the purr of Emilio's black Ford sounded clearly in the quiet, as it drew up before her house. She rose quickly, went inside and opened the door for him. He was wearing a light blue suit and smoking a pipe. As he kissed her, she noticed the deep creases which appeared in his leathery cheeks, then, dropping her eyes, she saw the modish tassels which decorated his highly polished loafers. He looks like a real man, she thought.

Taking his pipe from his mouth, he said, "Pleased to call on you, Senora Sally."

His eye fell upon the wine decanter and two glasses on the sideboard. He examined the decanter and said, "Waterford crystal, aren't they? A tribute to your taste, my dear."

"I can see that you're a connoisseur," Sally said. "It's always a pleasure to play hostess to a man who appreciates the finer things in life."

"I have plenty of this waiting for you at home," he replied. "And I'll get you additional ware if you like." A tremor of passion stirred in her. His taste—excellent!

"Couldn't ask for anything more, could I?" she commented with an appreciative smile.

"To give my wife credit," he then said, "she introduced me to many of these niceties of life. I owe much of my cultivation to her. But to live with her—whew!"

"Have you spoken with your father about your divorce?"

"Yes. He seemed to be non-committal. He has, as I've already told you, two reasons—a material reason—a financial one—and an emotional one to oppose my divorce. However, he knows Carlotta and I are ready to separate so I don't think he'll oppose me too strongly."

"And how is your wife taking it?"

"I've discussed it with her and, to be frank, she doesn't care. She's as sick of me as I am of her. Of course, I can only give you my side, but my dear, let me tell you how avaricious she is! Hell, I thought she was all sweetness and light when I married her, but it slowly became apparent to me that she has the instincts of—what can I say—a shark! She wants everything and gives nothing. And temper—My God! No waiter ever escapes her vituperativeness. She's a shrew. You have an expression in your navy which I picked up when I was in Texas and which just describes my wife—it's 'Pull up the ladder, Jack. I'm on board.' She is very demanding. So, after a settlement plan is worked out, our divorce will be uncontested, as was yours."

"There seems to be no serious problem, then?"

"No."

"What do you think if I can't offer you a dowry?"

"That would help down here. But—," he shrugged his shoulders, "you have enough going for you to make the right impression. Now I've already told my father about you. He's undoubtedly waiting to see what kind of a girl you are before supporting me strongly."

"When have you arranged for me to meet him?"

"I told him I'd have you out to the hacienda very soon after our trip today as Carlotta is going to Monterey to visit her parents for a month at that time."

"Well—I'm looking forward to meeting him. I liked him when I first met him, although I didn't do much more than shake his hand."

The Ruins at Uxmal

On the drive to Akumal, they stopped for lunch at an outdoor restaurant, situated at the edge of a small lake. Sally saw that she could look out from her table under the thatched roof and see a couple of small fishing skiffs gently rocking, about fifty yards offshore.

"Try this wine," said Emilio, motioning to the waiter to fill her glass. "It's made from a flower—the hibiscus."

"That's a new one on me," said Sally, raising her glass. To her the wine tasted like cherry soda, minus the fizz. "It's really excellent," she said approvingly.

Emilio proved a charming luncheon companion. He told stories with a droll air and gave Sally humorous advice about investing what money he would give her in the Mexican stock market. She enjoyed him immensely and was reassured that her inclination to accept him was right. He also showed that he was no cheapskate by ordering for them the most expensive item on the menu—lobster with rice and tomatoes accompanied by a bottle of excellent Mexican wine with guava dessert. Over the entree he became intimate again, telling Sally all about his personal life before he went to the University of Texas and afterwards the joys of living in Mexico City. She was fascinated by these experiences and regarded the life she could expect to lead as a Senora with increased enthusiasm.

They arrived in Akumal about 1 p.m., secured lodging in a small Maya-styled hut and changed into their swim suits for an afternoon on the beach. Sally knew that her shapely figure was very favorably set off by her black bikini which fitted her like a layer of skin. She was also pleased as she saw Emilio nod approvingly as she hitched up her suit to show half of her buttocks. She experienced another similar reaction as she surveyed his trim, muscular, well-proportioned figure. Her judgement—handsome.

They took two deck chairs on the beach. Looking back, her survey of the arrangement of the huts was unfavorable—and amusing. They were irregularly placed, having no symmetry to their order, and there were no walkways from one building to another nor directional signs pointing out a restaurant for guests. It was very haphazard, as if done by amateurs.

"Things will improve as tourists learn of this," said Emilio.

The beach, almost completely deserted, as the storm had caused people to stay home, did not live up to her expectations. It was, instead of a long broad, clean, white stretch, only a narrow, seaweed-littered "playa" of dun colored sand which, while finer than the sand on the beaches back home, looked a lot worse. And the water was the temperature of bath water—near ninety degrees. Too warm for her. But she gave no intimation of her thoughts to Emilio.

Later, in repy to further probing, Emilio continued telling her about his wife. "If anything," he said, "I've been too passive. I'm not really a commander, even in my own house—that's unheard of in a Mexican family. Possibly it might be better if I'd knock her around a bit, but I'm not mean enough to bring off that sort of thing. She wants—and needs—a more typical Mexican husband, someone who's more commanding. I suppose she has just become fed up with what she takes to be weaknesses on my part and is contemptuous of me."

"Your situation strikes me as more pathetic than anything else," remarked Sally, feeling an upwelling of sympathy for him.

"That's true," said Emilio. "But only in the domestic area. In my professional life, I've been quite successful." Then he changed the subject.

"Listen," he said, "how about going out to look at the beautiful tropical fish by a coral reef out there? We'll do it from a small boat which I'll rent from the club rental station."

"Isn't that sea pretty rough from this morning's storm?" Sally asked a bit fearfully. "I heard of an accident a few weeks ago when a boat overturned in rough water."

The Ruins at Uxmal

"I read about that accident too." replied Emilio. "It occurred because they weren't wearing life jackets. Furthermore, handling a craft in rough seas requires what none of them had—experience. But don't worry. We'll get jackets, and inside that reef it'll be relatively calm. I've done it a number of times." He paused, then continued. "Our boat will be small. That's easiest for one man to maneuver in rough water. Now do you see the rental station—over there, about a quarter of a mile away? Let's go."

"Don't they have prohibitions on that sort of thing when it's dangerous?"

Emilio laughed. "Look, they don't even have lifelines for any bathers."

"Ok," she said, nodding assent. "Now, let's enjoy this glorious day." She took Emilio's hand. As they walked to the rental station, they passed a construction site where a large stack of wooden pilings had been placed on the beach close to the water. Sally surveyed it and the surrounding area with interest. Yes, tourism would cause this place to develop; it would be exceptionally nice to return to when it had grown. As it was Saturday, the site of the pilings was deserted, the setting was utterly calm, and she became entranced by the repose of the region.

After securing their boat, tied up near the end of a small pier, Emilio wistfully remarked that he wished he had his children with him. To that Sally thought, be a good mother, and your chances of being a satisfactory wife for Emilio will be cinched.

With Emilio manning the oars, they got underway and soon were riding the waves about a hundred and fifty yards offshore. Looking landward, Sally surveyed the entire shoreline and on either side saw the flatland, covered with the same scraggy, bushlike scrubby growth she had seen on the truck ride to Chichen Itza.

"Not very pretty," she announced to Emilio. "But I've never seen greener water. It's truly an emerald sea. But God, it isn't calm at all. It's really rough!" she cried, as their tiny boat was lifted high on a comber.

"Much rougher than I thought," cried Emilio.

But then the thrill of mounting the waves replaced her fear as she watched Emilio deftly ply his oars to maintain their equilibrium. He may be temperamentally passive, she thought, but he's no coward! He's a real man, yes, he is, a real man! How wonderful it will be to be married to a guy like him—rugged, dependable and kind. She felt a sudden surge of passion for him and realized that feeling that way was really being in love.

Suddenly, with absolutely no warning, there was a sound of scraping—Emilio yelled "Look out!" and Sally just glimpsed a wooden piling, floated away from the beach by the high tide from the storm, under the bow before it overturned the craft and threw them into the water. The thing seemed almost to seize the boat in the vise of its split-pronged base. "Emilio!" Sally screamed as she fell overboard; she saw him hit the water and then lost sight of him.

She came up gasping for breath, gripped by a terrifying fear that the beach jacket and slacks she had donned were weighing her down and making her too cumbersome to swim. God! I'm going to drown flashed through her! She became aware as the air release cord of her life jacket brushed her hand. Agonizedly she grasped it and pulled. Jesus, thank God! She then tried to swim, but vainly, in panic, realized that the current was too powerful and was carrying her rapidly out to sea. She feared again that she was going to drown—Oh God! —and then thought that if she hadn't fallen in love, this wouldn't have happened.

The Ruins at Uxmal

Something bobbed up against her—she recognized first an arm, then a man—a head—Emilio! She quickly grasped the form, realizing that something was wrong as it made no threshing movement and then slid her arm around it to support it.

Suddenly a dark object blotted her vision; it came up alongside her; she became aware of being grasped by hands and pulled across a gunwale; she found herself lying on the floor of a boat. The next thing she did was shout, "Emilio!" One of her rescuers stared at her for a second, said something in Spanish and put his hand to his mouth indicating silence and pointed to Emilio, also lying on the floor, unconscious. Sally leaned forward and bent over Emilio. He did not stir, but she could hear his breathing. There was a gash on his forehead.

They reached the shore. Somebody handed her a cup of coffee. She was numb from shock and reeling from dizziness. Then she stumbled over to where Emilio had been laid out on the ground. She took one look at him. "Why did this happen?" she shrieked. His head was half covered by blood. She fell on her knees and grasped him in her arms. "Emilio," she screamed, shaking him, "Wake up! For God's sake, wake up, will you!" Then hands pulled her away from him. "Get some help!" she cried.

For about ten minutes, Sally lapsed into hysteria, crying and weeping, her words unable to coherently express her grief, then a doctor arrived and examined Emilio. Sally calmed down and intently observed what was transpiring.

After bandaging Emilio's wound, he muttered a few words to the proprietor of the club who, speaking English, translated what he said to Sally.

"The Senor will be taken to the local hospital," he said. "His head apparently struck something. The doctor, who was staying here, will order an ambulance."

"It must have been that log in the water," said Sally.

The proprietor nodded. "He has suffered a concussion. The hospital is just a short distance away. If he is allright, he will be released."

In the next hour Sally taxied to the hospital to see Emilio. On the way, she just trembled. She thought, what a terrible accident! What had happened to Emilio? In a welter of feeling, she realized the depth of her compassion and how much she cared about him. Yes—she had fallen deeply in love. God, if he should die! —she couldn't stand it! She sat back and looked, uncomprehendingly, out the window at the passing roadside scene, her wild thoughts only on what had happened. As the taxi drew up before the door to the building, she prayed for the safety of Emilio.

Her fears were short-lived. After a terribly tensional, brief wait in the emergency room, Emilio appeared before her, in a wheel chair, with a broad smile on his face and a bandage on his head.

"Just a concussion," he said, smiling. "No fracture. I'll be fine tomorrow."

"No celebrating, though, for you tonight." she emphatically cried. "I'm putting you straight to bed, back at the inn."

At her insistence, he ate a meal which she ordered from Room Service, and they passed the early evening chatting quietly about the day and thanking their good fortune that nothing worse had happened. Then, later, she lay in the bed by his side, reading until it was quite late—and just thinking. She was so thankful, because while their accident was of a monstrous order, nothing had happened to disrupt their future. What if he had been killed? Or seriously injured? Thank God, nothing like that had happened. She felt very grateful as she looked at him lovingly, while he slept.

Chapter 26

Sunday morning dawned. A rising sun shone in a clear blue sky, and the temperature was in the low nineties. Sally sleepily watched as Emilio rose and walked out in front of their hut, facing the beach. He gazed south over a calm ocean, then west to face the flatland, his view of both being bordered only by the horizon. "We shall have a fine day," he said to her with deep satisfaction and then returned to bed. Enfolding her in his arms, "Starting right now."

"Nothing better than pre-marital sex," she said jokingly. Yes—this was the man she felt she would choose—she was rapturously satisfied with her choice. He was so perfect— handsome, virile, masculine and romantic. And he loved her. And she him—so passionately.

When he kissed her, she felt the most perfect rapport with him. As he gleefully pressed against her full belly, squeezed her fat buttocks she sensed he would be an extraordinary sexual partner and responded eagerly to him. And when he took her, he was so gentle, yet so forceful, she couldn't imagine a better lover. Then, ecstatically exclaiming as she reached a peak with him, "Oh, you're good, you big guy, damn you, you're so good—Ohhh!!!"

After an hour they rose, dressed and went to the restaurant for breakfast. Over eggs and pancakes Emilio told her that they would see a couple of small towns on the way to Valladolid. "It may interest you to see what an inland town in Yucatan looks like," he remarked. "Not like those in the states. I want to show you typical Mexico."

When Sally saw one she was unimpressed. Drab looking homes and shops and occasionally a small restaurant, all colored red, yellow, white or ochre lined a narrow dirt road with no sidewalks at all. It reminded Sally of an alley. Dogs in abundance, none tethered or on a leash. Outside the town, fields of hennequin. But, no surprise by this time to Sally, the pedestrians were all neatly dressed in spotless clothing, and there was no garbage littering the streets or the yards of the homes.

"The cleanliness of these people, isn't that something?" she remarked to Emilio.

"It surprises me, too," remarked Emilio, "especially when you consider the scarcity of water in Yucatan. The rainfall in this part of Yucatan is extremely light."

"Well, where does their water come from? There are also no rivers in this part of the country."

"From cenotes. Cenotes are underground wells. They are places where the surface limestone has collapsed and exposed the subterranean water table. That is what we are going to see today. You will see something beautiful."

After a two hour trip, they arrived at the Cenote Dzitnup. At the entrance to the cenote was a restaurant where they stopped for lunch. Sally had her second meal of chili con carne, assumed that it would be excellent as she thought it so typically Mexican, but, contrary to her expectations, it was the worst meal she had had since coming to Mexico. Undeterred, however, by this culinary experience, when confronted by the flight of rather perilous stairs leading down into the cenote, she bent low and, with one hand on the guardrail, made the descent of about fifty feet to the level of the underground pool. It was about fifty feet by fifty feet and reminded her of a painting of the famous Blue Grotto on the isle of Capri in Italy. It was worth the difficulty of the descent, even the last few feet, when she had to jump from slippery rock to slippery rock to get to the best place on the rocky plane to witness the full beauty of the pool.

"Truly stunning!" she breathed to Emilio. "I've never seen such water in my life. It's a brilliant royal blue."

The Ruins at Uxmal

They were alone in the cenote. Emilio put his arm around her. "Allow me to say, in this romantic setting, why I proposed marriage and how I feel about you. I know I was very rash in asking you to marry me—after all, we hardly know each other, and I have, of course, some idea of the difficulties you'll face—there's the problem of marrying a foreigner and living in a foreign country, dropping out of the kind of a life you've always known, but, regardless, it was how I honestly felt that made me do it. I am very anxious to become your husband. Again, will you marry me?"

"I'm a risk-taking type." Then calmly and joyfully, "My answer—yes."

"Oh thank you, darling, thank you! I am so delighted! You pull me like no on else ever has—I know you're for me."

"I'm glad I'm so attractive to you," she murmured, inwardly ecstatic. They kissed.

"You're beautiful. As I see you now, dressed in your shorts and halter, which exposes such a pretty expanse of white skin between your breasts, your reddish brown hair reaching to your shoulders, your lips a lustrous red and your blue eyes, half closed, expressing a mood of ease under the brim of your white sunhat—I swear I am absolutely taken with your looks."

"You yourself cut no mean figure," she replied, smiling sweetly at him, "on the beach, trim, naked to the waist, tanned golden brown by previous exposure to the sun, your white shorts...you reminded me of nothing so much as a handsome lifeguard."

He smiled appreciatively, "Let's go back to the top now," he said. "There's a fine jewelry shop up there, and it's time to make a purchase or two, don't you think?"

"I'm amenable," said Sally, taking his arm.

When they sauntered into the shop, Sally was amazed to find such a quality store outside the limits of a city. "I wonder, how come?" she asked Emilio.

"Many tourists come to this cenote," replied Emilio. "Business is usually quite brisk."

"Snaring the rich Americano," laughed Sally. Emilio nodded.

"How do you like this?" said Emilio, as he picked out a ring fashioned of two intertwined gold bars with six tiny diamonds set in a row along one of them.

"That," said Sally excitedly, "is one of the most unusual rings I've ever seen."

"Neither have I ever seen anything like it," also remarked Emilio, "and, darling, I want it for you. It's a perfect engagement ring."

"And how about this for you?" asked Sally, indicating a handsome black onyx ring with an embossed gold insignia. "It's perfectly beautiful—just right for you. You can afford another thirty-five hundred for it, and I think you should get it to commemorate this occasion."

"I'll flash it before Senor Gutierrez's eyes when next I see him," laughed Emilio. "That gentleman has an eye for excellent jewelry."

"Do you see him very much?" asked Sally. "I wonder how he's doing with Kirke?"

"I've been seeing him quite frequently. My father has increasing use for me at the hacienda, so much so that he wants me to give up my job and go to work for him. So my contact with Kirke and the Senor has also increased over these past few weeks."

"Have you told the Senor about us?"

"Yes. He's an old friend of my father's and keeps up with all our activites. He warmly congratulated me when I told him I was hoping to marry you."

"What do you think he thinks of Kirke and Consuelo?"

"Because this is Mexico, he undoubtedly just accepts it."

"I'll probably be seeing a bit of him now and then."

"Very likely. We'll be having him out to the house every so often."

"Tell me, when have you scheduled me to meet your family?"

"In five days. I can be with you then. It'll be Friday, and that's a holiday. Does that suit you?"

"Yes. I'm most anxious to meet them."

"Fine.

"Well, that's about enough about Kirke, business and your father. I'm ready to journey home now. It's been a lovely weekend."

"I, too, have enjoyed it famously. But, as you say, it's time to be going."

Arm in arm they walked to Emilio's automobile. As they got in, Sally took a good look at Emilio and felt her opinion was confirned. "He is handsome," she said to herself. "And, I think, quite a guy, as well." She considered herself most fortunate.

Chapter 27

A suprise awaited her a day later. There was a knock on her door and who should be standing on the landing but Senor Gutierrez.

"Buenos dias, Senora," he said. "No doubt my visit is a bit unexpected, eh?"

"No matter," replied Sally gaily. "I'm delighted to renew our acquaintance; you are most welcome."

The Senor bowed, placed his sombrero on the console table in the hall and then entered the living room.

After seating himself, he folded his hands, took a deep breath, assumed a serious mien and began speaking.

"I'm here to see you on Kirke's behalf," he said. "But before I say what it is, let me explain why I am here. Because as you are now divorced, you are undountedly disinclined to meet him; you would only do so to discuss matters of very serious importance. But it would be difficult for you to grasp all the complications and significance of such matters in a conversation over the phone. You simply might not be prepared to hear him out. You might not listen to him. So I am here to persuade you to see him."

"So you know about our divorce?"

"As his employer, I naturally have to know. Also he could hardly keep it from me, considering my proximity to him—and to Senorita Lopez—and to the fact that he wanted me to do this thing."

"What is this thing? I have nothing further to discuss with him. Visitation rights have been settled as well as alimony, etcetera. What would we have to talk about?"

The Ruins at Uxmal

"He told me he has something to say which may cause you to change your mind about the custody of your child."

"We've been through all of that. I presume you know that the matter was settled—in my favor—at our divorce which was executed four days ago."

"That is true, but let me say something new—and very pertinent—has come up."

"Something has? Something which could change my mind about my baby? I doubt it. I greatly doubt it. What could it be?"

"You will have to discuss the matter with him. That is why I am here—to persuade you to do so. I have an inkling what it is—and it seems to be serious enough to cause you great concern. It has to do with the family of Emilio Gonzalez.

"You see, Kirke knew of your relationship with Emilio, knew what your intentions were. He told me this a few days ago, when I told him of Emilio's engagement to you. Now, astounding to me as it will be to you, he has recently acquired some legally incriminating information about Emilio's father—exactly what it is I don't know. But let me say that what he has told me does not appear to be hearsay—it seems to be pretty well substantiated by Consuelo Lopez—Kirke told me she was an eyewitness. As he feels that you would trust me, he asked me to speak with you first so that I could attest to the validity of what he will tell you, so that you would not disregard him—that you would not consider his statement a trumped up lie."

Intense worry greatly whetted Sally's interest. Frightened, she burst out with a flurry of questions.

"What on earth could he know about the family? How did he learn of it—whatever it is? And what the devil does he think he can do to change my mind—threaten me in some way?"

"Threaten your marriage is more like it. But I really can't say anything more because I don't know any of the details. But what he has told me seems to be true. However, my concern is about you. But let me say further that although I am concerned, I can do nothing whatever to stop what he has in mind. I have no influence over him. And I have no influence with the law. But I was anxious to help you so here I am—to ask you to be patient—and above all, rational about all of this."

"You've got me terribly mystified. And greatly upset."

"I am sorry to cause you so much anxiety. But I should not say anything more. That is up to Kirke."

"Well, I scarcely know what to do..."

" You must see Kirke. Do that, of course. But please be rational about this. Although it seems to be serious, regardless of what you may be forced to do, I don't want you to go crazy and read about you in the paper blowing your brains out or doing some equally lunatic thing."

"I won't do that Senor. But, as you say, I will certainly have to see Kirke. Will you tell him that I will see him tomorrow morning?"

"Most certainly, Senora."

"Thank you, Senor."

"Be calm, Senora. And remember, you have a friend in me. If I can do anything to help you, please call on me. And now, I must go."

How nice of him to do that. His genuine concern for her was most gratifying. She felt he was a true friend—and a perfect gentleman.

"Senor, I feel I could trust you utterly. Is that so?"

"Indeed it is, Senora. With anything."

"Adios, Senor Gutierrez."

"Adios, Senora Sally. And may your welfare be in the hands of God."

Chapter 28

Sally was very nervous the following morning as she awaited Kirke's arrival. What could he possibly have learned that would cause him to resume his aggravating demand? When the rapping on the door sounded at ten, she felt almost as if it signaled another court hearing.

She opened the door and Consuelo Lopez stood before her, poised, well groomed, excellently dressed and as Sally stood dumbfounded, extended a disdainful salutation.

"Good morning," she said as cold as a fence-sitter, then maliciously, "Now aren't you surprised to see me?"

Amazed and aghast, Sally could barely utter a word. "I-I-I..." she stammered.

"May I come in?" queried Consuelo. Sally, recovering, admitted her.

Inside, Consuelo, without being asked, seated herself on a divan and waited patiently for a moment, allowing Sally to ready herself for what she had to say. Then, speaking in a very authoritative voice, she explained.

"Kirke was unable to make it."

Anger replacing surprise, Sally bluntly asked, "Why?"

Consuelo disparagingly remarked, "He was afraid—he felt he was taking on too much risk so I took over for him."

"What do you mean?"

"I said he felt we were taking too much risk—I don't—that's why I'm here."

"And what do you mean by 'risk?'"

"Well," drawled Consuelo, avoiding Sally's vigilant observation by surveying the room, "possibly I should say there's a bit too much responsibility involved—for him. You might be inclined to refuse to cooperate—and if you don't, there would be complications. I, however, am used to taking risks—and don't mind responsibility."

"You don't, eh?"

"No. I don't. I feel that we are within our rights."

"From that, I take it, you're the instigator of whatever trick the two of you are trying to play on me."

"I might be. And you could call it that, if you like."

"I'm not afraid of you. The law is on my side—I'll stand up to you."

Consuelo drew herself up. "With this little complication I'm going to tell you about, you'll find that the law will not be on your side. As a matter of fact, it only concerns you indirectly. But I think you'll cooperate, nevertheless."

"I will, eh?"

"Yes. You will."

"Well, now, suppose you tell me what you're here for."

Consuelo leaned back, extended an arm over a wing of the divan and, gazing directly at Sally to enjoy watching her squim, began delivering her message.

"It's this. You have learned, I presume, that down here in Mexico, it's not uncommon for a girl like me—with my attractions and will—to become the—ah—companion of a man even though he may be married, have children and all of that. It's quite different from the setup—to use an American term—which exists in your country. Down here, we have no Puritannical influence, and our mores are quite diffferent."

Her speech awed Sally, its delivery was so unhesitant. But she rallied her strength, nevertheless, and showed fight. "So I have learned—first hand from you."

Consuelo ignored this thrust. She continued.

"It so happens that a well-to-do old man induced me to become just that a year ago—before I met your husband. As Kirke told me you knew that, I presume you learned it from his son."

"Yes, I did. The old man was Senor Hector Gonzalez."

Consuelo thought for a moment, then resumed. "It's understandable that in the course of your conversations, his son would tell you that, since you are about to become his wife."

"Your supposition is correct," replied Sally evenly.

"But whether or not you know of it does not matter," continued Consuelo smoothly. "What does matter is this. As his mistress, naturally, I learned a lot about him—a devil of a lot—you know a man is more liable to unburden himself while in the arms of his mistress than he would anywhere else—," she laughed—"so I kept my ears open while he kept his mouth open."

"And?"

"I learned a lot."

"About what?"

"About the more private aspects of the Senor's life."

"You did, eh?"

Consuelo leaned forward and tensed herself somewhat, but continued to speak easily. Sally, in spite of her feelings of animosity, marveled at her self-command and the flow of her language.

"Yes. You see, contrary to what you and the world believe about him, the Senor has recently developed a second side to his character. The original side, which is apparent, so open, so sunshiny and frank and generally indicative of a somewhat ingenuous nature—is not, surprisingly, a true picture of the real man now. Rather, it is a clever concealment—a screen—for a devious and—er—sinister—that is not too strong a term—characteristic which is his present nature."

"Well, I could hardly know that—or anything else about him. I've only met him once to shake his hand. But his son has never told me anything like that about him—only that he's extremely religious, is fond of money and quite clever at getting it. There's nothing sinister about those traits of character."

"He probably didn't attach much significance to the change—maybe attributed it to his father's years. Perhaps he just thought it was business worries. And the old man tried to keep it from the family, of course. Or it could be that the devious and sinsister aspects are not apparent to them because, up to a year or so ago, the hacienda has been quite prosperous with no financial problems."

"I see. Go on."

"But, as you may know, the development of synthetic fibres since World War II has started to destroy the market for hennequin upon which, even though he is subsidized, Hector Gonzalez is dependent for his livelihood, not to mention his great wealth. So this change in the market had led to a change in the character of our once carefree, happy Senor Gonzalez."

"What if the family does become aware of this change?"

"Even if they do become aware of that and perhaps this—what I am about to tell you—will not change any of their attitudes toward the Senor. As they are women, with the exception of Emilio, they will just accept this as necessary for their survival. None of them are very educated and, you know, of course, that men rule the home down here. Emilio, being a young man and having attended school far away from home, if he becomes aware may see things a bit differently. He may be quite worried, but still would not dare oppose his father. And he wouldn't tell you, not now anyway."

"Well, what is it that the old man does?"

Consuelo lit a cigarette and took a deep drag before speaking further.

"Pay close attention as I tell you this, Senora, as it is of especial interest to you, and I don't wish to have to repeat myself." Then she stretched, leaned back again, and the tone of her voice became steely with satisfaction.

"The Senor has recently become involved in the growing drug trade down here. He knows the market for hennequin is declining; nothing else on which money can be made can be raised in Yucatan so what else could he do? He knew he would not be too deeply associated so the risk, although the law forbids it, would not be too great. And the authorities are inclined to wink at trading in drugs, anyway. So when opportunity knocked, he took it and has been at it now for a little over a year."

"Good God!"

"Hear me out, Senora. He has become the silent partner of some gang operating in the state of Oaxaca. He contributes by using the obsolete, empty bins on his grounds as storage places for loads of drugs enroute to various ports for shipment to the United States. These bins are useful as hideaways because of their location—in an out of the way part of the peninsiula where no drugs are grown nor where there are any other drug operations. That is what he does."

Sally shook her head in disbelief.

"We imagined you would be quite surprised."

"I don't believe it."

"Let me show the records I made of a couple of the Senor's dealings. I knew where he kept the key to his private desk. When I left him I made copies of two of his records to insure that I had a financial hold on him in case I ever needed money."

Sally took the records and, after scrutinizing them for a few minutes, looked at Consuelo and said, levelly, "You devil."

Consuelo merely smiled. "I have to take care of myself."

Sally shook her head again. "Poor Kirke."

Consuelo laughed. "We'll get along. He'll do as I say." Then, very sarcastically, "You've trained him well."

Sally, utterly bewildered, made a further query. "Don't the people who work for him know about this?"

"The gang always sends its own men to handle the loads, of course. A load of the drug is always very small, can be contained in a few large boxes so just a couple of trusties can handle the shipment. They do their work at night. The Senor rents out the space to them—his involvement is slight. But he gets a lot of money for it."

"At some risk?"

"Not much. Although the law forbids it, drug usage is widespread in Mexico. The law is broken constantly. And the Senor could say that he is just an unknowing renter. But there are penalties; although the Senor would most probably not go to jail, he might be heavily fined."

"Tell me. Why did you cut out being his mistress? You were well set up."

"I suppose there's no harm in telling you. He was always complaining—the strain got to him, and I tired of it—and his otherwise demanding ways. I wanted more independence. Furthermore, the family didn't care for me. So I cleared out. I am educated and can make my own way in the world.

"Yes," said Sally. "You have all the equipment—in all ways."

Consuelo smiled. "I can take care of myself," she again said.

Sally then made a pertinent surmise. "You're telling me this to disrupt my marriage?"

"Only if it were made public. If it were, you'd have second thoughts about marrying—wouldn't you? Your're the type that avoids publicity."

"But what is your reason for doing this?"

"If you give us the child, nothing will be done to you, like informing the police about the Senor's involvement with drugs.'

"I see. You're trying to blackmail me."

"Only if you refuse to cooperate with us. If you are willing to give Bill to us, there is nothing whatever to interfere with your plan of marrying Emilio. You can become the wife of the local financial baron and be a queen in the society of Mexico City—if you don't mind being mixed up with drug-dealing—or else you could go off with Emilio alone." Then she paused to emphasize the threat in what she was going to say.

Sally waited, then, "Well, I see what you intend. If I don't..."

Consuelo stubbed her cigarette out in an ashtray on an end table. "Otherwise your hopes for an unsullied marriage will be squashed as quickly as I have put out this cigarette."

"Now that makes it perfectly clear."

"Releasing the information we have to the police will result in an investigation. The outcome of it will generate a lot ot the most unpleasant publicity for the family. Think of this as a headline in the journal in this city! Promininent Haciendado Indicted in Drug Scandal! Ah! —the results will be most ominous for the social standing of the Gonzalez family. Now

The Ruins at Uxmal

you wouldn't like to see that said about the family you were going to marry into, would you?"

"Hardly."

Consuelo laughed. "You see we have you."

"Let me see if I understand you—if I assent, you will leave all of us alone."

"Yes—we'll leave you alone. We do not intend to run afoul of the law by blackmailing the Senor. We'll have the child—that's all we want."

"There's just one hitch in your plans, Consuelo. You haven't figured on this—I don't think you have the courage to blab to the police. What about retaliation from the gang? Drug dealers are not people to fool with."

"I said before I was not afraid of responsibility. I say now, I have a lot of nerve. I've had to. It's hard for a single girl in Mexico to make her way. And this outfit is very small. They would not dare commit murder."

"They might."

"Of an American citizen? Or even of his Mexican girlfriend? Not much chance."

Sally's shoulders fell in despair.

"Furthermore," continued Consuelo, "we may be going to the states in a short time. So I don't think I have anything to worry about."

"You have everything figured out, haven't you?" said Sally, her anger rising. "You bitch! You're the shrewdest, coldest—and one of the most ruthless, calculating humans I've ever met!"

"So?"

Sally hesitated just a moment before giving full voice to the fury which welled up in her. She then uttered the vilest epithet she could think of.

"You know," she said, her voice edged with anger, "I can think of one term to describe you. The standard terms in the English vocabulary are insufficient—they're used too often to adequately express what I think you are. The term is 'offal.' You might not know it—it's the euphemism for the commonly used vulgarism—it means excrement! That is exactly what you are—offal, offal, offal! You're the lowest thing on two legs I've ever met."

"Why you bitch! You stuck-up vermin! To call me that! I know your kind! With your false notions stemming from your over-protected existence, you think you're above everybody else! Well, you're not! Say I'm beneath you! Be contemptuous of me will you! Call me offal! You have your nerve! I know your type! You do that, because you've undoubtedly never had to fight to get what you have—it's always been handed to you. So, you take what you wish, run off with it—and then hold yourself above everybody else—condemning what they do to make out. You have all the useless values of the idle rich, and when need comes for action, they're as superfluous as the lectures I received at the Catholic girls' school I attended when I was growing up. God damn you for what you've called me! Kirke and I are going to get what we're rightfully entitled to, and if you get in the way, we'll take care of you in the most appropriate way!"

"Yes," said Sally, speaking calmly, "You'll take care of things allright—in any way you can."

For a moment Consuelo stood, thinking, then her face showed nothing but malice. "I'll make you pay for what you've called me," she hissed. "Mark my words, I'll get you if it's the final act of my life—what we'll do to you unless you cooperate."

"I suggest you go now," replied Sally haughtily.

The Ruins at Uxmal

Consuelo went to the door, then turned and faced her.

"Well, what is your decision?" she demanded. "Are you going to give us Bill? Or," she said, leering, "face the consequences?"

Sally remained calm. But not knowing what to decide, she had to temporize.

"I cannot say, right now. I need some time to think this over. Give me a week or two."

"Very well," replied Consuelo. "But no more than two weeks. We'll be waiting to hear from you." She turned on her heel and strode through the door.

Chapter 29

After Consuelo had left, Sally sank into the sofa, shocked by the revelation she had just heard, utterly overwhelmed. But then, after more than an hour of tumultuous reflection, a need arose in her, a need to confide in somebody. Slowly this revived her. Then she thought, but who? Suddenly the notion of Senor Gutierrez popped into her head. Yes, she thought thankfully, he was the one to see. He had said that if she ever needed any help, he would be available. Yes, he was the one, he would tell her what to do. Then without further consideration, she picked up the phone and put through a call to the office of Amer-Mexico.

Next day, as there was a knock on her door, Sally thought, at least I'll have some idea of how to conduct myself during that visit to Emilio's family—which will be awful!

After entering, the Senor sat down in a leather armchair, leaned back and said gently, "I assume that what you have learned would be most disturbing."

"Indeed it was, Senor," replied Sally, seating herself. "You said that if I needed any help, I should call you. I desperately need your soundest advice. This situation you spoke about has got me up a tree." Her tension eased slightly; the Senor looked as if he would be helpful.

The Senor nodded and lit his pipe. "I refrained from inquiring too closely when Kirke first told me, as I figured it was not my business. But when I got back to the office, I was so worried about you I took the liberty of asking Kirke what he was going to do. As it's perfectly legal, he had no objection to telling me in complete detail."

"So you know the whole story? And who's really behind it?"

"Yes. Nervy devil—and clever, isn't she?"

"She certainly is. She is most formidable."

The Senor rose to his feet and walked the length of the room.

"Well, what do you think you should do about this?"

"I don't know. I'm at my wit's end."

The Senor took his pipe from his mouth and scratched his chin.

"Well—now, let's see—there's one possibility."

"What?"

"I think you should avoid any further entanglement with the Gonzalez family."

"Give up Emilio?"

"Yes."

"Just break up and leave? Go back to the states?"

"Yes. Things have gotten too complicated for you to handle—much too complicated. You're a young girl, alone, living in a foreign country, and you're not the kind to have had anything as difficult as this to cope with."

"And give up the kind of a life I want to lead?"

"Is that so important to you now?"

"It is important, but to give up to them—a worthless ex-husband and his mistress—damn them—that's worse! And furthermore..."

"What?"

Sally rose to her feet and paced the floor. She burst out.

"Senor," she cried, "there are three reasons—more important ones—why I cannot do that." She let her words sink in, then continued.

"The most important, of course, is that if I kept my child and ran, Emilio would still be exposed to whatever Kirke and Consuelo would do to him."

"Well, he would be—that's true."

"By hurting him they would hurt me—they know that, of course."

"Yes."

"Secondly, I have a damnable problem with my family back home—which also prevents me from clearing out."

The Senor peered at her intently.

"My mother has written me recently and told me my father is very sick and is expected to enter a convalescent home—a place where he will be cared for medically. That raises financial difficulties for us as, thirdly, I have a physical disability which prevents me from working. As there's not much money in the family, all I would do if I returned home would be to add to the problems of my mother. And I wasn't raised that way."

"Well, if you cannot do that, what's next? My dear girl..." the Senor then implored.

Sally stated the problem bluntly.

"I really don't see any way to avoid the embarrassment of scandal."

"Really—well, what are you going to do?"

"I'm just going to have to bite the bullet."

"And just how are you going to do that?"

"Senor, speaking about this with you has got me to thinking hard. Emilio, I don't believe is aware of his father's association with drug dealers—at best, he may just suspect it. So what I will do will be to break the news to him. I don't know how he will take it—I have reason to believe he is very obedient to his father—he only dared propose to me when he felt his father would not oppose him. I also believe he is a loving son. Nevertheless, I will have to convince him that his father is implicated in drug dealing."

"And then?"

"I'll simply ask him to face the music and elope—that's the term we Americans use to describe a runaway marriage in defiance of parental wishes. We can't save the family from scandal, and we won't have much money—Emilio will lose the gift of money his father promised him now and later on, his father's estate. I will have neither prestige nor money, but I will have Emilio—who will take care of me as I cannot work..." Her voice was desperate as she said this.

The Senor stopped walking, faced her and spoke point-blank.

"Unless, of course, you were willing to make a great sacrifice."

"Senor, giving my child to Kirke in company with the kind of woman he has taken up with would be the worst kind of action I could possibly take. Kirke is a weak-willed bummer, and that woman is so immoral and strong-willed—I really dread the kind of upbringing little Bill would have. No, I cannot sacrifice my child! Don't ask me to."

"The Senor paused a moment, looking out the window, reflecting.

"Well, my dear," he eventually said, "I suppose you are right. I guess your plan is the best you can do." But he shook his head.

"It is, after hashing over these other possibilites. I'll just have to steel myself for this ordeal I'm going to have to face."

"When do you see Emilio?"

"I was going with him to visit the family in five days. But as matters have gotten so complicated, I'll ask him to see me tomorrow. He's important enough to take a day off from work."

"The Senor looked thoughtfully at her, appreciating her.

"And, after that, we'll be on our way—hopefully—to live our own lives," continued Sally.

"I think you're doing the right thing. And now let me say, you're the most magnificent young woman I've ever met. It's a pleasure to meet and help you in some small way—I am grateful for the opportunity."

"Thank you, Senor. I am grateful for your help—and your sympathy."

"And however you end up, keep in touch. I wish to remain in contact with a remarkable woman." He picked up his sombrero from the table and, after making a deep bow, left through the door, a look of admiration on his features.

Chapter 30

She met Emilio the following day in a most determined mood. As he sat in an easy chair, she wondered how she should begin. But his attitude of affability did much to reduce her tension and restore a semblance of calm. After first asking him not to interrupt her, she forthrightly told him the whole story.

While she spoke, she observed him anxiously, noting how his demeanor changed. At first incredulous, he uttered an exclamation, but she raised her hand to prevent him from expostulating further and continued. When she had finished he sat for a long, solemn moment, then leaned back and released his breath slowly in a sigh.

"My God," he then said, "what you're telling me is almost unbelievable."

"Yes. But it's true, nevertheless. Consuelo's story is very convincing."

"Yes—and what it does is explain the change I noticed about a year ago in my father. At that time, he seemed to me to become worried, more depressed—I thought it was business worries, as this decline in the market for hennequin—but what you have told me—now the reason is very clear."

"Your family is in a heck of a jam which will only be avoided if I give up Bill. And I absolutely refuse to do that."

"And that isn't all of it. What is to prevent Consuelo and Kirke from blackmailing my father indefinitely?"

"She and Kirke haven't quite got the nerve to attempt that. The law is the law. So I think your father is allright."

"Well, that's good."

"We have ourselves to think of. I can see only one thing to do. Leave your family, do not let your life be tainted by your father's guilt and come with me—I will have Bill, we can marry and live somewhere else—either in Mexico or the states—preferably the latter. You are a professional agriculturalist, you might not have much difficulty in getting a job. That is really what you should do."

"I am not going to desert my father. He needs me desperately at this time. I know he is essentially a good man. I am certain he has been forced to do this thing out of economic necessity."

"That's undoubtedly true."

"I have my familial obligations as a loyal son. And besides, think now of the gift—five hundred thousand! If we run off, even if he does approve of you, we will not get it. For that money, if this thing comes out, I will try anything to help him! He may need advice, counsel, someone to lean on, and I am his son. I will not leave leave him. I will stand by him, although the publicity attendant on the case will be most embarrassing."

"Emilio, you are something to admire. But I question your judgement. It would still be better for you—and our future—if you left home and came with me."

"No. I will not do that. There's too much at stake."

"What about our marriage?"

"Later on, maybe. In a year."

"A year? Emilio, what difference will that make?"

"Dear—don't raise that question now. At this time, you must come, no matter how you feel and meet my father."

"Must I?"

"Remember. Five hundred thousand dollars."

Sally succumbed, feeling she faced the inevitable. "Well—very well. I will meet your father."

"You must act friendly toward him. And when he offers to take you up the pyramid at Uxmal, you must accept. You see, anyone joining the family is requested to go through that climb with him. It is with him a test of character—it takes some nerve—more than many women and some men have—to go up those pyramids, and my father wants women of courage in the family. He is a lion, my father, and kind of even expects deference from others out of politeness—call it subservience, if you like—to him."

Sally then could only say, in hope, "Maybe something will turn up to change things, I just mustn't give up."

Chapter 31

When Emilio picked her up on the day she was to meet his father, he told her that he would accede to her wish if his father would release him from his familial obligations and promise him his gift. "Our hope—after he meets you, is that he might."

"Oh, if only he would!" cried Sally. Her hand tightened its grip on his.

After the morning drive from Merida, as they came to the hacienda outside Valladolid, they turned off the highway, entered the cobble-stoned driveway lined by tall pepper trees with yellow spring blossoms, and drove up to a great wooden door—a zaguan. As they stepped out of the automobile, Sally looked around and saw what she had only noticed briefly on her previous visit: on both sides of the driveway, behind the pepper trees, were gardens. Purple and red bougainvillea and blue plumbago filled them. These were bordered by stone walls. Before her, vividly recalling her previous remembrance, loomed the massive hacienda: two parallel buildings separated by an inner courtyard.

Yes, thought Sally, Emilio had been previously assured he was going to get a gift and later an estate, but would he if her wishes prevailed? She gritted her teeth: under them she might just have Emilio. All for love—and security—ha! But think not of that now. Keep your mind on what has to be done. Then, "How does your father get such beautiful gardens? Is there some cenote nearby?"

"Irrigation," said Emilio simply. "He's favored by the local government because he is a power around here. And these trees and plants grow in our inhospitable soil."

The Ruins at Uxmal

The elder Senor greeted them at the door. After exchanging salutations, he escorted them into a big room (called a 'sala,' Emilio told Sally) and indicated chairs for all of them.

"I thought, after you have met the family and we have lunch, that I should show the Senora the place—and especially our gardens," said the Senor, playing the hospitable host. "They are very beautiful at this time of the year."

"That would please me very much," acknowledged Sally. "I want to see the whole estate this time." She thought—Emilio had said, "Maybe—after a year—marriage?".

"Before that, I'd like to see you in private for awhile, after dinner," said Emilio. The Senor nodded assent.

"But now come and meet my wife and daughter," he said. Then he called, "Delores, Adela." At his summons, two women entered the 'sala'. "My wife," he said, taking the older woman's hand. "This is Senora Sally Parks. Senora Sally, meet Senora Dolores."

Senora Dolores was a plump, firm woman, about fifty, in a dark voile dress, but what Sally noticed most was her small, slim hands and when she smiled, tiny teeth.

"Buenos dias, Senora," said Senora Dolores. "I am ver pleased to meet with you."

"Mamacita speaks English, but not as well as I," said Emilio, by way of explanation. "She has never been to the states."

"And Adela," said the Senor. Adela, a young woman about twenty with black hair and lively eyes, gave Sally an affectionate smile as she said, "Pleased to meet you. I am charmed," and spontaneously extended her hand.

"Nor has Adela," went on Emilio. "But as you see, she has studied English in school. And," he remarked jokingly, "you can see she likes to show it off."

After asking Sally about the pleasures of the drive and indicating chairs for everyone, Mamacita then called, "Jose," in a sharp voice. A servant hurried into the room. After Mamacita said a few words in Spanish to him, he left but returned almost immediately bearing a liqueur, glasses and small cakes on a silver tray.

The next question Sally answered, over amaretto and polvorones de maizena (which she learned were cornstarch puff cookies) was how she liked Mexico. She responded with marked enthusiasm, and Mamacita seemed very pleased. Adela then said she was going to visit the states, and Senor Gonzalez remarked that he had promised to send her there next year as a graduation gift from the University of Yucatan. Then Mamacita formally announced, "Let us now go in to dinner. The servants have it ready."

She turned and led the way through a long hallway to a large dining room. As the courses were served, Sally saw that it was to be a feast. First there were appetizers of tacos, chile and guacamole, then the main courses: enchiladas made of chicken, cheese and tomatoes and tortillas filled with beans—a very sumptuous Mexican meal—and on the sideboard stood a cake with white icing topped with shredded carrots.

Sally commented on the luncheon. "It's quite formal—with servants."

"Mexico, darling," said Emilio. "Usually, even when there are a lot of people—no buffet. Unlike what you have in the states. The affair at Senor Gutierrez's was an exception."

"In Mexico, meals are served by servants—at least in the upper class," said Mamacita.

And fine Mexican wine, thought Sally, as she took a sip from her glass. Absolutely de rigeur, of course, on an occasion like this.

At a pause in her conversation with the others, Sally took a brief but thorough look about the room, noting its luxurious furnishings, indicative of the wealth of the Senor. It was appointed with the best furniture, made in Czechoslovakia Sally learned in politely mentioning the chairs to Mamacita who also then told her the china and glass were English. The tablecloth, Sally also observed, was of fine damask weave, and the rug was Persian.

The luncheon was quite long, lasting about two hours, during which Sally answered questions about her experience in exploring the Mayan ruins at Chichem Itza. Then the Senor commented.

"You have seen the ruins at Chichen Itza, but those at Uxmal are more beautiful, and the temple there is higher," he said. "I will take you up it in the near future and give you a thrill."

"That's a date," said Sally with little enthusiasm.

She thought sadly that she would like very much to marry into this family, but for the outrage which threatened it. Something, she wished, had to be done. But what? What on earth?

After lunch the Senor excused Emilio and himself by saying that they had something to discuss of a private nature, and Sally was left with the other ladies in the 'sala.' Through all the following conversation which was chiefly about how the hacienda had prospered and how the Gonzalez family lived, Sally's mind kept recurring to the other vital conversation taking place between Emilio and his father in another room. She controlled her anxiety, although on pins and needles, until, after half an hour, they returned.

After Emilio and the Senor rejoined them, they sat sober faced, saying very little. Sally became restless, waiting for the gathering to break up. At length, the Senor said, "Now, Sally, I will show you the hennequin field and the gardens in the rear."

Jeremy S. Wood

As she rose to a accompany him, Emilio took her hand, said "Just a minute, Papa," and led her into a small anteroom just off the dining room.

"As you are crazy to know..." he began, but his grim face told her the outcome before he could unburden himself. Anticipating him, she said, "I can tell by looking at you that he will not allow you to go."

"That is true, you are right," said Emilio. "Meeting you did no good whatever." He sighed. "When I asked him about leaving, he said he was considering another line of work—he was very vague about what it was, because he said he didn't exactly know his part in it—it involves several companies—but he was clear that he wanted me to help him in it. He said he would not give me my gift if I refused—so, obviously, I didn't dare mention the fact I wanted to leave because I knew he was involved in drug exporting. He said I was the only man he could trust and that is vital to this operation—he needs me and that is all there is to it."

"Coming Senora?" called the Senor from the other room. Sally turned to go, thinking confusedly about what to do next.

The Senor took her down the long hallway and through a rear door out into the back of the hacienda. He then indicated the open field before them, covered with spiny, purplish stalks of hennequin. "My living," he said matter of factly. Then he looked at some tall trees at the end of the field, naming them as he pointed. "Those are cypress, those are jacaranda. Spider monkeys are at play in some of them." He laughed. "Don't get under the trees. The monkeys will throw excrement at you."

They walked down a dirt road, the Senor pointing out the extent of his holdings. They must, Sally thought, cover several acres, as the field extended for about a mile on all sides. After about ten minutes they came to a large barn standing on top of a tiny hill. Sally asked what it was for.

The Ruins at Uxmal

"We slaughter our own meat," replied the Senor.

During this walk Sally did some rapid thinking. Emilio was afraid that his father might deprive him of his gift if he were insubordinate. She herself felt cautious about what to do. She, of course, surmised the reason why the Senor was keeping his son—it certainly was not just to embark on a legitimate business enterprise. She felt he was retaining his son because he was sure he would not betray him. Then she thought and thought—would she really be endangered in any way if she dared to confront the Senor—to tell him, frankly, that she knew about his drug exporting. Risky! But then he could not brush her aside, and the way would be open for her to plead for Emilio's release. But her own security? God! She took a deep breath and thought further. She considered the options. Most importantly, she felt certain, as an American citizen, the Senor would not dare to harm her—although he might threaten. Also, she would not be bargaining with a hardened drug lord—she would just be speaking with a person who had seen no way out of the financial plight circumstances had put him in and had taken to cooperating with some small time drug dealers because he was desperate for money. He had not seemed tough or brutal to her at all—rather a nice, well-spoken old man. But nevertheless—God—it was risky.

Summon up all your courage, girl! Come on, she thought grimly, the stakes are worth it! She tried to figure out every move she would make and then, on the way back, made up her mind, decided to confront him—it was now or never—she would—God help her! —make the attempt! Nerving herself to her absolute limit, she stopped, faced and put the vital question to him.

"Senor," she said, "why did you refuse to let Emilio leave your family and come with me?"

The Senor, surprised by her temerity, looked at her sideways out of the small black, beady eyes which Sally noticed grew suddenly very hard.

"I was puzzled when he asked me the same question," said the Senor. "Now why do you ask? Didn't he tell you the reason why in the little anteroom before we came out here?"

"All he said was that you asked him to stay because you needed his help in business."

"That is true. What else is there to say?"

"What kind of business, may I inquire, would demand that your son stay? Why can't you get other men; they would be as good as Emilio?"

"No," said the Senor sharply. "Emilio is the best."

"Why?"

"Because, as if it were any concern of yours, the reason is that he has to learn it thoroughly as he is going to inherit it. So he should stay. And, I understand that you expect to become his Senora—his wife. Why aren't you pleased? You perplex me. Let me ask you a question—why should you be so desirous of taking him away from the source of his future large income?"

"To stay was certainly my intention when I originally accepted his offer of marriage. But circumstances have changed—that is why I want to leave—with him—and, Senor, you know what they are."

"What do you know?" The Senor looked at her intently again through his black, beady eyes, his bushy brows drew together and, as he frowned, very deep lines creased his forehead. "What are you implying?"

Sally looked down from the Senor's face to escape those questioning eyes, then, on lifting her gaze slightly, noticed that his hands were spasmodically clenching and unclenching. She hesitated before speaking, but when she did her voice was low, slow and steady.

"Senor, I know the real reason why you are refusing to let Emilio go. It is because you need a man you can control—a man in the family—a man who is your own son and who is devoted to you—who would not betray you to the police because of his devotion and who is too afraid to leave because you might not give him his gift. You need him to help you run the end of the drug business in which you are involved."

The Senor looked at her as if he were a jaguar about to pounce on helpless prey in a jungle, then replied very deliberately, very slowly—Sally felt that he was deadly.

"A business with drugs. What the hell are you talking about? Of all the nonsensical notions..."

"It is not nonsense. It is the truth. I learned it from an eyewitness to your activites."

The Senor regarded her shrewdly.

"You are making quite an accusation. An eyewitness to my activities?"

"I know what I am talking about. Senorita Consuelo Lopez—know her?"

The Senor was startled. He stepped backwards in utter surprise, saying, "What the devil—how do you know...?"

"Yes, I know her. She entered my life—to disrupt it—now yours. I learned it all from her."

The Senor attempted bluster. "Ridiculous," he cried angrily. "You have some nerve. Why, damn you, you're just making this—this ridiculous accusation—what do you think you're attempting? —oh—getting me to let Emilio go. Is that it?"

"I am not lying, Senor. I had the dope straight from her. Just two days ago."

"That whore! How did you come to know her?"

"When she became my husband's mistress."

The Senor's brows knit in curiosity. "But why the devil—why did she tell you? How did you come to learn of it—to get involved...?"

"She told me about you because you were involved in her scheme to blackmail me. She and Kirke wanted my child—which I refuse to give them."

"What reason would cause her to tell you about me?"

"To disrupt my marriage to your son."

"Explain." The Senor was short.

"Because I am in love with Emilio and wish to marry him. By scandalizing your family they can disrupt my marriage—they are threatening to tell the police; they can do it that way. Unless I turn my child over to them—and that I will not do."

"They will attempt to spoil your marriage to my boy by exposing me to the police, eh?"

"Yes."

The Senor exploded. "Well, damn them—if they intend, they won't succeed in damaging my reputation. This won't create such a stir. I have firm friends. And I won't see the inside of a jail. The government and police are very tolerant of drug use—hell, more than half the population use them. And if you worry about a scandal concerning me, your fears are groundless. Rest assured—my so-called crime is only big in your eyes. It really doesn't amount to a good damn! But I see—it's you they're after. Your ex and his girlfriend are just playing on your fears. A-r-r-gh! Now, look here, my dear girl, why don't you just accept my infraction for what it is—a minor peccadillo down here, if not in the United States. Don't think I'm a big time criminal. I have to do this in order to hang on to what I have. So if I have caused you calamitous worry—forget it."

He took out his pipe, lit it and grinned at her. Then he went on.

"Emilio wants to marry you, and I have no objections—you seem an ideal type. That is, if you become like a typical Mexican housewife and don't interfere with the men's operations in the house. You will make him a good wife—I can see that. But no interference, at any time. I know how to handle myself."

"You will not relent and allow Emilio to come with me?"

"No. I will not. I have control over him, and—I warn you—I generally don't like people who oppose my will!..." He broke off. "But I do admire your courage, I can see that you have nerve—you have Yankee gall—but Emilio stays with me."

"You sound threatening."

"I can be."

"Senor, although I am afraid of you, I am an American citizen, and I know you would not touch me. I am quite certain you would not dare."

"Humpf..." The Senor smiled grimly. "Although you are right, I still control Emilio."

"Senor, please, what is Emilio for? To engage in an occupation which breaks the law? I cannot accept that! Please relent, and let him live away from all this—with me—probably in the states. Your reputation will be blackened terribly in my eyes, and Emilio should not be tainted by it. I cannot marry a man who is engaged in such activity. Please! Release him! Let him come with me!"

The Senor looked at her with contempt. "Your appeal has no effect on me." He looked harshly at her. "Now come with me," he said in a more menacing tone. "I want to show you something I think you should see."

"Carlos," he bellowed, turning towards the barn. Then he shouted some words in Spanish.

A man came out of the barn, holding a piglet in his arms. The Senor then led them all the short distance back to the swimming pool in back of the hacienda.

The Senor then commanded Sally, "Watch." He turned and nodded to Carlos.

Carlos tossed the pig into the pool.

What followed froze Sally. The most agonized, deafening squealing swept over her as the piranha fish attacked the animal. The water boiled and swirled, blood red, as the flesh was torn from the poor beast; its death struggle was so violent it splashed water on the spectators at the edge of the pool. Sally, utterly transfixed by the grisly episode, watched, horrified for the half minute it took, involuntarily lifting her hands to her cheeks and gasping! The Senor calmly watched her emotional display, then, when she dazedly looked at him, picked up a gaff by the pool's side, dipped it into the water and retrived the skeleton of the animal. The piranha had stripped it bare.

The Senor then remarked in a manner which brooked no disregard, "Emilio will stay with me."

Sally was utterly cowed. My God—would this man kill his own son? Her head slumped to her chest, she barely dragged herself back to the hacienda behind the Senor. There he turned and said to her, "You will, of course, give me the pleasure of taking you up the Mayan temple at Uxmal. It is something I think you should let me show you, since you are going to become a member of the family, and Emilio asked me to be sure I do it only when he comes here in two days. Now, you're not afraid, are you? You have courage, I can see that. And after all," he said with a touch of sardonicism, "I have to show it to my future daughter-in-law as a courtesy."

Sally, utterly depleted by this afternoon of horror, could only nod. She thought, my God! Emilio! What would happen to him if?...It was too dreadful to contemplate. Now, for God's sake—she said to herself—do nothing to antagonize his father. He is cruel, yes, he would even murder. No, do nothing to antagonize him! He is too dangerous. My God! Do you still want to marry into this family? No! Do you have to? But her circumstances! Christ! But for now—in a flash she perceived—just get away from here, away from this awful old man—and, when—and if! —you recover—think, great God! —for an answer!

Chapter 32

On the drive home, Emilio immediately noted the distraught condition of Sally. He worriedly inquired what was wrong. Losing her last shred of composure, Sally broke down completely and told him what his father had done. Weeping, she said, "He is an absolute beast—a cruel, vicious man. Emilio, you must watch out for yourself, he might have you killed."

"No", said Emilio. "He would never do that—at least, so long as he is the man I know. He is devoted to his family; I know he loves me."

"But to do such a thing to a helpless animal!"

Emilio shook his head. "This drug business must be driving him to behave like that. It is most unlike him. He must have felt some great urgency to impress you—to make you afraid." He shook his head again. "I just don't understand his behavior."

Sally could stand his expostulations no longer. She threw back her head and blurted a desperate plea.

"Emilio," she cried, "will you leave your father and come with me? The gift can go to the devil! We'll make out some way! I cannot face the prospect of living in the same house with your father. No! I cannot do it. I simply cannot. I just cannot bring myself—that man..."

"Dear," he replied, "this with my father has greatly upset you. Please try to calm down. Be rational. I cannot, I must not leave my father—my God, five hundred thousand dollars and the emotional reasons you already know. Now why don't you take until tomorrow to think this over?"

"God! I certainly will! I need that—time to think it over. I need solitude—and then your advice. Yes, it would be best to leave me alone for the evening. We'll discuss it again tomorrow—yes, we'll do that and reach some decison. But one thing—I will not go up that pyramid with your father."

"My dear, you must impress him favorably—think of the money. Adela and Mamacita also would not understand you attitude. They think you are on the best of terms with him. Furthermore, you said you were willing. They would not understand your sudden timidity."

"The devil with that, Emilio. I simply cannot go up."

"We'll talk about that tomorrow," he said as he kissed her good-night.

That night, exhausted, she fell into bed. But she could not sleep. Her anxiety made her nearly frantic. She thought again and again, what shall I do to escape that climb? —then she saw her book on the ancient Maya on her bed table. She seized it and thought, in desperation, it's the only thing I have to read. It'll be interesting—it's on the Maya; I'll try it for awhile. It may help me to sleep.

The section she opened to dealt, however, with a grisly topic; the sacrifcial rites of the Maya. Morbidly, nevertheless, she began reading—was she, sort of, being sacrificed? It seemed that her whole life was being destroyed by this predicament she had gotten into.

She began reading "...human-sacrifice rituals were performed in several ways: The most common manner...was the removal of the heart. Women and chilldren were sacrificed as frequently as men. The intended victim—stripped, painted blue (the sacrificial color) and wearing a special peaked headdress—was led to the place of sacrifice, usually either the temple courtyard or the summit of the pyramid supporting the temple. When the evil spirits had been expelled, the altar, usually a convex stone that curved the victim's breast upward, was smeared with the sacred blue paint. The four chacs...also painted blue, next grasped the victim by the arms and legs and stretched him on his back over the altar. The nacom advanced with the sacrificial flint knife and plunged it into the victim's ribs just below the left breast. Thrusting his hand into the opening, he pulled out the still-beating heart and handed it to the chilam, or officiating priest, who smeared blood on the idol to whom the sacrifice was being made. If the victim had been sacrificed on the summit of the pyramid, the chacs threw the corpse into the courtyard below, where priests of lower rank skinned the body, except for the hands and feet. The chilam, having removed his sacrifical vestments, arrayed himself in the skin of the victim and solemnly danced with the spectators. If the sacrifical victim had been a valiant and brave soldier, his body was sometimes divided and eaten by the nobles and other spectators. The hands and feet were reserved for the chilam, and, if the victim was a prisoner of war, his captor wore certain of his bones as a mark of prowess."

Sally put the book back on the table. No respite from reading this, she thought. She decided to try sleeping, put out the lamp and closed her eyes. Overcome by the trials of the day, she eventually fell into a slumber, but did not rest; a vivid nightmare about the slaughter she had witnessed ensued.

With the arrival of morning, a letter came. It was special delivery form the states. It overwhelmed her. It was from her mother and contained nothing but bad news. Her father's condition had worsened so much that they had decided that he should enter a nursing home. The additional cost entailed by this move would take all their income. Nothing would be left over. Her realization of this action left her with absolutely no avenue to escape, no option to return home. It tore at her. Sinking into the deepest despair, she thought and thought, but could come to only one conclusion; her only course was to marry Emilio and accept his father.

Emilio arrived. She told him the latest news.

The Ruins at Uxmal

"Well," he then said, after a long minute, very slowly, "this—what you just said to me—you cannot return to your family—I must stay with my father—what shall you do?"

"It looks as if the only thing I can do is marry you—regardless of the circumstances," she said. "And I must go to the pyramid with your father tomorrow. It is impossible to turn him down now."

"Well, let us pray our luck will turn," said Emilio. "We'll just have to hope for the best. Now let us spend the next hour in prayer. Then, perhaps we can go for a walk?. It may be of some help in getting our minds off our troubles. And we still have each other."

That was true. She nodded.

"And I'll call for you tomorrow real early. At my father's request to avoid overcrowding from many tourists and so you won't get sunstroke from your exertions."

Chapter 33

Rising at six the following morning, Sally prepared a big breakfast of ham, eggs and pancakes for herself and Emilio. "I know I'll also need this," she then said resolutely to herself as she poured her first cup of strong Mexican coffee.

She had dressed in shorts and her lightest blouse for the climb as the weather was ideal, being cloudless and sunlit with low humidity for Yucatan and a temperature only in the nineties. That's about the only good thing which will happen today, she thought.

Emilio arrived, nodded approvingly when he saw that her attitude was determined and then offered some comfort. He said that he would try to convince his father that his changed behavior was evidence that he was destroying himself. Then he might eventually persuade him to get out of his ruinous activity. He also beseeched Sally to try to understand the strain his father was under. And after they had embarked on their trip, he elaborated on his father's basic virtue when they passed the sixteenth century cathedral in the zocalo as they drove through downtown Merida on their way to Uxmal.

"When my father came to town he always went to Mass," said Emilio. "He was very religious. He is not a savage man. I cannot understand his cruelty. That drug business—it must be driving him to behave in such a sadistic manner."

"Don't make excuses for him," said Sally, unconvinced. "He is utterly vicious now. And," she finished, "that is whom I will have as a father-in-law."

In the country outside Merida, Sally recalled how supremely ugly the landscape was—a condition suitable, she thought, for the day. But although the day had just begun she, trying to be heroic, bravely faced up to it.

They arrived in the vicinity of the temple at Uxmal at seven. Senor Gonzalez had not yet come. After a twenty-five minute walk from their car, they came to the exact site. There, Sally just stood and gazed at the temple, called in the book, the Temple of the Magicians.

It looked most formidable, looming high and steep over the surrounding flat landscape. It was dissimilar, to some extent, from the one at Chichen Itza, much taller and with an eroded temple roof-comb—the latter a masonry backdrop for front-facing decorative elements that added to the height of the building. The structure was, according to Emilio, 120 feet high with a climb at a seventy degree angle up very tall steps—about thirteen inches high but only four inches deep.

"I can see why your father regarded this as a test," Sally remarked dolefully.

Emilio avoided responding to her comment, then said, "When you get to the top, you should survey the surrounding countryside. My father expects guests to enjoy this. Better take some binoculars with you."

"Obedience demanded," said Sally grimly. Then, "They're in the car. But I really don't want them."

Emilio shook his head. "He wants you to remember the whole experience. He says it'll give you something to look back on."

As he says, thought Sally resignedly. Then, "Will you go back and get them for me?"

Emilio nodded again. "You wait here for my father. He said he would be here by eight o'clock. It's seven-thirty now." He then left.

Senor Gonzalez arrived where she was, however, in five minutes, nattily dressed in whites and a banded sombrero.

"Where's Emilio?" he asked.

"He went to get some binoculars which I left in the car. He'll be back in twenty minutes, or so."

"We shouldn't wait even that long, as the sun is already up and will grow much stronger. Already there's a tour group gathering at the base of the pyramid. Let us go on without the binoculars. And leave Emilio behind. Climbing these pyramids is hardly a novel experience for him."

It's like him to be unfeeling like that, thought Sally. You'd think he would have some compassion and realize what it would mean to me to have Emilio along. Heartless—yes, cruel, terribly so.

A tour of twenty people had gathered at the base of the pyramid, muttering among themselves in low tones as the Senor and Sally approached. All appeared to be American tourists. Two were children. In the quiet, she could overhear several comments as she and the Senor came up behind the group..

"If you won't tell anybody, I didn't go up, I won't tell anybody you didn't go up," remarked a very pretty brunette to a tall well-built man, who stood looking obdurately at the pyramid and then, although she looked no more than fifty, revealed her age by saying, "I'm seventy-one."

The man looked at her, then said, "I'm going up that damned thing."

"If you do, you have a lot of nerve," said an elderly white-haired lady, standing next to them. "You're as old as we are." Then to the other, "How about you, Emillie?" The woman looked undecided.

Another older man grinned and said, "Cameras at the ready," and drew a ripple of nervous laughter from the crowd.

The Ruins at Uxmal

The director of the tour then addressed the group.

"I want to emphasize that nobody has to go up, if they don't want to. If you feel you're not up to it, don't go. You can sit over there." He indicated a shady grove about a hundred yards from where they were standing, with benches scattered about under the trees.

"Ever lose anybody?" the man who had spoken with the women then asked.

The director, avoiding direct comment, answered, "Oh, just a few around Merida."

The questioner persisted. "Not anyone at all, eh?"

The tour director then said, "A lot of people have fallen off this pyramid, but only four have been killed. But never anyone from this tour."

"Oh," said the man and then half-humorously, "Care to give us any statistics on the number of broken backs and limbs?"

The tour director smiled and indicated the pyramid with a nod.

Several people exchanged glances, and then seven, after milling about for a few seconds, made up their minds, separated from the group and migrated, willy-nilly, toward the seating area.

"Well," said Sally to herself, "four people—and others. This is going to be no picnic."

About half of the group going up looked to be in their sixties and seventies. The others, she noted, were in their forties. They all must be adventurers, however. Possibly most of them were experienced climbers.

The man who had spoken to the attractive lady then took a few paces to the foot of the pyramid, where there was a chain stretched over the steps from the very top to the bottom of the structure. He mounted the first step, bent over, seized the chain at his feet and, in a stooping position, began mounting. The attractive woman, to her credit, Sally noted, followed right behind him.

Eleven members of the tour trailed behind the first two. Sally and the Senor followed them, with the Senor leading. At the foot of the steps, Sally's initial apprehensiveness was greatly intensified as she looked upwards. My God, she thought, this looks from here as if we're going to climb, not at an angle of seventy degrees, but in a convex manner, like scaling the inside of an eyeglass lens. It's like being a fly on a wall. Christ! What had she consented to?

She put her foot on the first step and, following the Senor, bent over, grasped the chain and began to climb. As she got about forty feet up the incline, she was tempted to look down and see how far she had come. Dizziness hit her—the shock of gazing down almost vertically made her, for a moment, too unsteady to go on. It was like looking into a deep well. She was aware of the dull shine of the limestone steps, terribly steep and grayish white, stark against the backdrop of greenish brown earth at the base of the pyramid, appearing to her in her dizziness, in a vivid whirl of color, like a kaleidoscope. For a moment she almost tumbled from her perch and dropped to the ground. Instantly she averted her eyes from this terrifying sight and looked then at the step directly before her, muttering "fool, fool,' under her breath and, at that instant, thought never again to risk looking down while either climbing or descending from the pyramid. She was so depleted by this experience that she paused and rested, sitting on the steps, for a full minute, noticing that her knuckles were white from her heightened grip on the chain and thought, how in God's name can I go on?

"Come on, Sally," said the Senor from his vantage point, several steps above her.

The Ruins at Uxmal

"I can't," said Sally. "Let me rest a few more seconds." The Senor nodded.

After a half minute, Sally resumed her climbing position. The Senor turned his back and proceeded slowly.

As they climbed higher and higher, Sally felt under greater and greater tension. God, she thought, this is taking time! It seemed to her like forever! Her fear was so intense that all she could think was, steady girl, steady! Take your time, you're not in a race with anybody, there's no need to hurry. Just keep going!

Knowing that if she made one mis-step or if she lost her grip on the chain, which was her sole anchor as she clambered up the incline, she would plummet headlong over the side three feet away or tumble down the stairs to the ground utterly overwhelmed her with terror. She could scarcely lift her legs from one step to the one above, so steep were the narrow ledges comprising them. She had to place her feet at a 3/4 inch angle to avoid slipping. Just one false step, and she would be a goner! She had the feeling of being drained, that every bit of courage she had was being used, not used up, but just being completely used every instant. She had to fight, every moment, against the thought of making a mis-step.

When they had almost reached the summit, they paused as the group just ahead had stopped to listen to the tour director as he addressed them from the top level of the pyramid. Standing on the two feet wide area before the entrance to the temple, which rose to a height of about fifteen feet above his head, he issued a direction which simply appalled Sally.

"You have to walk on the ledge along the sides of the building to get to the stairs on the other side," he said. "The stairs there are less steep which is better for going down. You shouldn't use the ones you are now on to descend."

For a moment, the group stood, crestfallen. Then one of them asked, "Which side is wider?"

A wag broke the anxiety. "I'm awful glad you asked that question, Ralph," he said, causing the group to break into laughter.

The director indicated the right side with an extended thumb.

The next thing Sally saw were the two children who had reached the top level—she just gasped, cried, "My God!" and grasped the Senor's elbow—the crazy young fools were jumping from the top and straight down three steps below.

The Senor just looked at them calmly and said, "Don't worry. They're allright."

Sally could only ejaculate, "Children have no fear."

The director of the tour was addressing the group, giving a brief talk about the temple and its purpose. He went straight to the point of his discourse.

"The significance of human sacrifice, performed on the sacrificial altar in this temple was to express the Mayan creation belief—a belief that rebirth is possible only through sacrifice. It is a metaphor for life after death and symbolizes the greatest life force for the Maya—which was the sun, which descends into Xibalba—the Mayan underworld, the Greek Hades, our Hell and emerges from it every morning."

Sally did not want to hear more. She had read enough about Mayan human sacrifice from the book at home to satisfy any curiosity she had. "Let's go on," she murmured to the Senor. It was enough for her; she felt as if she were being sacrificed. Her recollection of the book caused her to think of the Mayan ritual preceding it. She thought in her imagination that she had been led across the clear, four hundred yard grassy square below, separating the temple from the surrounding scraggy brush woods, between rows of dancing Indians taking long war steps to

The Ruins at Uxmal

the beat of a drum, according to a religious rite, not one dancer in more than eight hundred being out of step, after fasting for the period immediately preceding and burning pom incense made from the resin of the copal tree.

They passed through the group to the top of the pyramid, then turned and stood facing the two foot wide ledge the director had indicated. The Senor turned to her.

"Hug the wall." He stepped out on to the ledge.

Praying as she turned to the wall, Sally extended both arms full length and clawed at the limestone side, desperately searching for a place where she could get some grip on the rocky surface. With her muscles tight as her hands tenuously gripped it, she took one small, hesitant step out on to the ledge and then, breathing a trifle easier, another and another, very slowly. As she approached the corner, she turned her head and, in spite of her fear, chanced a look outward, seeing, in a bird's-eye view, the clear area at the foot of the temple and beyond that, two other Mayan structures set in the forest of brush trees extending to the horizon.

Then she reached the other side. Gasping in relief, she stepped on to the wider terrace at the rear of the temple. Utterly ready to collapse from strain, she looked dumbly at the Senor; he regarded her with approval and said, "You're doing ok, as they say in the states. Emilio will be proud of you."

Feeling only hatred for him, she made no comment, just regarding him with a what's next? attitude. But she had made it this far; her ordeal was half over.

Then she realized her hatred for him had become even deeper; it had turned into a cold, hard, bitter contempt for him. This dog, she thought, should be killed. He's worse, far worse, than Kirke was—or would ever be—he's worse even than Consuelo Lopez.

Where was Emilio? Where was the man who loved her—and she him! —the one for whom she was undergoing this awful ordeal—the one for whom she was making this great sacrifice? Where was he?

"I want to find Emilio," she then said.

"Well, look for him," said the Senor with contempt in his voice. "He must be down there on the ground."

She compared the Senor to these Maya. Her rage welled up! Look at them—they had killed—they were cruel—yes, very cruel, but no worse than he! Even better—they had killed, yes but for a noble purpose—rebirth of life!

She braced herself. Stepping into the rear entrance ot the temple, she turned and faced outwards, pressed her hands hard against its walls and looked first out towards the horizon, then swung her head from side to side for a survey of the broad scene. Then gritting her teeth, she took a deep breath and lowered her gaze to survey the area immediately below. Carefully, slowly she performed this action.

Emilio was nowhere to be seen, although she expected him to be at the base of the pyramid or else standing back on the grassy square.

"He's not there," she said to herself, wondering why in God's name not?

She repeated the procedure. Still no Emilio.

She stepped back out on the area next to the Senor. Yes—these Maya, they had killed—but for a noble purpose—rebirth of life! And chance had put her here—now it was time to act!

Yes, chance and necessity—to kill for a noble purpose—a rebirth, hers and Emilio's; it was time to act! In a flash, she suddenly moved—she stepped behind the Senor, put up her hands and pushed—against him—hard!

The Ruins at Uxmal

Without even a grunt of surprise he fell, tumbling precipitately head over heels down the stairs, not stopping because of the force of her shove until he hit the ground, 120 feet below, coming to rest face up with one arm flung out from his side, his head now hatless, blood covering it from a smashed skull. Sally, frozen into immobility by the shock, thought in the first second of nothing but the drama of the action, then, awareness returning, felt suddenly immensely weak; she sank down on her knees, then rolled backwards, her face to the sky and thought, God, what have I done? and began to shudder.

Too drained to move, she only became aware that the first of the members of the tour had arrived when she perceived a man's face looking into her's in utter surprise and consternation.

"Where's the fellow?" he asked. Then as Sally, too insensible to answer, just waved vaguely, he ejaculated, "What are you indicating? My God—he didn't fall, did he?"

Sally did not even nod, just muttered, "He fell," weakly.

"Jesus Christ!" he cried, then looking down, "My God!"

As the next members of the tour arrived on the side, he turned to them, gesticulating violently and crying out, "This woman, lying here, has just indicated the man she was with fell off the steps." Then he pointed. "See him there, lying a the bottom—My God, what a thing to happen!"

The remaining members of the tour now arrived, in single file around the corner of the ledge. Displaying concern and consideration when they saw only Sally and the other members of the tour, they immediately began speculating about what had happened and then excitedly asked questions, largely incoherent, of the first man. On gleaning an emotional reiteration from him, they then exploded in ejaculations of horror and began to mutter confusedly and animatedly among themselves.

The tour director addressed the Mexican officer who, as the official guide for the tour, had been the last to arrive. "Better hurry down there," he said, pointing to the ground.

The official put his foot over the first step. "I'll get the police," he said.

"Look—there's somebody coming," said a youngish, black-haired woman, standing in the area before the temple and pointing to the woods, at some distance from the base of the pyramid. "Not the police. He's not wearing a uniform."

"He may have seen what happened," said the director. He then knelt over Sally, speaking nervously to her in a controlled manner, asking questions in a low voice.

Sally was unresponsive. Although she was trembling with emotion, hardly knowing what to say, she still realized she must not tell the director the truth. She just babbled incoherently for a few seconds; the director, feeling she was incapable of speaking sense, rose to his feet with words of comfort.

"Just lie there for a few minutes, dear. They'll come up and take you down in a little while."

Sally lapsed into obliviousness, being conscious only of the hard surface of the pyramid and the blue sky above; then a minute later, closed her eyes and tried desperately to shut out all thoughts from her mind.

She was finally disturbed by a strange voice speaking a few words in Spanish she could not understand; then, as she opened her eyes, hands gently laid hold of her by the shoulders and feet and lifted her into a canvas stretcher.

A slow decent down the pyramid began.

Sally felt herself being inclined, head low, as her bearers took the first step down the pyramid. The sudden lurch, even though slight, frightened her; she involuntarily clutched the sides of the stretcher. Soon it will be over—this terrible climb and then the fearful thought—what will be next? God—you've killed Hector Gonzalez! What would happen to her?

Feeling all was lost, she succumbed to despair, thinking just give up and confess. Maybe her punishment wouldn't be too harsh—after all, you're a terribly wronged woman and then, in an emotional surge of feeling, felt, God! —didn't you have great justification!

Yes, justification! She clung to that reason desperately, as they carried her, swaying up and down, being very careful as they slowly progressed down the incline. Sally looked skyward, hoping to avoid the reality of danger and then lapsed further into a near catatonic state.

Finally, as they regained level footing, she came to and realized she was on the ground. She looked and saw Emilio running up to her together with two policemen from where the corpse of the Senor lay.

"Emilio," she murmured as he came up to her and reached out her arms to him.

He grasped her hands, then made a curt inquiry of her bearers. "How is she?"

The bearers shrugged their shoulders; then one of the policemen who acted as if he were in charge, said, in English, "She's undoubtedly in a state of shock. But we'll have to ask her some questions now."

Emilio gave her a long intense, questioning look. "No, I don't think that would be a good idea."

"Who are you?"

"A close friend. I came with her, but did not go up the pyramid."

"It's necessary to make an investigation—at the scene of the crime," said the officer. He bent over Sally. "How did it happen?"

Sally, fearing the law, summoned up the remnants of her strength and answered coherently "I hardly know. We got around the corner and before I knew it he fell over the edge. He must have stumbled—or tripped over something—maybe his feet—I don't know what."

"That's true," chimed in Emilio. "I was standing on the ground, back in the woods to get out of the heat and saw the whole thing. It happened in a flash—they arrived on the place just before the temple entrance, stood there maybe for a minute, and then before I knew it, he suddenly lurched forward and fell—God—what a sight!"

Jesus, thought Sally. He saw the whole thing. He knows.

"It happened like that, eh?" said the officer.

"Yes," replied Sally weakly.

The officer then addressed the crowd of people from the tour who had been up the pyramid. "Anybody see what happened?"

"No," answered the tour director, "we were all on the other side."

"Any of you see anything?" the police officer asked of a small crowd of other tourists who had just assembled.

One of them answered. "No. We're from a tour that has just arrived right now."

The officer nodded. "Very well." Then, "Only you two saw it?" to Emilio and Sally. Emilio nodded his head affirmatively.

"Nothing to prove suspicion of murder," the officer muttered under his breath. Then he said to Emilio.

The Ruins at Uxmal

"Give me some time. I have to ask you a few questions about names, family relationships, you know." Emilio nodded and moved a couple of yards with the officer away from Sally. Sally ignored them. Then, after a minute, the officer and Emilio returned to her.

"You can have her transported to the hospital now." said the officer. "It looks to me, as if she needs to go."

"Will anything else be done?" asked Emilio.

"Most probably not. But you'll both hear from the police office by tomorrow as they'll want to question you. But I don't see any reason to take either of you into custody right now. However, after you, we'll have to interview everybody else more closely. It'll take a week." He paused, then continued, "An ambulance will be here in a few minutes. They,"—he indicated with his hand—"two officials from the park force called it from the booth at the front gate, the same time they contacted me."

Suddenly alert, "Who contacted them?" worriedly asked Sally.

"The guide from the tour," said Emilio, as the officer moved a few feet away to make some entries in a notebook. "Now hush," he continued, "just keep quiet; they're about to take you to the hospital."

A medical attendant approached them and briefly examined Sally as she lay in the stretcher. Then he reached into the bag he had with him and took out a syringe. Then he spoke to Emilio briefly.

Emilio then spoke to Sally. "This is a very strong sedative which will put you to sleep for a few hours. You're suffering, of course, from shock."

The medic administered the drug to Sally who immediately lapsed into unconsciousness. She was then loaded in the ambulance with Emilio riding with her, and both were then driven to the hospital.

When she awoke she looked about her room. She noticed first that it was quite small, painted white, and that she was in an iron bed, clad in a hospital shirt and covered with a sheet. Then she saw Emilio sitting in a chair a few feet from her bedside, calmly watching her.

She managed a wan smile. He looked at her with compassion and then asked, "Feel any better now?"

"Oh, Emilio—I am calmer—from the drug, I suppose, but problems..."

"You'll have nothing to worry about from the police," said Emilio. "No one but us saw it, so proving anything against you will be impossible."

"I'm so glad you thought so quickly," she said gratefully. "You didn't say anything..."

"I am virtually certain that you'll get off free. They can't prove a thing against you."

She heaved a sigh of relief. Emilio continued.

"If asked anything, I'm just going to repeat I saw him stumble and fall. And, of course, all you have to say is the same thing. I'm pretty sure you won't be touched."

"Well, I'm glad to hear that."

"I'm certainly not going to turn the one I love over to the authorities—you'd face the death penalty or life in prison—possibly"

She nodded. "Yes, it was awful—what I did."

The Ruins at Uxmal

He burst out, leaning forward and throwing out his hands. "But for us...how in the devil could you do such a thing? Admitted, you had reason, but..."

"Emilio! I did it for us! You know that! I couldn't stand the possibility of having to live with that man—and have you dragged into drug dealing. You know he was wrong—terribly wrong—your father is a cruel, vicious, utterly unfeeling person. How could I have had the nerve? —God, I don't know—some force, something foreign—something alien to me made me do it. There I was, on that pyramid—confronted by this vicious monster—who would destroy not only us but hundreds of others to satisfy his lust for money. I thought—the Maya—the reason for their ritual of sacrifice—they killed, yes, but for a noble purpose—your father, he would destroy you—and me—to satisfy his lust for money. Wasn't I justified in killing him? We're better off—the world is better off! He could have done something else—I don't know what—but did he even try? No! He took the easy way—the swine—with no regard for the evil he was committing. And I felt chosen to pay him off. So I did!"

Emilio sat for a full half minute, looking bemusedly at the floor. Then he folded his hands across his lap and raised his eyes to look at her with sympathy.

"Yes, I can understand why you did it. But..." He took his eyes off her and looked at the wall, summoning up his nerve to continue.

"What I have to say is going to cause much pain and grief—to both of us. It is very hard for me, feeling the way that I do about you, and it will be equally hard for you feeling the way you do towards me."

Terribly anxious, she remained silent, waiting for his pronouncement.

"Dear," he said, speaking most tenderly, "we cannot go on together..."

"What do you mean?" she gasped.

"Dear, what I mean is that I cannot marry you."

Stunned by this statement, she remained silent. He continued again, speaking very quietly but very emphathically.

"I cannnot marry the murderer of my father. Regardless of what you say—and there is—maybe—considerable truth in what you say, I still cannot marry the murderer of my father."

"Emilio!"

"No. I cannot. I cannot marry the murderer of my father."

A gulp as she was shocked to her roots.

"No," he repeated, "I cannot marry the murderer of my father."

She lay back as the realization of what he had said broke over her. She thought for a few moments of something to say, then raised her head on her elbow and spoke in a tone of apology.

"I didn't think of the consequences of my action when I took it. I didn't think about the police or the consequences of murder. I just acted."

"I know. But that doesn't alter the consequences—the long term consequences. I could never be happy with you."

She began quietly to weep, reaching for a paper wipe by her bedside. Then, drying her eyes, she said quietly.

"I do see what you mean"

"Yes. There is no alternative. I was devoted to my father."

For a long moment she thought, then said, "Very well, Emilio, if that's what you want. If we must separate, we must separate."

He looked fondly at her, then spoke wearily.

"Yes. We must. And it had better be now. But please take comfort in this—the police will talk first with you. Tell them nothing, of course. You'll receive a formal notification of your release from any suspicion of murder—after they complete their interviews with the rest of the people there." He rose to his feet and turned to go.

"Good-bye, Emilio," she said very sorrowfully.

"Good-bye, dear. You'll be released in an hour or so from the hospital. It is better. though for me to leave you now." He walked slowly to the door, quietly opened it and departed.

Chapter 34

Feeling very depleted—very depressed—and very worried, Sally left the hospital by taxi at five o'clock. Depleted because of the terror she had faced, depressed by the fact that Emilio had left her and worried because the decision by the police was not yet final. One more trial to face, she said to herself wearily, thinking of the inquiry. Well, she then thought further, buoying herself, there's small chance of being indicted. But still it was something to face.

Emilio? Sorrow welled up in her. She had so loved him—she had even killed for him. And what had she gained? —nothing! Although she was a criminal in the eyes of the law, he knew better—he knew she had acted for her own idealistic standard of justice and out of her own sensibility for human life—especially her own and his! But he, he was unworthy of her! So—she must be through with ever thinking of him.

But her thoughts were suddenly disrupted by an overwhelming sense of wickedness. Her conscience struck with the force of a maelstrom! She <u>had commited murder!</u> God! Would she face the tortures of hell for her crime? Staggering into her bedroom, she collapsed on the bed, ready to break!

For an hour she succumbed to despair, but then slowly realized she had the will to think. Immediately she began to consider: there are cases where murder is justified, there are cases in which people are justified in taking the law into their own hands when, as in this instance it would not have been enforced and rightfully enforcing it—in the very name of justice!

She felt, then she knew she had been right—the Christian ethic, "Thou Shalt Not Kill," in her case was not applicable. Put it aside! She summoned her will again—determined to do it.

The Ruins at Uxmal

Yes—so much for the way she had been reared. She felt she was strong; she felt she had the strength to put aside conformist behaviour and act individually—and nobly—in a just cause. Yes—she did have the will! And she would do it.

And so—that would be over, that would be finished. Yes, that would be over. It would be; it should be finished. Even if the slightest traces of it remained, her will would eventually eradicate them.

But would it? Terrified—her conscience—God—if it didn't leave her alone? Desperately she put that thought aside.

But it persisted. She tried to think of something else. Ah—it was obvious—what to do! If she were not indicted, it was to pick up the pieces of her life and carry on—and live on her alimony as an expatriate American in Mexico. Yes—that was it! She could only hope that with the possible threat of the law Kirke would not welsh. He could not be trusted. She had to live—and slowly recuperate—in Mexico.

Being totally exhausted from her ordeal, she undressed quickly and fell into bed. But she did not sleep soundly, and when she awoke at eight the following morning, she was very tired. Bad dreams had not left her alone.

Her mental torture continued. Then a call after two days to report to the police diverted her. Although thorough, her grilling was done courteously. But after she had repeated her statement, made at the site, the presiding officer said, "You may go," with a smile on his face.

While she waited during the days that followed, she tried to preoccupy herself with her immediate problems—Kirke and the law—but the recurrent thought of what she had done was always present, worried her constantly and made her very restless.

Maria arrived daily with the mail. Finally, a letter came—a notice from the police department. Her elementary Spanish enabled her to read it. It did relieve her somewhat. Nothing incriminating her had turned up in the interviews the department had conducted. She was completely free. Being temporarily restored to a modicum of indomitablity, she was able to eat a good breakfast that morning and devote considerable attention to considering the future.

After a second cup of coffee, she turned to thinking about Kirke for a long period of time. She had to do something to safeguard herself from him. But what? Unable to work and unskilled in any trade useful in Merida, or in all of Mexico for that matter, what could she do?. Finally, after cogitating further, she made up her mind as to a plan of action.

She rose and went to her writing desk. She pulled her best stationary from the drawer, picked up a pen and wrote a long thoughtful letter. She reread it very carefully after she had finished it, then deliberately put it in an envelope, slowly sealed it and walked in measured steps to the kitchen.

"I'm going out for about an hour," she said to Maria. Then she walked to her bedroom where she carefully dressed herself for her trip, carefully tucked the letter in her bag and said adios to Maria.

Arriving at the post office she posted the letter with a slight smile, as she studied the name and address on the envelope. Then she turned and with a preoccupied air walked back home.

After telling Maria she could have the afternoon off, she spent the rest of the day playing with Bill and then, after putting him in his crib at 6 p.m. just sat in an armchair, thinking over what she had done. At seven-thirty, she prepared a light meal and then went to bed early, wondering if there was any hope in what she had devised...

He came the next day and knocked loudly on her door As she opened it, she saw that he was handsomely dressed in blue pants, a white shirt with ruffles and embroidered waist band and a white sombrero. Anticipating his appearance, she had dressed in her best sport dress, fit for an outing in the land of sunny climate and greeted him cordially.

"Ah Senor," she said, attempting gaiety, "How nice of you to come to see me in reply to my letter. You have taken the day off to be with me—I am flattered."

"My pleasure, Senora Sally," said Senor Gutierrez.

"And—it is always my pleasure to see you, Senor," she rejoined. "You look so handsome in your fine outfit, complete with sombrero. The color combination—it is both striking and beautiful."

He smiled, came in and sat down at her invitation and crossed his legs.

"Before I ask you to go out for the day, Senora, let me tell you this: I am only struck with admiration at your independence of spirit—and your bravery. Your letter told me your reasons most adequately, and I am in complete agreement with you. For you, I have only respect—and," he smiled again, "affection."

Sally's heart leaped.

"It's so nice to hear that, Senor, from you. Especially after being rejected for only doing what was right."

"So correct you were. Again, what you did was most eminently justified. And that is the reason why I am here today—to congratulate you for what you did. I am in complete accord with it."

"I am so glad you are. I so hoped you would be. I am greatly relieved." She felt like kissing him. "Now let's celebrate today. Shall we go? I want to get out of the house."

He rose. She strode up to him, put her head on his shoulder and melted in his arms.

"How could he give up a treasure like you?" said the Senor. He then looked straight in her face.

"Senora Sally, may I kiss you?"

She surrendered herself to him further.

"I regard this as the opening of what will be a long relationship," he then said.

"I am so glad that you do," said Sally, her face breaking into an expectant smile.

"And," he said with finality, "may it become a permanent one."

Sally smiled very broadly and nodded her head, acquiescing.

"And now," said the Senor, "Shall we do as you say? I am delighted with the honor of taking you out on this entrancing day."

She took his arm.

"And if there is anything I can do now, to ingratiate myself further with you, what is it?"—he paused—"my darling."

"Just one thing," she said. "Because I have been so cruelly hurt—you know whom I am talking about, of course—would you do me a favor?"

"What is it?"

"Would you discharge Kirke from his job and leave both him and Consuelo to shift for themselves?"

"As good as done, Senora Sally," he said as he took her arm and led her down the steps to his waiting automobile.

But in the car, her worry returned. She then knew—the sense pervaded her—that even under the sunlight which would shine on her all her days, was the ever-present cloud, signifying the gloom and penance that would always be a perpetual accompaniment to her, even in her happiness.

Jeremy S. Wood

Bibliography

Coe, Michael D. The Maya New York, Thames and Hudson, c. 1993

Collier's Encyclopedia New York P. F. Collier & Sons, c. 1964

Fodor's Travel Guide, Mexico New York, Fodor's Travel Publicatios, c. 1991

Fodor's Travel Guide, Mexico New York, Fodor's Travel Publications, c. 1993

Gugliotta, Guy and Jeff Leen Kings of Cocaine New York, Simon & Schuster, c. 1989

Price, Berkeley Trafficking New York, Charles Scribner, c. 1989

Riding, Alan Our Distant Neighbors New York, Vintage Books, c. 1986

Sharer, Robert The Ancient Maya Stanford, Stanford University Press, c. 1994

Trevino, Elizabeth Borton My Heart Lies South New York, T. Y. Crowell, c. 1953

Walker, William O. Drug Control in the Americas Albuquerque, New Mexico, University of New Mexico Press, c. 1981

Wyman, Donald Wyman's Gardening Encyclopedia New York, MacMillan, c. 1971

Jeremy S. Wood

About the Author

The author has attended three major universities and holds degrees in English Literature and Library Science. His experience has been principally in library work, but also to some degree, in business organizations. He has traveled extensively in the United States and, more recently, has also done some foreign travel. He is unmarried and now participates enthusiastically in life in Springfield, Missouri.

Printed in the United States
52694LVS00001B/6